SCANDALOUS
Prince

——— A MAFIA ROYALS ROMANCE ———

by
RACHEL VAN DYKEN

DEDICATION

To my readers, this entire series is for you. I hope it gives you some normalcy in 2020 and I hope it feels like coming home, and also, I'm sorry in advance, HAHA just kidding, stop freaking out...
it's the mafia after all.

Blood in. No out—pour some wine!

AUTHOR *Note*

This is a standalone within a brand new series; I know you probably already know that since you picked up this book, but hey, let's just repeat it again! ;) If you recognize some of the names in this book, it's because back in 2010, I wrote a series called Eagle Elite, and the parents in this series are the OG's of Eagle Elite. That series got extremely long (as you can imagine), so I decided we needed fresh blood back at Eagle Elite University, and that started with Ruthless Princess and continues the saga with Scandalous Prince.

If you are an EE fan, then this is the part where you may nerd out and want a family tree; I have that on the very next page, NEVER FEAR! If you're new, just scroll on by, it won't matter to you, haha, and you'll be like yeah, I don't care. And you don't NEED to know any backstory, because again, this is a new series (do you like how I keep repeating that), oh by the way, it's a new series.

PHEW okay so… this one is a bit different than Ruthless Princess, and if you're new to the series or my mafia books, know that the research I do is extensive—to the point that for ten years, my research into the Italian mafia has matched how long it takes to write the books as well. I also rely on my Italian readers, HEAVILY, to make sure that things like family dinners are authentic (Eat, EAT! Lol). Know that this book came from a place and a story that I felt needed to be told. Like I said, it's different, but in a good way, it's not like the other EE books; then again, I don't think it should be; the last thing you guys want is the same thing over and over again. I hope you enjoy the story!

Pour a glass of wine, maybe a cup of gin, HA kidding… it's just Breaker's favorite, and please, escape for a little bit into the world of the Elite.

Blood in, no out. Let's meet our Scandalous Prince, Breaker Campisi, aka Breaker of Hearts Keeper of Souls…

WHO'S WHO IN THE
Cosa Nostra

Nixon and Trace Abandonato. Nixon is the boss of the Abandonato Family; he's a bit psycho, has a lip ring, and in his mid-forties, looks like a freaking badass. Think if Jason Momoa and Channing Tatum had a baby. SURPRISE, Nixon! Trace is the love of his life. Nixon's daughter, Serena, is his pride and joy; she's the heir to his throne and in love with Junior Nicolasi. His adopted son Dom is ten years older than Serena. At thirty, he's ready to step in if he needs to, but he really doesn't want to, not that he's thinking about a family of his own. Nixon's youngest, Bella, was a most welcome surprise.

Phoenix and Bee Nicolasi (formerly De Lange) have one son, Junior, and he's everything. The same age as Serena, he has only ever had one thing on his mind. Her. And now he has her. Pursuing her was like signing his own death sentence. The one rule that the bosses gave all the cousins, all the kids, no dating each other, it complicates things. They all took a blood oath. But he risked it all, for just one taste—and is still here to tell about it.

Which brings us to Chase and Luciana Abandonato, their love story is one for the ages. He had Violet first, gorgeous, Violet Emiliana Abandonato. And then he had twins, God help him. Asher (Marco) and Izzy. All are attending Eagle Elite University. Violet is more into books than people. And the twins, well they are polar opposites. While Izzy is quiet and reserved, taking after her uncle Sergio in the tech support part of the mafia, Asher was an assassin at age twelve. He takes care of everyone even though he's younger than Serena and Junior. He feels it's his job to make sure everyone is safe, so when he was unable to do that for his girlfriend, Claire—he was inconsolable. She was his soul mate, and he'd do anything for her. And don't forget the baby of the family, Ariel, who everyone dotes on.

Tex and Mo Campisi. He's the godfather of this joint, gorgeous, he's a gentle giant unless he's pissed, and his wife, Mo, is just as violent as he is. They have two sons, Breaker and King. Breaker is in his sophomore year at Eagle Elite, and he can't wait to release his own flirtations onto the campus. He's a force to be reckoned with, just walks around with chicks and shrugs. King, on the other hand, is vying for top whore at his own high school; I mean, they say high school is supposed to be memorable, right? He just can't remember any of the girls' names, so he calls them all Sarah. It's a thing.

Sergio and Valentina are also Abandonatos. While Val is quiet and reserved, Sergio is the resident doctor of the Families. He's also really into tech and loves spying on people. They have two gorgeous daughters. Kartini has her daddy wrapped around her little finger. He just hopes he survives her last year of high school without shooting one of her boyfriends. With Lydia, he knows she can take care of herself. She already beat up the class bully, making Sergio quite proud.

Dante and El don't have things easier; they're one of the younger mafia families, he's the head of the Alfero Family. And he has two twin girls at age ten who are making him pull his hair out. Raven and Tempest are adorable, but they're feisty like their mom. He lets them have more screen time than he should, but they say he's their favorite in the world, sooooo… he lets it pass.

Andrei and Alice have been through a lot. Their name single-handedly brought the Russian Mafia into the Italian fold. Andrei is both Petrov and Sinacore, meaning that the oldest Italian mafia family is now part of the Cosa Nostra. Forever. Their son's name is Maksim, and weirdly enough, he's a total flirt; he takes nothing seriously but can flip a switch in a minute if someone he loves is threatened. Anya is his little sister, and he would do anything for her; she seems fragile but studies Krav Maga, so nobody messes with her.

These are the Families of the Cosa Nostra.

Welcome to the Family.

Blood in. No out.

MAFIA
Royals

Mafia Royals Romances

Royal Bully — *Royal Bully is a prequel novella*
Ruthless Princess
Scandalous Prince
Destructive King
Mafia King
Fallen Dynasty

BREAKER'S
Lullaby

I am so thrilled to bring this original song to you!
I had an amazing time working with Indi Anderson as she
put music to my words.

Breaker's Lullaby is the soul of this book!
Listen and dive just a bit deeper into his psyche!
Listen to Breaker's Lullaby on my website:
www.rachelvandykenauthor.com

Two roads diverged in a yellow wood, And sorry I could not travel both, And be one traveler, long I stood, And looked down one as far as I could... —Robert Frost

PROLOGUE
One

I loved her against reason, against promise, against peace, against hope, against happiness, against all discouragement that could be.
—Charles Dickens, *Great Expectations*

Valerian

I watched her often.

Sometimes I imagined I was her guardian angel, or maybe her avenging knight, the fallen hero who would never have her but could watch from afar.

Watching, after all, didn't mean touching.

She was wearing white again, so pure as she did a twirl under his hand and then threw her head back and laughed as he bowed, she curtsied, and then the rest of them joined in, the cousins of the Italian mafia.

The royals.

The untouchables.

They had no idea how lucky they were to grow up in a

house where parents loved you rather than told you that you shouldn't have been born. Of course, that was after, but that didn't lessen the effects of those words.

Bastard.

Liar.

Fool.

For years, I thought that my middle name was Bastard until one of the men took pity on me and told me it was just Valerian.

Imagine a ten-year-old, introducing himself as Bastard and not understanding why everyone around him laughed and mocked him in Russian.

Her laugh brought my thoughts back to the present as I stood behind the tree and continued watching, hiding my face in the shadows like I always did when I watched.

She may as well be a siren.

My siren.

And I, the pathetic sailor, begging for her to just let me drown in her arms.

My phone buzzed in my pocket, interrupting my stalking. I quickly answered it. *"Da?"*

"Pora Umerit."

I hung up.

I had always known the day would come.

"Time to die," he'd said.

Was it so wrong to hope to see her in my dreams?

"One day," I whispered, my accent thicker than usual. "I will have you, Violet Abandonato, and it will be my name you scream… not his."

I turned on my heel and walked off.

Because sometimes, dying meant you were finally going to get a chance to live.

PROLOGUE
Two

The Beginning...

Some say the world will end in fire. Some say in ice.
From what I've tasted of desire, I hold with those who
prefer fire, but if I had to perish twice, I think I know
enough of hate, to say that for destruction ice, is also
great, and would suffice
—Robert Frost

Breaker

Christmas 2019

I tapped the thick red invitation against my thigh. My all-black suit felt like it was choking the life out of me; at least I didn't have to wear a tie. With my free hand, I adjusted the red mask on my face. You could see my un-naturally green eyes, square jaw, and full lips, but that was it.

And wasn't that the point?

Secrecy.

Power.

Greed.

Smokescreens.

"Sir." An attendant dressed in an all-red suit and black mask held out a tray of red wine. I almost rolled my eyes. Were we fucking mafia vampires now?

Bad enough that I had to even be there when every one of my cousins got a free pass—everyone but Chase's kids who were probably bored to tears and ready to set fire to the place.

So many politicians and celebrities to rub shoulders with. My presence alone should make them feel uncomfortable. I was armed to the teeth, ready to act if needed, and prepared to do the one thing I promised Chase I'd do.

Make sure Violet didn't try to sneak off.

They'd gotten in another fight about the facade of being both a politician's daughter and underboss's daughter and feeling like a fraud every single time she wore her white dress and perfect nude heels and smiled for the cameras.

She would be easy to pick out in the crowd.

Her sleek black hair was the envy of literally every female I knew, and that matched with her light blue eyes, seriously hot body, and high cheekbones and full lips made her look like a fallen angel.

One I would desperately like to corrupt. Not that we hadn't had our moments, some of them embarrassingly fast, but most of them firsts because—regardless of how she treated me in front of her dad—she trusted me, and I was in love with her. The shitty part was that she never let me get that far, almost like she knew the minute we crossed that line, there would be no going back and only death in our future.

Delivered from Dear Old Dad himself.

I smirked to myself.

Right, the last thing I needed was Chase Abandonato murdering me for touching his perfect daughter.

After all, my blood was no good, according to him.

He didn't know though—none of them did—how easy it was for me to play the dumb sheep when I'd been a wolf since birth.

Ready to devour the innocent.

Corrupt the powerful.

And take my rightful place on the stolen throne.

I was running out of time.

This year I would need to choose.

This year would be the year my adopted dad would find out and force me to make a choice.

I downed the wine in one gulp.

"Gulping wine, how savage of you," came Andrei Petrov's rough voice from behind me.

I steeled my expression, chased away the easy-going smile and wink for the cameras as I shed every last emotion and turned to give the boss of both the Russian Petrov Family and the Italian Sinacore Family a cold look.

"Vodka does go down better," I commented.

"That's the spirit." He put his hand on my shoulder and gripped until his fingers dug into my muscle so miserably hard that I winced.

Sick bastard liked to torture people by dangling them in a fucking tiger cage; the last thing I wanted was to get on his bad side.

"Did you need something?" I asked in a bored tone, jerking out of his reach.

Those passing by gave us a wide berth, their ill-concealed whispers drifting to my ears.

"Monster…"

"Murderer…"

And then, of course, "Gorgeous," from a few women who watched with rapt fascination even though he was married.

"A favor." He licked his lips and grinned over my head.

Slowly, I turned.

There she was in all her stunning glory, dancing with her father and smiling. Violet Abandonato, my mission, my curse, the one woman I wasn't allowed to touch, like the pretty crystal you save for special occasions, the silver you only polish during Christmas.

I might as well be dirt beneath her fingernails.

Chase shot me a wink that just dripped with fake enthusiasm.

I nearly flipped him off in return.

"What's this favor have to do with?"

"Some… associates."

"So, some assholes? Awesome, where do I sign up?"

"Rich assholes." He grabbed a glass of wine from a passing waiter. "It won't take long. My sources say a group of women were trafficked from Europe late last night. They'll bring them to the club as per usual. I'll try to get as many away as possible and as for the remaining ones…"

Bile rose in my throat. "Can't save them all."

"I'll let them choose, I always do."

They either chose service or death.

The only choices given, so it didn't look suspicious, so Andrei could control the trafficking underworld without as much of a hint of goodness. They had to believe he was the demon he claimed to be when people closest to him knew best—he was their dark knight—their savior.

The ones that stayed weren't allowed to be beaten, but being sold in prostitution, no matter how high profile, wasn't usually what little girls grew up wanting to pursue.

"Wish I could help, but I'm on babysitting duty."

Violet did another twirl with her dad. The lights overhead caught the shine in her hair, which was pulled into a bun so tight that I wondered if she had a throbbing headache. Diamonds dripped from her ears, sparkling with each turn, and her white form-fitting strapless dress did nothing to hide the curves I was itching to palm.

Andrei snorted. "Perfect little Violet looks ready to run away screaming. One day she'll snap. I hope it's you who gets to see it happen."

I cursed. "Are you insinuating that I should bring her to your club, where several high-profile people will be bidding on women? Are you insane? Besides, they know who she is."

Andrei rolled his eyes. "Nothing happens in my club without my permission. We'll let her sit at the bar and drink away her sorrows."

"Yes, because that won't make Chase want to murder me, getting his daughter drunk on guard duty," I spat.

"Grow a pair," Andrei growled and then crooked his finger at Violet.

She seemed relieved that the devil wanted to chat with her.

Never thought I'd see the day when Violet was happy to see Andrei. He was like the horror story you tell small children, the monster who lived under your bed, the demon that hovered over your lifeless body at night.

She gave her dad a kiss on the cheek and then made her way over to us. Her perma-smile made *my* face hurt.

"Gentleman." She leaned up on her tiptoes and kissed Andrei once on each cheek and then gave me a cold stare.

Deserved.

She hated that the one guy who got under her skin, the one person who knew her better than she knew herself, was forced to watch her while she pretended to be what Chase needed her to be. I swear every single time I stole a heated glance in her direction, I prayed she'd remember our first kiss or dry humping like idiots with raging hormones in her dad's pool house.

I blew her a kiss and winked.

She clenched her teeth like she wanted to bite me and then turned her attention to Andrei, flashing him a shiny bright smile. "Did you need something?"

"I think…" Andrei grinned. "…it's you who needs something. We're going to let you escape, though you'll need to make a small detour at the club."

Her eyes widened. "Really?"

"Really," I said dryly. "I'm going to help Andrei. It won't be long. You can drink your weight in cosmos, and I'll even carry your ass out the door when you're too drunk to walk in a straight line."

She flinched. "My hero."

"I try." I smirked.

She seemed to shudder, and then she gave Andrei a curt nod. "Sounds fun. Let me just let my dad know I'm not getting kidnapped."

"I wish," I muttered under my breath, earning a sharp heel slamming into my right foot.

I winced.

Again, deserved.

Candles flickered around the room as more people started to dance and drink. Hell, it felt like a cult; the way they worshipped Chase wasn't right.

He was too rich.

Too powerful.

Too good looking.

And he had the ear of the United States President.

Hell had indeed frozen over for the state of Illinois. If only they knew who wielded all the power now that he was in office, now that he could put who he wanted into the cabinet, now that he'd helped pick advisors.

I sighed as he made his way over to us.

"Keep her safe," he snarled under his breath.

"My blood for hers." I gave the pledge I always did since I had first started following her last year.

Chase leaned in and kissed my right cheek then whispered, "Make sure she has a bit of fun. She's pissed she's had to wear those heels for three hours."

"When is she not pissed at these things?" I wondered out loud.

"It's necessary," he said coldly. "And remember the rules, no touching her, no looking at her and fantasizing, absolutely nothing that could mean I'll have to kill you."

"Got it." I stood back and winked. "Plus, I have enough female attention, the last thing I need is one who'd probably suffocate me with a pillow just to see my legs twitch."

Chase grinned. "That was a good day."

"Yeah, it really was, nearly dying." I rolled my eyes. "Have fun. Give Luc my love."

"My wife," he barked.

I made a face, "I'm eighteen, don't be weird."

Andrei just chuckled under his breath while Violet returned with her matching white coat.

Sometimes I wondered if Chase did it on purpose.

Made her wear white to make himself look less covered in blood.

Made her wear white to remind me she was an untouchable queen.

And I? I was the slave. The adopted bastard son of someone he didn't even ask to know.

Wouldn't that be the shock of his life?

I almost laughed.

"Let's go." I put an arm around Violet and attempted to keep my body from reacting like it always did when we were this close.

But it was like holding your breath.

You last thirty seconds, maybe more, and then you're gasping for air, greedy for it; my hands trembled a bit as I lowered my palm down her back and held it there.

She sucked in a sharp breath but didn't look in my direction.

And when we got into the waiting limo, she kept her expression blank as she stared straight ahead.

Classical music turned on.

I groaned. "Tchaikovsky? Really, Andrei?"

He smacked me in the back of the head. "It's called culture, I'm almost insulted to call you—" He hesitated. "Human."

I exhaled the breath I hadn't realized I'd been holding.

Nice save asshole.

Violet shifted in the leather seat, drumming her fingertips along her tanned thigh.

I reached for her hand and scowled. "Red fingernail polish how scandalous, next thing your dad knows, you're going to start having sex and watching porn."

She jerked her hand away, her cheeks flushed. "Could you keep your lewd thoughts to yourself, Campisi?"

"I could. Will I? No, no, I won't. I like pushing your buttons". Pushing, touching, caressing, really, I didn't discriminate when it came to her or any other girl. I gave her a chipper grin. "Besides, who else is going to teach you about the birds and the bees. See guys have these things called cocks and—"

"Andrei, if you don't muzzle him, I'm going to pull out my knife and shove it against his scrawny throat!"

"There she is." I slow clapped. "Welcome back to earth, princess. You're not in front of the cameras; people aren't hanging on your every word while you discuss global warming and the need for true leadership in America. You're so damn uptight I wouldn't be surprised if those diamond earrings came from your ass."

Andrei chuckled and looked up from his phone. "I approve of this message."

"You're both impossible." She crossed her arms and then moved against the leather again and sighed, pulling down her skirt.

"Knife." I held out my hand.

After some hesitation, she dug into her purse then handed it to me; it had the Abandonato crest on the hilt and was sharp as hell.

I tore into her expensive dress and made quick work of creating two slits on either side of her dress. "Better?"

She swallowed uncomfortably and nodded. Shit, she was

still thinking about the party, still wondering if her performance was good enough, probably going over every mistake that nobody even saw.

I sighed and handed her the knife back. "The pointy side goes—"

She let out a shriek then held the pointy side dangerously close to my dick. See? All she needed was a bit of encouragement.

"You better pray to God we don't get in an accident or slam on the brakes because you'll lose the smallest appendage you have."

I barked out a laugh. God, I loved her like this. "Yes, because that's what girls say when I fuck them. You were on vacation with us last year. Did you hear any complaints?"

Her face fell.

Best friends that can never be together.

Fun story.

Tell me more.

"Children." Andrei yawned. "Put the knives away. Please."

Violet jerked away.

I flipped her off.

And the universe naturally restored itself to rights.

With Violet ready to impale me.

And my body wishing it could impale her.

Fantastic.

The car finally pulled up to Andrei's club. One of his giant bouncers was already opening the front door to let us in.

People waited in the freezing Chicago cold with the hopes to gain entrance when it was nearly impossible after eleven at night.

Shrieks were heard when all three of us made our way to the front of the line. They knew what we were, who we were—

the whole world did—but nobody could really prove shit, and when you had people in the FBI, CIA, NSA, and the highest levels of government on your payroll, things just naturally went missing.

Files.

Hard Drives.

People.

We ducked into the club; the techno was a welcome change from the classical music in the car.

We wandered over to the bar, I pulled out Violet's chair, and then I crooked my finger at the bartender. "Keep her hydrated."

"Whatever you say, Breaker." Tank winked.

Not only did the guy work for the FBI, but on really busy nights, he took on a shift at the club to learn people's secrets, because alcohol tended to make you loose-lipped and because we still had lots of enemies.

"Think you'll be able to survive without me?" I whispered in Violet's ear.

She shot me a glare. "Must you stand so close?"

"Must you be so fucking tempting?" I snapped my teeth and then ran a bare knuckle down her shoulder.

Her skin immediately broke out in goosebumps. "Not here, Breaker, don't."

"I love it when your innocent little mouth lies while your body shakes for me... literally," I growled. "One day, I might lose all self-control. I hope to God I'm the one that gets to watch you come undone."

She gave me a hard shove, but her eyes said something completely different; they always did, they always had, they always would. "If I wanted syphilis, there are more enjoyable ways to get it! And people to get it from."

I cackled out a laugh. "Yeah, okay, don't go running off, I'll be right back."

I was gone maybe twenty minutes, helping Andrei with the girls as they were introduced one by one, given numbers instead of names—his idea to keep it all about business. Money exchanged hands. And then the announcement was made.

The auction would start in four minutes.

Men of all shapes and sizes started shuffling into the private rooms to watch the women, to watch the show. They couldn't touch, but they could bid, and all their money was going into setting the women free that we could.

It was a shit show.

All in all, about half the women decided to stay as long as they were given citizenship.

The others wanted to go back.

I yawned behind my hand as I watched it all go down and then nearly shit myself when a group of five men walked into the room who were most definitely not Team Andrei.

Or team Italy.

"Drei," I barked as my worst nightmare walked into the small room, holding my everything hostage, including my heart. "Problem."

My life would not be the same after this.

Neither would hers.

For once, I understood the feeling of being completely powerless as I looked into her eyes and knew.

This moment would alter us forever.

And there would be no going back.

I moved to grab her, to kill every last one of those bastards that held her in their arms, but Andrei held out his hand, stopping me instantly in my tracks. "No."

Rage pulsed in cadence to the heavy drum of my heartbeat as blood roared inside my body.

They had no right to touch her.

Violet locked eyes with me and slowly nodded as if to say, stop, it's okay, but she didn't know what these guys did, and she had no clue that the look she was giving me would haunt me into the next life and maybe more.

It wasn't a look of war.

It was one that said to keep the peace.

And she would be the first sacrifice.

CHAPTER
One

The way a crow shook down on me. The dust of snow,
from a hemlock tree. Has given my heart. A change of
mood. And saved some part. Of a day I rued
—Robert Frost

Violet

I should have stayed at the bar like I was told. Instead, I
decided that I wanted to dance a bit, or a lot, since I was
only ever allowed to dance with my dad at political events.

I'd never even been to a club that wasn't owned by someone
my family owned—and they rarely let me go to Andrei's by
myself, for good reason.

I knew the sort of depraved things that went on here. As
much as my dad tried to protect me. You can't protect your
eldest daughter from the horrors of a sex club you helped
protect day in and day out.

My dad was both a hero and a villain; he played whatever
role he needed to in order to keep the Family safe, and now

that we were even more in the public eye, I worried about the toll it would take on the great Chase Abandonato. Other politicians called him the Dark Horse.

They had no clue how right they were because the minute he threw his hat in the game, it was already over, already won, a parade already planned.

Because he was Chase Abandonato.

And they would always be beneath him—beneath our Family.

I wasn't able to dance long. I held my rum and coke in one hand and tried to maneuver my body through the sweaty people to get to where I saw some space when it happened.

A hand over my mouth—leather gloves protecting his fingers.

And an arm around my waist picking me up like I was a rag doll he'd just purchased and was in a hurry to get home.

My drink fell to the floor with a loud crash.

But nobody heard it break.

Just like nobody heard my scream.

Because the people in that club were used to that sort of thing. The way they saw it, I was probably already bought and paid for by whomever had just taken me.

"You won't get away with this!" I yelled.

"Muzzle it." He snapped back, his breath was foul as he yelled in my ear, he smelled like old cigars, whiskey, and something tangy that made me gag.

He carried me kicking and screaming past the dance floor, meaning Tank didn't see a thing, and neither did my favorite bodyguard of Andrei's, Ax.

"My father's going to kill you!" I added in for effect because he would, and the fact that he'd make it painfully slow was the only thing that calmed me.

Because even if I died like this.

His death? This man carrying me?

It would be unimaginable.

That was a fact.

Something my dad promised me over and over again when I was a child expecting a fairy tale—he always swore he'd avenge me in the most bloodthirsty way, and for some reason, that's what put me to bed at night with a smile on my face.

My daddy's bloody promise.

My daddy's oath of honor and revenge.

We made it to one of the metal doors, he knocked twice, and when it opened, it revealed both Andrei and Breaker in a room with five other men.

I breathed a sigh of relief when Andrei's expression turned hard. "What the hell are you doing?"

"I want proof." He set me on my feet and then wrapped a blindfold around my eyes before I could memorize the faces of the other four men, one of them was younger than the others; he had brownish hair and was muscular; that stood out against the older men's wrinkled faces. But that was all I noticed.

"Proof?" Andrei spat. "Careful, you do realize who you're speaking to?"

"I do, and that's why we need proof." A deep Russian accented voice spoke up. "You say you're still in the trade, and yet, your alliance with the Italians is, shall we say, extremely disconcerting."

A laugh erupted from someone, and then Andrei voiced. "And I should be concerned that you're uncomfortable because…?"

"Because there are whispers of the great Andrei Petrov going soft, being, how did they put it... oh yes..." He laughed. "...fucking domesticated."

This was bad.

Really bad.

I jerked against the man again but flinched when something sharp pricked my arm and then went deeper.

"What the hell did you give me?" I roared.

"Just something to make it easier to hold onto you... Jacko's getting old, and you're struggling isn't helping," a smooth voice said.

I didn't recognize that voice, but it sounded... friendlier...

My body suddenly felt like it weighed a thousand pounds as I slowly slumped back against my captor. It was like he'd put me in a dreamlike state.

I was there.

But I was also somewhere else.

I didn't like the lack of control, and I hated that the voices were even harder to focus on now.

"...it has to be a Petrov," one said.

"...you know the price must be paid, pure of blood..."

What? What pure blood?

"He will do it."

"I need proof, damn it!" someone yelled.

I shook my head. *Focus. Just focus on something familiar.*

I couldn't see anything but the blackness in front of me and could feel nothing but the warmth that continued to weigh down my muscles, my bones.

My head lolled to the side.

The man holding me cursed. "So, it has been confirmed?"

Confirmed?

"Thirteen minutes, one camera, this will be the best day of his life, fucking mafia royalty, being her first."

My first?

My brain told me to panic.

It told me to fight.

Run.

But all I could do was inhale, exhale, measure my breaths as I was slowly handed over to someone else.

He had rough hands.

Hands that made me wonder about what sort of man would take a girl's innocence without a second thought.

My heart dropped when I was suddenly picked up and carried somewhere. I couldn't control my head as it fell back, exposing my neck.

"Beautiful." The accented male voice whispered.

Maybe he would be kind.

Maybe he wouldn't take what wasn't his to take.

Maybe he would save me.

All the things I thought and prayed as my sluggish body tried to alert itself to what was about to happen, clearly my anxiety was pumping whatever drug they gave me through my system fast enough to start to clear my head.

I should have just asked one of the guys to take my virginity, one of my friends, though the only one who even tempted me was currently outside with Andrei allowing this horror to take place.

I would have given Breaker everything and several times almost did only to realize that my dad would murder him and I couldn't have the death of my best friend on my conscience no matter how annoying he was or how he paraded girls in front of me like he wanted me to know he was getting it somewhere else.

Funny, how when you're about to lose, you realize how precious that one thing was to you, you realize that you really did want to give it away to someone, but that that someone wasn't a hero.

Never had been.

Breaker Campisi was as hard as the rest of them, with a steely glint in his eyes that told me I should have just listened to him because he knew more than anyone, how fast a person's life could change.

I focused on Breaker's bright green eyes when I was dropped onto a soft mattress. I imagined that he was touching me, not this Russian monster, whoever he was.

I imagined that he was dying with jealousy.

That he was seconds from breaking the door down.

And yet, no sound was heard beyond my own panicked breathing, and the man's rustling as clothing was moved around.

Hands gripped my wrists as they pinned them at the top of the bed, and then he lowered his lips to my ear, causing a chill to erupt down my body as his heavy accent broke out in English. "I'm sorry it has to be like this."

"No, you aren't," I rasped.

"You have no idea." He said something in Russian and then pressed a small kiss to the corner of my mouth. "I have thirteen minutes with you. I'll make it fast, but I don't think I can make it painless."

I could make out the smell of mint gum on his breath as I tried to focus on things that would calm me down, familiar things.

Most of the men I'd seen were old—except one.

This one, I imagined, because, despite my ability to reach for him, to feel the softness of his skin, I knew he was young.

And I knew he wasn't going to stop.

Tears filled my eyes, one slid down my cheek past the blindfold. "Please, I'll do anything. Just please."

His body tensed over mine, and all he got out was an accented. "Sorry."

"Don't lie!" I snapped. "You're not sorry. You're going to take and take and take from an innocent woman while she lays numb and drugged. Does that make you feel bigger? Better? Like more of a man?"

The room spun behind my blindfold as the familiar scent of my favorite cologne hit me square in the face. How dare he smell good? How dare he ruin the Gucci that Breaker, King, and Asher all wore!

My stomach rolled.

I tried to jerk against him, but my body wouldn't follow my brain's instructions; my brain screamed, my body stayed asleep.

And I was trapped.

I let out a scream of frustration. "Just do it already! Fucking do it!"

He didn't say anything.

"What? Now you can't get it up?" I expected him to slap me, but he stayed still over me. "Afraid I won't feel anything?"

"Stop." His voice had a rough warning edge to it, but I already felt dead inside. "Stop."

"No!" I roared. "So get on with it, fuck a helpless girl, go back to your little Russian friends who will, for the record, never defeat the Abandonato Dynasty, and tell them how you took a girl's virginity without her permission, without her pleasure, with nothing but pain!"

"You're wrong..." His voice was deep, rich as his lips nipped my right ear, his tongue sliding out as he pressed an erotic kiss to my neck. I wanted to buck against him but was immobile, and I hated that his kiss felt tender when it should have felt like a thousand needles burying inside my skin. "You will feel pleasure, or I'm not doing my job right."

"I'd prefer you not do your job." I spat. "At all!"

I felt something cold against my thigh, and then he whispered, "Scream again."

I didn't need any encouragement.

I screamed, and I screamed, and I screamed until the sound of the door opening and closing filled the room. I still couldn't move very well or see.

"No games," another Russian voice said; it was deeper. "You do this, or her entire family dies."

The door shut again.

"I'm sorry." The smooth Russian voice was back and then the weight of his body as he sat next to me. "I thought—I imagined they wouldn't come in and look, the blood..."

"They can't die." My voice shook as another tear slid down my cheek.

"Regrets." His voice was back, this time it felt guttural like the room had turned into his own personal Hell or maybe he'd just joined mine. "We all have them. And I can promise you, this will be mine, something that will be at the top of the list will be this very moment, taking what wasn't mine to take, what was only yours to give."

Tears burned my eyes as my lips parted to say something like. "Good."

Instead, I felt nothing but pain.

My own.

His.

"Will they really die if you don't do this?" I asked softly.

He was silent and then. "You die, possibly the new Sinacore boss, definitely your father, they have a gun trained on him right now at the party along with your mother and younger sister."

"It seems such a small sacrifice." A knot of emotion lodged in my throat. "One small thing I give, you take, and everyone lives."

"There is living—" he agreed "—and there is surviving. You're doing the second right now, but one day, not tomorrow or the next day, you'll live again, you'll smile without pain, and you'll know you did your part in saving your family when you were given the chance."

"Who are you?" My heart slammed against my chest. I'd never heard a person speak like that before or have such insight like he'd lived a thousand lives and only taken the wise, meaningful moments and collected them for a time like this.

"Valerian." His voice shook. "Valerian Petrov."

"That doesn't sound like the name of a monster."

"And yet... it is." His hands cupped my face, my lips trembled as he brought his mouth to mine in the most tender, confusing kiss I'd ever received in my entire life.

My brain said we had to give in.

And my body pounded with confusion as his tongue slid past my lips. I could barely kiss him back; I was too tired, too drugged.

"Every kiss," he whispered against my mouth. "Should feel like this."

"Like I'm getting raped?" My voice trembled even though his body was warm as it hovered so close to mine, I could feel the skin from his chest, his neck, the short intake of breaths against my mouth.

"Like you can't help but feel everything even when you know you shouldn't." He said softly, his hands dug into my hair, and then he was kissing me again. Hands shaking, he palmed my thighs and then slowly slid my skirt up around my hips.

He hesitated again.

A soft knock sounded at the door.

My lips trembled. "What does the knock mean?"

"Three minutes left."

Three minutes until I was a different person.

Three minutes until I was undone.

Three minutes to give myself to save the ones I loved.

"Valerian?" I gulped.

"Yes?"

"I'm giving you my permission." I had to do this on my terms, so I had control even though it was a lie.

He cursed.

"Please."

He was gone, and the sound of breaking glass had me internally panicking, and then his hands were back on my legs, spreading them open as another hot kiss pressed against my lips.

"Imagine him."

"Who?" I wasn't dating anyone, clearly had never been with anyone, just lusted after Breaker then wanted to murder him when I heard of every single sexcapade.

"Whoever you dream about at night." His voice was

filled with so much pain that it almost felt like the roles were reversed, that I should be comforting him. "Whoever holds your heart, imagine him, his smile, his eyes, imagine his hands." He removed my thong as he spoke, gently encouraging me, seducing me with his tenderness.

My heart was at war between right and wrong.

A trembling hand slid between my legs.

I could barely move, but it didn't matter, because he seemed to be doing all the work as he worked me into a frenzy I couldn't even fight against while his other hand dug into my hair, his mouth met mine in a painful kiss before he whispered. "I'm so fucking sorry." Against my lips and then searing pain hit me so hard that I cried out.

He was inside me.

This stranger.

"Are you doing it? Imagining him?" he asked tenderly, not moving, but throbbing as my body clenched around him, unsure if I should feel good or bad, angry or sad. "Imagining the man who holds your heart?"

My vision flashed.

A memory of Breaker in the car with me.

Arguing.

And then the heated look across the room that I knew I would never get used to as he watched me dance.

I instantly relaxed. "Yes. Yes, I'm imagining him."

"Good." He slowly started to move. "You're giving this to him, not me, the one who owns your soul, he gets this, not this monster, do you understand?"

"Yes." Hot tears slid down my cheeks as his hips moved in a slow cadence that replaced the pain with enough pleasure that I was helpless to do anything except lay there and wonder how my night had gone from a boring party to a complete stranger taking my virginity, and Breaker Campisi's name in my head and on my lips.

I would hate him forever for not stopping this.

Just as much as I would love him for being my imaginary hero during this nightmare.

"Damn it," Valerian groaned. "You're so tight."

My body exploded with pleasure on his next thrust, and then he was quickly pulling away.

The rustle of clothes was like a bucket of ice water getting thrown over my still naked bottom half.

Another knock sounded.

"Shit." A rip sounded, and then he was cleaning me up as much as he could, and gently pulling my dress down, sliding my underwear back up, and then lifting me into his arms.

Twenty seconds later, the door burst open.

I kept my head high even though I knew they were making jokes about the sheets, about my virginity, about the price I paid.

And then I was getting handed off to someone else.

"Are you okay?" Andrei's low voice whispered in my ear.

"Yes." I gulped. "No."

He let out a string of curses that had me tensing in his arms. "Breaker is taking you immediately home. I need to talk to your dad."

I almost laughed. Dad would kill me, kill him, even if it meant saving him, he would rather die than know this story.

"Don't," I commanded. "Don't tell him."

"Vi—"

"Promise me."

"Damn Abandonatos will be the death of me." He sighed,

and then his mouth was pressing a kiss to my forehead. "I will avenge you."

"I know you will." And he would, he was terrifying. You didn't cross the Sinacore-Petrov boss and live to tell about it.

"Go with Breaker, he may need to carry you until the drugs wear off. I'm going to deal with this... situation."

I felt myself getting passed over to another person's arms, familiar arms, arms that I'd dreamt of just minutes ago. "Breaker?"

"Yes." He sounded like he'd aged twenty years.

"Tell him to use the Tigers."

"My fucking pleasure," he spat and then, still blindfolded, I was carried to the waiting SUV.

Once inside, Breaker jerked it off my face and pulled me into his arms.

I didn't cry until we left the parking lot.

And then the sobbing didn't stop as he pulled me into his lap and rocked me back and forth like it would somehow fix what had just been broken and return what was just taken.

CHAPTER
Two

Nature's first green is gold, Her harder hue to hold. Her earl leaf's a flower; but only so an hour. Then leaf subsides to leaf. So Eden sank to grief, So dawn goes down to day. Nothing gold can stay.
—Robert Frost

Breaker

With each quiet sob, I watched a piece of my heart dislodge from my body and plummet to the ground with a resounding crash, over and over, the crashing turned into a chaos of glass and blood. Should I be shocked that by the time we reached her still empty house—I had nothing left?

There was blackness where once had been life.

Blood still pounded.

And something still beat, but it was more rage than life, and it filled me to the brim with hatred for so many things that it would take years to assess the damage.

"C-can—" she hiccupped "—Can you stay with me?"

I often wondered how easily people were deceived by the light when, in fact, they were nothing but dark. This was one of those moments where lies and smokescreens existed.

Where loss and evil chuckled their win, while love and innocence mourned what once was.

"Yeah, Vi." My voice sounded like gravel as I spoke, and felt even worse; my throat was sore from keeping the screams in, my body was weak from desperately trying to take her pain in any way I could.

Take me.

Use me.

Hurt me.

Just leave her alone.

But the universe, as it often did, had other plans, didn't it?

I hadn't seen this one coming.

We were both quiet as we moved around her room. She went to the bathroom and turned on the shower.

It was the quickest shower any girl had ever taken, I was sure of it, because within four minutes, she was back in the room, wearing black silk sleep shorts and a white cami.

She crawled into her king-sized bed with its pure white duvet and white pillows and had my heart still existed—this would have ended it.

Her innocent face now marred by something else as she blinked her light blue eyes up at me as if to ask.

Am I still pretty?

Am I still worthy?

Am I still me?

On wooden legs, I walked over to her bed and sat on the edge of it; my hand trembled as I pushed some of her silky hair away from her forehead.

"I'm sorry—" my voice cracked "—that I couldn't save you."

"Breaker." She reached for my hand and squeezed it. "There are some things, even the great Campisi son, can't save me from. Like Valerian Petrov."

I kept my sob in.

The pain was unbelievable.

The guilt was unimaginable.

I would not come out of this the same.

Neither of us would.

"Still." I found my voice. "It's my job to protect you, to keep you safe, and tonight, I was just as bad as them, just as deserving of punishment—death."

"Tigers?" She offered with a small smile.

"How can you joke right now?" I couldn't stop my body from shaking.

"Because." She swallowed and looked away quickly. "If I don't, then I won't stop crying."

I lay down facing her, pulling her close. "How about I change the story?"

"What?"

"The story. How about I change it?"

"Do you suddenly have a time machine hiding in your pants or what?"

I smiled at that. At least some of her sass was still there, lingering beneath the sadness and fear. "Yes, that's what I tell all the ladies…"

"Knew it."

God, her smile was unreal. "You met him dancing."

"Who?"

"Your mystery man."

"Ohhhhh, so you really are going to tell me a story?" She bit down on her bottom lip and frowned; her ears were bright with unshed tears. "Do you think it will help?"

"I hope so," I answered honestly.

She nodded. "So, I met him dancing?"

"He bought you a drink, but you being the smart girl you are—"

"I dumped it and ordered my own."

I smiled. "Good girl."

"And then what happened?" She scooted closer.

"He kissed you—the best kiss of your life, books are written, sonnets are sung, and time stood still, the music slowed, it was just this kiss, existing between time and space."

A tear slid down her cheek. "I don't know what that sort of kiss feels like."

My story seemed to be making things worse.

Without thinking, because if I did, I would lose the nerve, I pressed a soft kiss to her mouth and then deepened it as I massaged my tongue against hers then pulled back on the pressure. A hand slid up her neck as I held her close, kissed her like she deserved.

When I drew away, her eyes were misty. "I think I get it."

"Good." I pressed one more kiss to the tip of her nose. "You kissed and kissed, just like that, and when you couldn't handle it anymore, he took you home, the end."

She frowned. "Wait, what?"

"That's all that happened," I said softly. "Just the best few kisses of your life with a promise for more. No dark rooms. No guns. No violence. No stealing. Just you, mystery man, and the kiss. Focus on that."

"Or," She licked her lips and leaned in. "I could just focus on you instead of mystery man."

My soul screamed no.

My heart, wherever it was, broken by my feet, used its last beats to say yes.

"Yeah, you could do that too," I agreed as a feeling of darkness wrapped itself tightly around my throat, making it nearly impossible to breathe.

"Thanks, Breaker." Her eyes closed while I kept watch over her, over a treasure I had failed to protect from the monsters of this world, from the darkness.

She fell asleep fast.

When her breathing deepened, I quietly got up from her bed and walked into the bathroom, shutting and locking the door behind me.

The scream was building so hard and fast that my entire body was convulsing. I ran to the toilet and puked everything I had eaten that day and maybe for the past week out of my body as tears streamed down my cheeks.

And then I kicked off my shoes and walked into the shower fully clothed, closing the glass door behind me as I stumbled against the wall and slid down to the tile floor.

Tears mixed with the water.

And then the body-wracking sobs came.

I pounded my fists against the tile until blood dripped down my fingertips and arms.

I deserved the pain.

All of it.

"God!" My voice muffled against my forearm, so I didn't wake her up as I rocked back and forth, back and forth until the water ran cold.

And even then. I sat there staring straight ahead, teeth chattering.

I could have saved her.

I should have saved her.

Why? Why? Why? I held my head in my hands, having no tears left to cry, nothing left to give.

I stood then, as memories pounded into my skull, and I walked out of that shower, no longer able to suppress the rage at Valerian Petrov and the secrets he held—the gift he held.

Vengeance would be mine, even if it meant my own death.

CHAPTER
Three

...And of course there must be something wrong in wanting to silence any song.
—Robert Frost

Violet

Present Day

I tugged on my tight black knit dress and searched for a pair of heels that wouldn't murder my feet.

My heart was heavy. Then again, it was constantly reminding me of all the scars it held and all the wounds that refused to heal.

I was pre-med.

So, you'd think that school would distract me.

It wasn't.

If anything, it was making it worse—because I still saw Breaker on a weekly, if not daily basis.

Things had shifted last Christmas, and they never righted

themselves the way they were supposed to. He had easy smiles and sarcasm for everyone but me, and I wasn't the only one who noticed how he was often just silent and protective, stepping into that role he felt he'd failed at last year without even really thinking about it.

But I wanted my friend back.

I wanted the guy who made me laugh back.

The one who caught my tears and told me imaginary stories about a mystery man who didn't exist but kissed like a god.

I licked my lips and thought of Breaker's example, how he held me like I was precious, and brought his mouth to mine like our lips were the only holy pure thing between us.

A knock sounded at the door before shoving open. "Vi, gotta hurry, they want us arriving as a family."

It was Breaker.

Because, of course, it was. I swear it's like I conjured him up with my own thoughts.

I didn't turn around. "I'm deciding on shoes."

He sighed heavily, his footsteps clicked against the wood floors of my room as he stopped at my side and looked at my two walls of shoes. "Do you even wear all of these?"

"What do you think?" I crossed my arms and grinned.

He didn't smile back. "It's a funeral. Wear black." He grabbed the closest pair, a black half-inch kitten heel that wouldn't make me look too tall and would actually be quite comfortable.

My heart pinched in my chest at his unreadable, blank expression. "All black…" I took the shoes. "Got it."

"Great." He shoved his hands into his black trousers; he was wearing a black button-down shirt and fitted jacket that was made just for him. With no tie, and the top two buttons undone, part of his Campisi Family Crest tattoo peeked out.

What was I even thinking?

I might be Chase Abandonato's daughter.

But he was the Capo's son— still extremely powerful regardless of his unknown bloodline.

Not to mention, drop-dead gorgeous and a year younger than me.

I mentally slapped myself. "I just need to grab my purse."

His green eyes flashed before I turned around, or was it just a trick of the light? His messy reddish-brown hair had pieces of gold in it that almost seemed fake they were so pretty, one piece was currently falling across his aristocratic forehead. We always joked that he dyed his hair, just making him more annoyed when girls commented on how gorgeous it was.

He looked nothing like Tex.

He didn't even look Italian, really.

His skin had a gorgeous tone.

His eyes were green, though.

His hair more light than dark.

With full bow-shaped lips meant to drive a woman crazy and high cheekbones, he was almost too pretty to be dangerous.

Even though he was lethal.

"Vi?" One eyebrow shot up. "Your purse?"

"Oh, right yeah." I quickly put on my shoes and grabbed my purse from my dresser. "Ready."

"Finally," he muttered under his breath.

I glared and then held out my foot to trip him.

He stepped over it with a heavy sigh like he didn't have time for games right now.

Which I understood.

We all grieved differently.

My brother Ash had just lost his soon-to-be fiancé in a freak car accident set up by one of the De Lange kids—we'd basically offered them our protection, our name, and the first thing that blotted-out family line of the Five Families did?

They killed someone.

It was meant to be Ash.

But Claire was driving Ash's car, so it ended up being her.

I'd never seen my brother so broken. So unwilling to be fixed. He was drinking more—not that I blamed him—since he'd found out days before her death that she'd been pregnant.

It wasn't just a nightmare.

But an inexplicable tragedy.

The funeral would make the news, which meant his pain would be on full display for the world to see.

It also meant I had to put on my fake politician's daughter smile.

The one I hated.

The one that made Breaker look at me like he was almost disappointed.

I hated all of it.

All of this.

I hated how out of control I felt when I was having trouble just putting one foot in front of the other—trouble just existing and at night, sometimes, trouble breathing without having a panic attack about hands on my body.

Some nights it was Breaker's face.

Other nights it was the stranger's accented voice.

Valerian.

I shuddered.

"You all right?" Breaker put his hand on the small of my

back as we walked down the hall and out of the house toward the waiting black SUV.

The bosses had left separately, ahead of the kids, and as instructed, each family heir had to ride in his or her own car just in case.

This left me alone with Breaker since Ash was technically the heir to our family and had ridden ahead by himself.

The fact that he was even able to sit in an SUV by himself without anyone to travel to Claire's funeral showed how strong he was and what he was capable of.

I scooted across the black leather seat and stared straight ahead as Breaker got in next to me and slammed the door. "You can go."

The car immediately moved.

Techno music was playing in the background, making my stomach roll with nausea. That was always a trigger these days since that was what had been playing when I got kidnapped.

"Change the station, please," Breaker said in a clipped voice.

I peered up at him. "Thanks."

His jaw flexed like he was gritting his teeth. "You're welcome."

Maybe it was the funeral.

The utter sadness I felt for my brother.

Or my broken heart shrieking in pain, dying to be noticed or fixed by the only person it recognized who had the ability to do just that.

"Breaker?"

"What?"

I scooted closer.

His chest rose and fell in a fast cadence as he sucked in breaths and released them, his green eyes locked onto mine.

"Do you hate me?"

He flinched. "No, Violet, I could never hate you. Why would you think that?"

"Because—" God, why was I starting to cry? "You aren't the same, and I know I'm not the same. Is it me? Did I do this to us? Did I mess up somehow and make it so that—"

"Shhhh…" He used his thumbs to wipe the tears from my cheeks. "You're going to ruin your makeup, and I know how much that pisses you off."

"I don't care about my stupid makeup!"

His lips pressed into a small smile. "Says the girl who lost her damn mind when her new eyeshadow palette broke as if she can't afford a new one."

"There was a discontinued color in that one, and you know it," I grumbled.

"Sure." He smirked. "All right."

"Don't be an ass." I glared.

"But it suits me so well." His eyes lowered to my mouth and then back up.

And then suddenly, it was all I could think about.

Kissing him.

Losing myself in him.

Breaking the one rule our parents made for us when we were young.

No dating within the Family.

And definitely no sex.

I wanted to break both of them. Repeatedly.

With him.

It wasn't like Serena and Junior were doing a great job of hiding all the sex they were having!

"What are you thinking?" Breaker asked. His lips looked delicious, plump, and I knew that Breaker was rumored to be not just incredible, but addicting in a way that made many a woman lose their heads.

I ran a few fingers through his messy hair, my nails scraping lightly against his skull.

He moaned as his head lulled forward. "If you're trying to seduce me, it's working."

"Good," I whispered.

His head shot back up. "What?"

"Wow, is that all I needed to do to get you to smile at me again?" I wondered out loud at his bright, happy expression.

"No. Yes." He seemed confused by his own feelings, and like flipping a switch, he jerked away from me, his expression dark. "It's—we... shouldn't. There are rules, you know?"

"Rules?" I wasn't giving up. "Trust me, I know all about the rules, all of us do, but I'm sick of it, I'm sick of all of this." I willed him to look at me, but he kept his face averted. "And I know you are too."

"I'm doing my job." He repeated it to me, maybe more so to himself.

Fine, I could do this, I could take things into my own hands—literally. I just needed a bit more courage.

Where was Serena when I needed her? She was the bloodthirsty one who had no qualms about punching Junior in the face one second then sucking him off the next.

I swear fighting was their foreplay.

I pretended to look out the window, took a deep breath,

and then without giving any more thought to it, placed my hand on his thigh and squeezed.

His eyes widened, and then he ground his teeth and looked away.

The minute we stopped at the stop sign, I hiked up my skirt and straddled him, shoving away any sort of protests with a heated kiss.

He went from being as still as a statue.

To being even harder than one as his hands dug into my hair and pulled, pulled my face against his as he deepened the kiss with a hunger that matched mine in its terror.

I cupped his cheeks, trying to keep his face in place as I kissed him harder, but he yanked me back by the hair and started kissing down my neck into the cleavage of my tight dress.

With a growl, he was licking the skin there and then cupping one breast while keeping his hold on my hair painfully tight.

"You need this?" he rasped, biting the sensitive skin he'd just licked.

"Yes." I clenched my thighs around his body.

His assault didn't end there. He kissed every exposed inch of me, finding his way back up to my mouth in a painful crush. Nerve endings pulsed and exploded over and over again with each sensation, each touch.

He was fire.

I was ice.

"Ahem." A throat cleared. "We're here."

Disappointed, I pulled back, startled to see Breaker's hardened gaze stare past me.

"How much time do we have?"

"Fifteen minutes."

That hard stare turned determined as he slowly pulled his hands away from me, righted my hair, wiped lipstick off his mouth, and then grabbed me by the hand. "Let's go, we only have fifteen minutes."

"Go?" I grabbed my purse and followed him out of the car, tugging my skirt in the process.

We sprinted up the cement cathedral stairs. I had no time to take in the massiveness of the church I grew up attending or the somber feeling that hit me in the chest, knowing that this time I was going for a reason that should never exist in the first place.

An innocent life taken.

Breaker jerked me toward the women's restroom and shut the door behind us.

The place I'd been baptized.

The place I'd come to worship.

And now the place I would sin.

We went into the first stall, and then he was kissing me again, lifting my skirt up past my hips, and I was letting him, letting him do it, begging him for it because the only other time I'd ever done this hadn't exactly been on my terms.

And it hadn't been him.

His mouth moved down my neck as his teeth grazed right where my pulse went wild. My hips bucked beneath his touch as he gripped my ass and then pulled my legs up around his waist.

"You still want this?" he murmured against my mouth, his lips wet from my tongue, his breathing ragged.

"I want this." And to prove it, I tugged his head back down and domineered that full, lush mouth of his, taking my time sucking on each lip before tasting him; there was something vaguely familiar about his kiss. Something in the deepest recess of my mind took me back to that day—that night, maybe because he'd tried to kiss away the tears.

And replace the memories.

But magic didn't exist in our world.

And no matter how many pretty words or distracting stories he sent my way—it had still happened.

At least I gave permission.

That didn't make it rape, right?

I had to tell myself that it didn't, because, in the end, I was in control, right?

Right?

"What's wrong?" Breaker broke our kiss.

Our chests heaved as I slowly looked up. My own breathing was so erratic I had to suck in another breath before I answered. "I'm fine."

Slowly he pulled one hand from my hip and swiped it under my right eye, showing me that it was wet with a tear, which only made my eyes fill up more as he started to ease away.

"No!" I was frantic, grabbing at his jacket, then at his shoulders, then locking my legs around his hips. "Please, Breaker, please!"

His eyes were wild. "You don't know what you're asking—"

I kissed away whatever else he was going to say as I undid the front button of his slacks, shoving them and his briefs down in one swoop.

His forehead pressed against mine, a sigh escaped his full lips, the bow on top was slightly swollen from all my sucking, making me just want to suck it more, to feel his hot mouth pressed against mine in so many wicked, sinful ways that I was sick with him, like a poison in my blood that caused a fever I never wanted to break.

Then again, his name was Breaker, right?

"Vi—" He gasped in an agitated breath. His green eyes glinted with a crazed expression. "I think that—"

"Stop thinking, thinking is bad when you want something selfish, let me be selfish, please? Plus, I know how you look at me…"

He swallowed slowly and looked away, asking, "How's that?"

I cupped his cheeks with my hands. "Like you want me to stay but need me to go."

His mouth attacked mine then, earning a groan from me as he ripped off the last barrier keeping us apart, a thin thong that found itself dangling from one ankle as he braced himself at my entrance.

"Look at me," he whispered.

It was impossible not to.

He was beautiful.

All aristocratic lines with wide full lips and eyes I could drown in.

"Look at me," he said again. "While I give you everything I can… and maybe, one day, this will take a bit of that moment away and replace it with something else, something you deserve even if I know it's not me."

I didn't have a chance to ask why as he slowly thrust in, sliding so easily inside me that I wondered how he fit and how it felt so amazing.

He moved his hips around, making me reach for his hair holding on for dear life as my body exploded with pleasure.

His mouth met my neck again like he needed to use his teeth and hands to hold on to my squirming, or maybe he just wanted to mark me the way I wanted to mark him?

Pleasure exploded as he thrust deep and then just stayed there, pulsing hard inside me while I clenched around him like I was afraid to let go too soon.

"It's me, you, it's us," he whispered as his lips slid back up and claimed my mouth in a kiss that set my world on fire as I clung to his shoulders while he deepened his movements.

"You're close…" he rasped.

I nodded frantically. "Yeah, yeah, I am."

"Look at me."

Our foreheads touched, and I watched Breaker Campisi love me; I watched him re-break me and hold me in his arms. I watched… and I felt reborn.

All because he'd said yes.

Maybe this holy moment was ordained.

It felt that way as my body soared higher and higher then let go as he shuddered inside me.

Chest heaving, I cupped his strong jaw with my fingertips and pressed a chaste kiss to his cheek. "You're one of the best friends I've ever had."

His eyes filled with tears, his jaw ticked like he was clenching it, and then he was pulling out and whispering in a shaky voice, "Vi, you're my everything. I hope you know that."

"Then stop." I slid down the wall and picked up my thong while he grabbed a tissue and ran it up my thighs without even saying anything. "Stop." I grabbed his wrist after he threw the used tissue in the toilet.

"Stop what?" He was shaking. Why the hell was Breaker, of all people, shaking?

"Stop giving me only the protective parts of you, the ones that act more like guardian than lover or friend."

He hung his head. "If you knew…"

"I do know." I smacked him in the arm.

"Ouch! What the hell, Vi?"

"Listen, I'm serious here, Breaker. I know what happened, I was there! But if I can move on, so should you. So what, you couldn't protect me one time? Your job on this earth isn't to be the bulletproof glass. Most days, I'd just prefer the ride or die."

He smirked. "Ride or die? You mean that as in—"

I rolled my eyes. "Men are impossible."

"We really are, you should know this by now, Abandonato."

I poked him in the chest. "Look, thanks for the great sex, but you know there's more here, and I'm not stupid, so if you want to start not being a giant asshole… I'll be in my room tonight, the code's 666."

He groaned into his hands. "Great, so your father's going to kill me after I type in the devil's numbers? The hell, Vi!"

I just shrugged. "Grow a pair, Campisi, or I'll find someone else who can."

He grabbed me by the arm and spun me around, pinning me against the stall again. "Do it, and I'll chop his balls off and feed them to Sergio's cow."

"Sergio still has that thing?"

"I'm glad that's what you're concerned about, the grandma cow that literally sleeps standing up and has been on her last leg for about a decade."

"She's sweet!"

"She chased me last year and made King cry!"

I laughed. "Weird, he's terrifying, and yet cows make him run."

"According to him, the mooing is a satanic chant."

I threw my arms around Breaker's neck, earning a smirk from him, one that I felt all the way down to my tall black heels. "Tonight?"

He grumbled a curse. "If he has me at gunpoint, I expect you to explain to the senator that I was only answering a siren's call, okay?"

I frowned. "He would never believe it."

Breaker eyed me up and down. "You know? I wish you could see yourself how I see you, all innocent, wicked perfection wrapped up in a package that I just want to rip open with my teeth and pleasure you inside out and then do it again. Then maybe you'd understand why your dad's been so fucking territorial and protective of you."

My cheeks heated. "It's because of his reputation—"

"No." He put a finger to my lips. "It's because you're irresistible and every sane man's kryptonite, hell, even the crazy ones."

"I don't want crazy, I just want you..."

"I'm not... good." He frowned and looked away.

"Holy shit, did you just quote Jacob from Twilight?"

He glared. "Speak of this again, and I'm choking you."

I rolled my eyes again. "Please, you'd probably like that too."

"Son of a bitch." He wiped down his face. "What the hell am I supposed to do with you?"

"Welllll..." I checked my watch and winked. "You have exactly three hours to figure that out, don't you?"

He blew out an exasperated breath. "Not sure if I should spank you or thank you."

"You can do both..." I blew him an air kiss. "You have

three hours to decide." I reached to open the stall door just as he put a hand over my fingertips. "Yes?"

"Does this offer have an expiration date?"

"What a great idea." I jerked away from his hand. "It does now."

"But—"

"Hey, we gotta go; we only had fifteen minutes."

"Vi, I don't think—"

"See ya!"

I adjusted my dress as I stepped out of the stall and nearly had a heart attack when Breaker's hand snaked out to snatch mine. He turned me around and pressed a heated kiss to my mouth that I hope translated into the word *"tonight."*

He pulled away abruptly with a smile on his face.

One I hadn't been privy to since last Christmas.

My first real Breaker smile.

His smile was bright like the sun, and beneath it, I felt nothing but warmth and security as he slowly started buttoning his shirt back up.

Movement caught out of the corner of my eyes. I whipped my head to the right just in time to see Junior wrap his arm around Ash and lead him into the church.

I exhaled in relief.

"You ready, Abandonato?" Breaker offered his arm.

I swallowed the ever-present ball in my throat. "Not ever."

"Shall I distract you?"

I snorted. "Watch it, or I'm going to start calling you Cocky Campisi."

His dark chuckle wrapped around me even though he was barely touching me as we walked arm in arm into the church to join the Families.

"Admit it." His voice lowered to a whisper. "It does have a ring to it. Plus, better you think about tonight than right now."

"Impossible." My eyes welled with tears. "Look at us."

He followed the direction of my stare.

Ash was trembling next to Junior, who was trying his best to keep his expression neutral, but every time Serena glanced at him, you could practically see the guy grab a knife, cut open his own chest, and offer his heart to her, with every stolen glance, every breath, and then there was my little sister, Izzy as she stole looks at Maksim, who was doing his best to burn a hole through the back of the church pew while his dad sat next to him.

"Shit, we're a mess." Breaker agreed. "Maybe this isn't—"

"Finish that sentence, and I'm going to find the first random stranger who smiles at me and invite him into my bed."

Suddenly Breaker's hand gripped my arm, tight enough to cause a stinging pain as we stopped walking. "One day, you'll realize how dangerous your threats are… one day, I may not stop myself." He released my arm, his eyes burned with fury as he waited for me to say something.

But I had nothing.

Because I liked the darkness that swirled behind his emerald eyes.

And one day, I would do more than push him over the edge.

I'd give him a shove and jump after him into the oblivion—and I'd worship at the feet of the fallen.

CHAPTER
Four

The fault must partly have been in me.
The bird was not to blame for his key.
—Robert Frost

Breaker

Claire's funeral was heavy with a sadness felt in the soul—it hurt to breathe, my lungs burned with the need to inhale more air, but every single time I tried, I imagined myself in Ash's position.

Standing up at that pulpit.

Destroyed.

Lost.

Un-fucking-repairable.

How easily our spots could have been switched. And the only people who knew were the ones who kept my secrets safe.

Phoenix Nicolasi, who was currently watching me like a hawk—for good reason.

And Andrei Sinacore-Petrov, who cheerfully sat directly

to my left with his wife and Maksim. Every few seconds, I saw the glint of the knife shoved down around his ankle as he purposely crossed his legs.

Message received, dick.

Ash's voice rasped as he continued the Eulogy. "All it takes is one second, and life can get ripped from you. I actually had a fight with Claire that morning. She wanted to go shopping, and I wanted to send security with her. She finally…"

His voice trailed off as I squeezed my eyes shut and tried to think about anything but that night.

"You have a choice," Andrei whispered as I watched the leering fifty-year-old looking man shrug out of his black leather jacket and grin at one of the idiots spouting off insults in Russian about how tight her body would be, how it was an honor…

"I don't," I hissed through my teeth.

"We always do. The choice will always be yours." Andrei put his hand on my shoulder and squeezed.

"And her?" I grit my teeth as her body slumped against one of the Russians. He was petting her hair, and I was seconds away from cutting every single one of his fingers off. "What about her choice?"

"Who do you think she would prefer, that piece of shit, or someone she sometimes tolerates?"

I snorted and felt my entire body go rigid. "I don't know how to do this, Andrei, I can't separate the man I am, and the man you need me to become to make this choice."

"I never said you had to pick one or the other—you've always been both."

"It's heavy, that moment when you realize your life isn't ever going to be the same," Ash continued. "When you realize your love created a life you'll never get the chance to see." A hush fell over the room. "She was pregnant. And we were still trying to figure out how to navigate this world, we were shaken with the brutal truth that bringing up kids in this atmosphere is anything but easy, anything but innocent, and we were broken with the absolutely horrifying idea that we would fail, but she reminded me, in a time when I desperately needed it, that our parents succeeded. They raised up a generation of warriors, of mafia royalty that would forever protect their blood until their last breath. She reminded me who I was."

My heart hammered against my chest; could they see? Could they tell? Could they smell my blood in the air? All of the mafia royalty around me with their perfect bloodlines? Resentment started to ooze into every pore of my body. Resentment for who they were, who she was, and who I was.

I didn't belong in this seat.

I didn't belong in this world.

I was meant to rule another.

And yet, there I sat.

With the Italian family I loved.

And another family I swore to die for.

I lowered my head as cold fury pulsed through my veins, because tonight I wouldn't be able to help myself, would I?

And eventually, they would all know my sins.

I'd have no choice but to confess them and do what my namesake said… *Break her*.

Break them all.

I was the snake in the garden.

I should have never dangled the apple.

Because now the one responsible was as equally damned.

"Blood in. No out… except death," Ash said.

It reverberated in my soul as my very short life flashed before my eyes, and then I saw Violet turn around and look at me as I whispered back with the congregation. "Blood in." I licked my lips and watched her eyes fill with tears. "No out."

One spilled over Violet's cheek.

I gripped the pew in front of me to keep myself from jumping over all the rows between us and pulling her into my arms—a liar's arms.

But a rustle of whispers interrupted what would be my own suicide as I frowned and looked around.

Andrei gripped me by the wrist like he knew I would come to Junior's defense as he very slowly moved toward Serena and rather than sit with his own family—something that even the most rebellious of us never even attempted—nodded his chin down at Nixon in pure defiance, moved down the pew grabbed Serena's hand, kissed it, and sat down.

He'd boldly just chosen the Abandonato heir in front of the Five Families, in front of our enemies, the De Langes.

But most importantly, she'd chosen him.

And they had done it on holy ground.

In front of the priest.

In front of God.

Junior, one of my best friends, had singlehandedly signed his own death sentence, and I'd never seen him look so relieved.

I was sick with jealousy over his boldness.

King tensed on the other side of me and whispered under his breath, "We have to do something."

"Shh!" Dad snapped from his other side. "He's made his choice. Now, he deals with the consequences."

I let out a snort. "Yes, God forbid we actually have hearts

that can't help but beat for each other—even in death, his choice was still his." I stood and walked past Andrei and was glad when I saw Ash get up and do the same thing until all the kids exited the church, together, united.

A family within a Family.

"I'm gonna take Serena home," Junior said once we were all on the church steps staring at him like he was already dead like we were already planning his funeral after finishing this one.

He might as well have been a ghost.

A walking corpse.

And Serena along with him.

"We can fix this," was my answer as my brain tried to conjure up every different scenario that led back to the house, back to the reckoning both Junior and Serena would face for breaking the one rule we had sworn in blood we would never break. Hooking up with each other. No messing around within the Five Families; it caused too much drama, too much jealousy, too much distraction. "Right? We can do something."

Ash's expression was hollow, his skin tone pale. "I'll think…"

"Oh good, Ash is going to think!" I roared. "Thinking isn't going to save his ass!"

Maksim's sharp blue eyes narrowed in on me. "If I didn't know any better, I'd say you're more freaked out than Junior. Any reason for that?"

Brilliant bastard. I hated him for seeing everything. "No," I lied. "But I kind of want to avoid more bloodshed. It is a Sunday."

"Actually, it's Monday," Maksim corrected with an arrogant tilt of his lips. He was lucky we were on holy ground—I was seconds away from aiming my gun at his kneecap and pulling the trigger.

"I'm hungry." King kicked one of the steps and yawned like we weren't in yet another life and death scenario.

I shot him an incredulous look. "Are you serious right now? Junior's about to drive his own funeral procession toward the house, and you're worried about your stomach?"

He just shrugged. "It'll work out."

Naive. Sometimes he was so naive.

I ran my hands through my hair and threw my arms up at Ash. "So, anything?"

His eyes narrowed. "Yeah, Maksim's right… what are you hiding?"

"How the hell is this about me now?" I wondered out loud while Junior jerked his head for me to follow them.

He'd driven to the church in his black Maserati; it was parked near a tree I used to climb in the park next door to the church.

Hell, was I ever that young?

"I'll wait in the car." Serena swiped at the moisture beneath her eyes and flashed us both a confident smile that I wish I could believe.

Once the door slammed behind her, Junior's teal-colored gaze locked with mine.

I lifted my chin and stared right back.

"You're shaking," he pointed out.

I noticed the tremble in his right hand. "So are you."

"So either we're both addicts…" He released a hollow-sounding laugh.

And then I cracked, lunging at him, ready to fight because

it felt so much better than this sick feeling in my soul that told me everything was about to come crashing down around us.

Because I was the spare.

And if something happened to Junior—the spare would be needed.

Since I was adopted, I was the Capo's spare.

I would take his place.

A place I didn't deserve.

A place I didn't want.

A place that would expose every sin committed before I was ever even able to ask for forgiveness or to confess to the one girl who held my heart.

He let me hit him in the chin, then ducked my next sloppy blow and pulled me against his chest. "It's going to be okay."

I hugged him back, not sure if I wanted to beat the shit out of him or cry. "You don't know that."

"This isn't about me… is it?"

"I—"

We released each other.

He loosened his tie and pulled it off, then leaned against the car, not making eye contact as he asked, "Is it love?"

I squeezed my eyes shut as the feel of her mouth against mine, my hands in her hair filled my head until I couldn't even think straight.

Junior just patted me on the shoulder, then pulled open his car door and got in.

"So, that's it?" I asked once the window came down. "You just get in the car and drive toward certain doom?"

"You forget one small detail," He reached over and grabbed Serena's hand. "Sometimes, all you can do is drive, Breaker, even if all roads lead to hell, I have my heaven, my heart, right by my side… the question is, do you?"

He pulled off, then, leaving me in a cloud of dust.

More confused than ever as I slowly walked back toward the waiting SUV, with the Abandonato princess inside.

Taking a calming breath, I crawled in and rasped, "Drive."

"Ash will figure it out," Violet said as she wrung her hands together in her lap. "He always does."

Ash, our leader of the younger generation, was my king, and I was more peasant than prince.

"Yeah," I agreed. "He'll figure it out."

The drive back to the house was as silent as looming death. And when we finally made it there, most of the bosses were outside waiting, my dad included.

I helped Violet out of the SUV and escorted her past her father.

"Violet, go inside. Breaker, a word," Chase said through clenched teeth.

I could tell Violet was ready to defy him, so I gave her a little shove past him in hopes she'd get the message. The last thing we needed was for them to find out we had sex minutes before the funeral—in the church restroom.

Or that I still had his daughter's flavor on my tongue and wanted nothing more than to tell him how good it tasted when his daughter came undone just so I could pick a fight, just so he could hit the fear out of me, the pain, and the looming dread of losing her before I even had her.

Shit.

Did he know?

I stopped and crossed my arms.

"Give me your eyes," he snapped in a harsh voice that

demanded respect even though I wanted to knee him in the balls and hold a knife to his throat.

Slowly, I pulled off my Ray-Bans and gave him a cold, unfeeling stare back, one I'd never given any of the bosses because it required something Breaker'd never had.

Defiance.

Arrogance.

Emptiness.

Abandonment.

The mask fell for one brief moment as the wind picked up around us like the universe was trying to give them a warning while welcoming me back into the darkness.

Andrei started making his way toward us.

"Better?" I said in a hollow voice. "Or do you want a kidney too?"

His blue eyes flickered. "You've protected my daughter since you could walk—don't make me regret it by putting you in a wheelchair."

I rolled my eyes. "You've got nothing to worry about. I'm not into spoiled princesses, and even if I was, I highly doubt she'd satisfy how dirty I would want to get."

"Breaker," Andrei said my name like a warning.

Chase was fuming.

I patted him twice on the shoulder. "Chill out, old man, we don't want our favorite senator having a stroke at forty-four."

He lunged, but I jerked back just in time.

And then he forgot all about me because the sound of the gates opening again announced Junior and Serena.

Without looking back, I made my way into the kitchen, my eyes searching for Violet.

She shot me a pleading look.

I didn't know what to do.

I couldn't pull her into my arms.

And I couldn't push her away for her own good.

So I just stood there, like a powerless idiot, while chaos raged around me. Fists were thrown the minute Junior and Serena made it inside.

Nixon was yelling for Serena to choose.

And a cold feeling settled over me as I watched her pick Junior, as she chose the man she loved, and as Ash gave me a look of horror while we numbly walked them both down to the basement where they would die.

Where their love would die with them as they took their very last breaths.

With each step, I lost a little more of Breaker Campisi. Bitterness pounded inside my skull because how dare they? How fucking dare they tell us who to love? When every other choice had already been taken?

They would take the one thing that might save us from damnation?

My blood roared with the need to spill more, again and again, and then again until my face was wet with it until my nose was numb with the metallic smell.

Hands shaking, I kept walking behind Ash as the rest of the cousins followed, all except the ones too young to see the horrors that Ash would release upon someone who had always been closer than a brother.

Junior Nicolasi.

A king among mortals.

And now he would die.

"This is wrong," Maksim said as Ash started tying both

Junior and Serena to chairs, back to back, first rope, and then chains. "You know it! So stop it! Stop it!"

I had never seen Maksim lose his cool.

There was a first for everything as his chest heaved like he was minutes away from holding a gun to Ash's head, but what he didn't see was that Ash had no choice. If he defied the families, he died, and it was a kindness that he was the one doing this so that the blood wouldn't be on Maksim's hands, or King's, even though I somehow felt like it would still be on mine for not preventing it, for not giving them something else to argue about.

Someone else to kill.

My head shot up.

That was it.

They needed someone else to kill.

Violet grabbed my arm like she could read my mind. I shoved her behind me and shook my head slowly.

"Don't worry," Junior gave me a sad smile. "If it were anyone else, they'd probably just get a warning shot in the leg, nothing fatal."

My eyes narrowed.

He shrugged. "Chase knew anyway—"

"What?" Ash stopped grabbing the chain.

We all lunged forward.

And then Junior slowly locked eyes with me as if to say, *does it really matter, man? I'm in fucking chains.*

"Let's go." My voice was hollow as I ushered the cousins out of the dark room full of death and took my own walk toward hell back up the stairs.

I released Violet's hand and approached the bosses. Nixon

didn't get up; he had his hands on his head. Trace was sobbing next to him, begging him to do something.

My dad, the great Tex Campisi, was pacing a hole through the floor while Phoenix just stared me down across the table like he knew what I was about to do.

"I have something to say." God, they were going to kill me.

Phoenix stood like he was going to jump across the table while Andrei started stalking toward me and then stomping like he was going to knock me out to keep me from talking.

"I'm—"

"You were so easily annoyed by everything, and then I was annoyed you didn't give me any attention even after that time I climbed the tree and threatened to shove you out of it," came Serena's voice over Maksim's phone that he held out in front of him, on speaker.

Junior let out a dark laugh. "Because boys aren't supposed to go, 'By the way you're pretty, whoops don't fall, don't fall!'"

Her laugh was part happy, part devastating, and my chest ached.

"Oh, shit, you were so pissed at me you ran to your dad crying that boys were mean. I'm sure that didn't help my stellar reputation with him."

"It's because I liked you, stupid. And you threatened to kill me!"

"Oh, hell, Serena, it was like maybe five feet."

A few snickers erupted around the group.

"I was short still!"

"And you aren't now?"

"Take it back, you bastard!"

Nixon stood, a ghost of a smile on his face.

"Stop moving!" Junior scolded with a smile in his voice. "And I would take it back like I stole all those kisses."

"Hah, you think you're sly enough to steal them, I gave those freely, willingly the day I told you I loved you."

A few of the moms gasped, while Nixon looked ready to murder Junior all over again.

"Fifteen is too young," Junior confessed softy.

"I argued with you until you finally gave in." She sighed. "You looked over your shoulder for a good year every time we had family dinner. But it didn't matter; you made me yours."

"Yeah." His voice cracked, "Maybe we leave all that part out, so your dad doesn't come back and kill me a second time."

"Let them know," she whispered. "You were so... gentle."

Violet covered her mouth with her hands like she was afraid she was going to scream, and I knew it didn't matter if they saw. But I saw her, I saw the ghosts, I knew the demons.

Hell, I was her demon.

And now I was wiping her tears and holding her close.

I was no saint.

I was the darkness that chased her. I was what haunted her dreams, I was her nightmare, and yet she held me like I was the knight that had ridden in on my white horse—she was right about one thing—the horse was white, but the knight was no servant to the king—he was fallen, and she'd singlehandedly resurrected him, not realizing something was very wrong.

Violet put her face against my chest as hot tears slid down her cheeks and across my button-down shirt.

"You took your time, you kissed my mouth like you worshipped me—you still kiss me that way," Serena confessed.

"Because I do," Junior said in a tender voice I'd never heard him use before. "Because I fucking worship the ground you walk on. Would sacrifice my body just to honor yours."

She sniffled. "And then the great disappointment."

"You mean when Chase found us having sex…"

"Awkward."

All eyes turned to Chase, who just smirked and held his hands up like he was innocent in this entire thing.

"It's not like he watched. I mean, it could be worse. Remember Claire and Ash? He was literally inside her, ass naked while his dad came charging in like a bomb going off."

"What?" Luc, Chase's wife, smacked him in the stomach and somehow lived to tell about it as he pulled her into his arms for a hug.

Serena laughed. "Okay yeah, that's worse."

"So much worse. I mean, have you seen Ash's ass?"

"Um… something you wanna share with the class?" Serena asked.

"I think you know one hundred percent that I'm all man, and I've only ever been yours."

"Despite your attempts to make everyone believe you're a manwhore."

Nixon's eyebrows shot up as he looked at the rest of the cousins. "Is that true?"

"Breaker's the slut, not Junior," King said in a proud voice.

Immediately Violet tensed beneath me.

Great, thrown under the bus by someone I actually liked.

"What?" He frowned. "It's true."

I was tempted to pull away from Violet when Chase sent a glare in my direction that promised all sorts of bloody torture. But she needed me, and God knew I needed her. And I would take as long as she would offer. That's what sinners did when given such a perfect gift. After all, it would be arrogant to turn away something so pure when my dark soul needed it so desperately.

Junior kept talking without realizing what was going on upstairs. "You know I've only ever given myself to you, only you, forever you."

"I shouldn't have—"

"You wanted to make me jealous. That was understandable after the incident."

"Ash turned our love to hate," Serena admitted. "But the thing about love and hate… the pendulum often swings all the way back."

"I couldn't stop my heart from falling, Serena, even now, know that it beats for you, until the very last faint thump against my chest."

Her voice caught on some of the words, and I knew without a doubt she was sobbing quietly, trying to be strong for him, for us, until the bitter end. "I love you so much it hurts."

The line went eerily quiet and then.

"For as long as we both shall live."

"For as long—" she hiccupped "—as we both shall live."

Nixon shot down the stairs along with several of the bosses and wives.

The wait was torture, but then footsteps sounded. And within minutes, everyone was back upstairs, including a very shaky looking Ash, a rarely emotional Nixon, and the happy couple.

It's like the minute the bosses knew that their love was real, that it wasn't just sex but something more, something rare in this life, they saved them.

So why didn't I feel happy? Why wasn't I breathing a sigh of relief?

The clock struck six, an omen perhaps, to say, jokes on you—you're next.

I watched Junior's confession, something that was so dark and hopeless, become redeemed and beautiful.

Even him, my heart beat. *Even one of the worst of us gets his happy ending.*

My heart skyrocketed into a gallop—I should have stopped myself. I should have tamped my feelings down.

Instead… I hoped.

And in that moment, I was able to shove memories of Valerian away with an F U look and embrace my adopted family and the life I'd been given.

Not the legacy I'd left.

Or the lies that stayed as a result.

CHAPTER
Five

Have clapped my hands at him from the door
When it seemed as if I could bear no more.
—Robert Frost

Violet

I ran home to change clothes since everyone had decided to crash at Nixon's again, and lucky me, I'd had my own personal escort who didn't even have to type in 666.

Breaker was back to his quiet, reserved self during the car ride. Then again, after this afternoon, how could any of us feel anything except relief and sadness at the same time?

"Pretty crazy, huh?" I asked. My small talk was the absolute worst, but I wanted to at least hear him do something other than grunt.

"Life is crazy… it makes you want to get high and shoot birds," he grumbled.

"Um, are *you* high?"

He snorted out a laugh. "I wish."

"Breaker?"

"That's my name, isn't it…?" His jaw flexed like he was clenching his teeth. Even in the darkness, I could make out the strong aristocratic nose, high cheekbones, and thick, shiny hair, which was a bit of a mess from him running his hands through it. "Shit."

"Breaker?"

"God, could you just stop saying my name for one second?" he snapped, his green eyes nearly feral as they pinned me in place.

For the first time in a year, I felt actual fear, but it wasn't from the men who had taken me. It was from the one who had saved me, and I couldn't figure out why I suddenly felt like puking, or why he looked so lethal when he was supposed to be the one keeping me safe.

I reached across the leather seat and put my hand on his muscled thigh, my palm pressed against his slacks, feeling the heat from his skin pulse through my body. "Something's wrong… you know you can talk to me, right?"

He hung his head and put his hand on mine. "I'm sorry, it's not you, I'm just—"

"Not good," I joked. "Gonna turn into a werewolf or something? Hope you brought more pants because you're about to just morph right out of those tight slacks you're wearing."

He smiled down at our hands. "First off, I told you what would happen if you mentioned it again, so prepare to fight me off, and for the love of God, get that eager grin off your face before I take my knife to your dress here and slice from slit to neck." He sighed. "Second, you'd know if I was a werewolf."

"Ohhhh right, because in the mafia we're raised to know

the difference between a mere mortal and a wolf, totally." I nodded in mock agreement.

"Ha-ha," He squeezed my hand then lifted it to his mouth. "You'd know because I would have bitten you already... we both know my self-control is at negative ten when it comes to you."

"Wow, negative ten, I had no idea you even knew how to count back that far, Breaker. Just full of surprises."

He nipped at my fingertips, then kissed the palm of my hand and brought it to the side of his face as he sighed and whispered, "You have no idea."

"Are you okay though?" I frowned as he held my hand there, keeping it prisoner as he squeezed his eyes shut like he couldn't bear to look at me.

"I'm tired," he finally said after a few tense seconds. "Just really tired... of everything."

"It's okay to be tired."

"Not when I'm trying to protect you, Vi, never when I'm trying to protect you." He dropped my hand softly and turned to stare out the window, ending the conversation and making me even more worried.

The SUV pulled up to my massive brick mansion. My dad had built it originally for his deceased wife, Mil De Lange. She'd singlehandedly destroyed the De Lange Family by doing a deal with the Petrovs without realizing that Andrei was playing both sides and that he was half Italian, meaning his loyalty was always to us and ours to him.

So when she got greedy and messy.

She was killed.

My dad didn't talk about that night, but the rumors said that her guilt was too great, that she was too wounded, and that at the end, it was Phoenix, her older brother, who had pulled the trigger so my dad wouldn't have to.

Because no matter how much you love someone, a rat is a rat, and you exterminate rats regardless of how much you like to keep company.

I sighed as the driver came around to open my door. Breaker slid out behind me, typing away on his phone like I didn't just have my legs spread for him a few hours ago like we didn't have a moment in the car.

What the hell was wrong with him?

I took two steps and stopped, and he ran into my back. "Vi? What's up? Your own personal werewolf needs something to drink."

"We have company," I whispered in horror as both Phoenix and Andrei got out of the black Denali and stared us down.

"Fuck," Breaker said, radiating instant tension from behind me. "Whatever happens just know—"

"What do you mean, whatever happens?" I hissed. "They're family."

He was being crazy, right?

A side effect of his exhaustion?

Of being a werewolf? I joked to myself to keep from panicking.

Because those two together did not mean happy endings or beginnings. We all knew that.

"Innocent little Violet Abandonato," Breaker sighed. "With her fuck-me heels, white dresses, and incredible smile—you know nothing."

Hurt knifed through me, so sharp it must have shown on my face, but he ignored it, shoving me behind him and approaching both men with confidence in his swagger.

Breaker had always been strikingly beautiful, too pretty for words.

But right now, he seemed like someone else, someone meant for pain, someone who was suffering, or someone who maybe just did a good job handing it out.

I rarely saw that side.

I thought he was protecting me.

Now I wondered if he was just hiding.

"Gentleman." Breaker shoved his hands into his black slacks. "Something you need?"

"More like…" Another person got out of the car. "Someone."

What the hell was going on?

"Violet." Nikolai Blazik, the smartest doctor in the world and the "doctor" for the Russian mafia, gave me a cold smile. "It seems like your number has unfortunately been called up, both of you, in the SUV, now."

"No." Breaker took a step toward him but was held back by Andrei.

"Yes." Nikolai's blue eyes fell a bit as he looked between us. "I'm sorry, but we can't forget that night happened, and because of that night, she's officially betrothed."

"The fuck she is!" Breaker roared. "It wasn't even him!"

"It doesn't matter," Nikolai snapped right back. "An agreement in blood is an agreement till death, and unless you want the world to know your secret…"

"What secret?" I asked in a shaky voice. "What aren't you telling me?"

"Never!" he snapped. "That would be more of a death sentence, and you know it!"

Nikolai shrugged. "That's your choice then?"

"It was my choice then, it's my choice now," Breaker ground out. "Protect her at all costs even if that means I protect her from me."

I let out a little gasp. "Stop being ridiculous. You would never hurt me!"

Andrei and Phoenix shared a look I couldn't decipher before Andrei stepped forward. "You have my word, you'll be safe, we just have a few things to discuss."

"Safe…" I gulped. "Where?"

"Besides," he added with a casual shrug, "it will be quick. It's just an alliance. We've drawn up the contracts, and once the ceremony is done, you can come back and visit. We'll let everyone know you're headed to Seattle for a few months to continue studying beneath Nikolai for pre-med. It's the perfect cover…" He nodded to Phoenix, who opened up a black file and held it out to her.

"Your fiancé."

"I don't understand." My hands shook as I accepted the folder. "I'm not marrying anyone!"

"You have no choice," Phoenix said in a sad voice. "We gave you close to a year, but the minute you walked out of that club…" He eyed Breaker briefly before saying. "You leave now to make preparations."

"But—"

"Now and then in a week, we'll host a going away party for the Abandonato Princess," Phoenix said in a voice that meant no arguing, and I stood there, black folder in hand, wondering how my life had spun so out of control, and so incredibly fast.

It was supposed to be that one time.

It was supposed to be okay now.

I was supposed to be safe.

Shaking, I stared down at the blurry photo, which was strange in and of itself. Why would the face be blurred out? My stomach dropped to my knees as I read the small amount of information in front of me.

Valerian Petrov.

Twenty years old.

That was it.

I knew nothing else except for the way his kiss tasted, and how rough his hands were as they pressed me into the bed.

The folder fell from my hands onto the cement.

I wanted to run, but I was paralyzed.

"What if I say no?" I whispered, staring down at the cement by my feet, a chill wracked my body. "What if I run?"

Nikolai was first to answer. "There is no running from this, Violet. For what it's worth, I am sorry. We all are, but it's the only way, and we need to keep the Petrovs in place; Andrei can only do so much here in Chicago. The Family is large enough that they're constantly trying to plan a coup, even with someone like Andrei in charge."

"Right." I licked my lips. "So, I'm going to be the ultimate sacrifice just to keep some greedy old men happy?"

Next to me, Breaker shook, his hands dangled at his sides, his fingers trembling like he was about to ball them into fists and punch someone, or maybe he would just pass out.

The wind picked up, worsening the sickening chill in my heart, sucking out the last pieces of my soul.

Nobody answered.

Which was my answer, wasn't it?

"We all make sacrifices," I said in a hollow voice, "for the Family. I guess this is mine."

"Violet—" Breaker grabbed my hand, but I gently pulled

away and looked up into the eyes of the men who'd sworn to protect me, the ones now handing me over to another Family.

"Anything else? Because I'd like to have some time alone to process." I sounded calm on the outside, but on the inside, I was twisted, a bit broken, and trying to figure out why my chest felt like it had been cracked in half and put back together backward.

"For now, just get in the SUV." Nikolai backed away, and I had no choice but to follow, hands shaking at my sides as a pissed off Breaker got in after me.

The car ride was fast.

And then I was staring up at Nikolai's private jet. "Why are we going now?"

"Because I can't keep you safe anymore here in Chicago, and your family can't know about any of this." He said sadly, his dark brows drawing together. "It looks less suspicious if Breaker's with you—you'll be visiting different Universities under the guise of studying in Seattle, he'll accompany you, and then you'll return decision made, ready to say goodbye to everyone and everything you've ever known."

My throat closed up as I reached for Breaker's hand.

He took mine and squeezed; by the tick in his jaw, I knew he was ready to fight, but I needed him calm because if he wasn't, I was afraid that I would snap, and if I snapped, I might not ever be able to put myself back together again.

"Fine." I licked my dry lips and made my way up the stairs of the G6 gripping Breaker's hand the entire way.

We were, of course, offered champagne once we were on board. I took two glasses, Breaker grabbed the bottle, and without even asking, we moved to the master bedroom.

He closed the door and locked it while I started chugging the champagne like it was water.

When I was done with both glasses, he handed me the bottle, left for a few seconds, and came back with another one of whiskey.

"Ah, starting in on the hard stuff already?" I tried teasing.

He said nothing, just stared down at the bottle in his hands. "This is my fault."

"Breaker, it's not—"

"—it fucking is." He snorted. "I didn't save you, Violet, why am I always too late? Why am I always in the wrong? You know why I've been different since that night?" His emerald green eyes met mine, blazing with fury. "Because I can't fucking look at you without feeling like I failed."

"You didn't fail me."

He opened the bottle and tipped it back, his throat moving making him look powerful, sensual as he drank deep and then wiped the back of his mouth with his hand.

I got up and walked over to him, then very slowly hiked up my skirt and straddled his lap. I gripped his chin with my fingertips and stared into his eyes. He looked so regal sitting there, his jaw tight, his eyes furious as he stared me down. "What do you need, Vi? What can a man like me give you that you don't already have?" He tried to jerk away from my hold, but I wouldn't let him, which just seemed to piss him off more. "Vi—"

I cut off his protest with a kiss.

He gripped my sides, digging his hands into my skin like he wanted to mark me as his tongue clashed with mine. He tasted like whiskey. He tasted like wicked, sweaty nights, and lazy days in bed.

"You can make me forget," I said against his mouth. "And you can make me remember why it's only ever been you."

He sighed, resting his forehead against mine. "We were damned from the start."

Panic rose in my chest. "Let's think about now, not about a week from now."

He picked me up and tossed me onto the bed, then hovered over me, his hair a mess, his eyes practically glowing. "You aren't mine anymore, Vi. Don't you get it?" He looked crazed. "You're not mine!" He jerked away from me then and went over to the wall punching it twice before falling to his knees. "Sleep."

"I can't—not without you," I whispered through the tears that slid down my cheeks. "Please?"

"I won't sleep next to you, Vi, my heart is having trouble processing what my brain is telling it, that no matter what I've always told myself, you've never been mine. If I sleep next to you, I'll want to hold you, I'll want to comfort you, I'll want to mark you, and then I'll make my second mistake when it comes to touching you, I'll wrong you, I'll wrong what you have…"

"Please, Breaker… Please." I broke out into a quiet sob.

He was at my side in an instant.

And what was supposed to be a torturous week of looking at different Seattle colleges and being photographed with Nikolai—went off like lightning.

Before we knew it.

We were landing back in Chicago.

Breaker hadn't as much as looked at me the entire trip. He did, however, manage to plan a going away party for me that night; we had enough time to go to my house to change after the plane landed, and then we were expected back at Nixon's.

My stomach sank.

This was it.

This was my life now.

It was built around lies.

Around a broken heart.

Around a broken Breaker.

Numb, my legs took me down the stairs and into the waiting SUV with Andrei waiting—and in his hands a black box as if to warn us that things could, in fact, get worse. Breaker sat next to me speechless, hard, like a complete stranger. Like he had no choice but to hate because the love was killing him from the inside out.

"I'll pick you up in the morning." Nikolai nodded once we were back at my house. "Pack light."

"Why? Because your G6 is hauling weapons or something and has no space?" Andrei joked.

"Actually. Yes. As you know, ammo is quite heavy." Nikolai examined his fingertips and then reached across the seat and grabbed the black box Andrei had brought into the car. It looked like a sleek tattoo gun.

He motioned for us all to get out of the SUV. Shaking, I did just that while he rummaged with the gun behind me.

Something clicked, making me jump as I took a step back and collided with Breaker.

"Your hand, please." Nikolai held out his palm.

"Why?"

"Breaker, grab her hand, please, the left." Nikolai ignored me, and of course, loyal Breaker grabbed my left hand and placed it in Nikolai's palm. "Don't move."

I was right.

It was a cordless tattoo gun, small, he turned it on, and suddenly needles were diving into my pale skin.

It was over in less than a minute.

Extremely small.

Hardly noticeable.

But I knew what it was the minute I saw the black swirl.

Valerian Petrov had just marked me without even being there—with the mark of a sickle.

The brand of the Petrov's.

I was no longer Violet Abandonato.

I was his.

"You should pack," Breaker said in a wooden voice. "Then, you should probably tell the rest of the cousins how excited you are to be studying in Seattle." He sneered as he paced my room, pulling out luggage and tossing shoes inside without even asking.

His steps were purposeful.

His eyes laser-focused on getting rid of me.

It stung more than I cared to admit.

That my protector, my friend, the guy I'd been half in love with for most of my life, was so easily handing me over to another.

"Breaker, can we talk?"

He breezed right past me toward my dresser. When he jerked open the drawer, he nearly knocked it over with his force. Then he started pulling out T-shirts, a few pairs of jeans.

"Breaker!"

He shoved the drawer shut, the few pictures on top of the dresser fell over and broke, including one of us together last Thanksgiving. It had been my favorite because it was the first time we'd kissed in a while, and that kiss had turned into a bit of a make out session that still made me hot.

"Wow. I take a shower and come out, and God decides to give me my Christmas present early?" He crossed his arms over his muscled chest; he had on low-slung jeans that were still unbuttoned as if he stopped the minute he saw me, and his blue shirt was open, revealing the giant Campisi tattoo on his chest with all its swirling glory. I never stared at it longer than a few seconds mainly because he always gave me shit when I did and because I was afraid I wouldn't be able to look away.

With a groan, I laid back on his bed. "I was trying to find a bed to nap in."

"Hey, I have one of those." He joked.

I smiled despite my need to throttle him; just two days ago, he'd had yet another girl dangling off his arm like a trinket, the jealousy had been unbelievable even though I knew it was impossible, my obsession with him.

My love for my best friend.

I felt the heat from his skin as he laid down on the mattress next to me, grabbing my hand and squeezing it.

We laid like that in silence.

It was what we did.

He let me think since, in a moment of weakness, I'd told him I think better next to him, and he was convinced that his hand holding made me smarter, so there we were.

"Where's Cathy?"

"Cathy?"

"The blonde."

"It's Katy, Abandonato, then again, you knew that." He nudged me with his elbow. "And we had a difference of opinion, so she had to go."

"Oh?" I turned to my side. "And what was that?"

He turned to his then pulled me against his chest. "God, you're so pretty it hurts."

I swallowed the ball of emotion in my throat. "So? What was it this time? She didn't like your shoes? Your muscles are too big? Hates cheese?"

He gasped. "First off, my muscles are perfect, you said so yourself that one time you were moaning in your sleep." I smacked him. "Second, we don't discuss footwear, and third who the hell hates cheese?"

I grinned. "Then, I'm out of ideas."

"Sure." He winked, and then he tilted my chin toward him. "I may have, maybe, accidentally, said your name."

I gave him a shove. "Stop messing with me!"

"No." He scrunched up his nose. "I swear on my life and on King's—I called her Violet, we're lucky I still have working equipment."

"Yes, all those girls are just so damn lucky your dick isn't broken." I sighed and then punched him in the shoulder; he grabbed my hand, rolling me to my back and hovering over me. "Breaker—"

"—just one taste." He lowered his head. "For old times' sake…"

"It's never just one taste with us." I licked my lips anyway, waiting for his kiss, waiting for the moment it would start so I could already panic about when it would end.

"That's the problem," Breaker pressed a soft kiss to my forehead. "I want it all—your dad here yet?"

"No." I wrapped my arms around his neck. "I came early, you know, for my nap."

"Nap my ass," he growled, crushing his mouth to mine as we rolled around his bed. He was so good at kissing it was almost annoying; he led with his lips, not his tongue, so every single kiss felt like a tutorial in how to get a girl to respond. I slid my tongue into his mouth; he smiled against me in triumph, as I grabbed the collar of his shirt and pulled him close.

He was rock hard against my thigh. I grinned and pulled away. "I see all things are in good working order."

"Maybe we should test that theory." He moved his body over mine, creating enough friction that my hips rose without thinking. "Mmmmm," His hands moved my dress up. "Just a little bit of foreplay... a little of this a little of that."

I dug my hands into his hair. "Just a little."

"It's not like we're crossing a line." But even as he said it, we both knew, one day, we would set the line on fire, and there would be no going back.

I don't know how long we kissed, but my mouth was swollen when he finally pulled away and laid onto his back, chest heaving as he whispered, "I wish you were mine to love."

Tears filled my eyes as I reached for his hand and then laid my head on his chest. "I wish you were mine to keep."

"One day, I may just storm the castle, also known as Chase Abadnonato's scary as fuck compound, and make my intentions known, do the whole rock to your window, hold up a boom box, maybe carry a rose in my mouth and declare my desire to court you."

"One day," I whispered. "I may just be waiting at my window for that proposal, but you better bring whiskey."

"My lady wants whiskey?" He grinned over at me.

I rolled my eyes. "No, I meant for all the blunt head trauma the King may just give out to my suitor, but hey, the door prize for winning might be me so… worth it."

"Vi—" he kissed the top of my head "—I would walk through any fire for you, just name the time and place so I can make sure I have my slow-motion hero walk down, deal?"

I laughed. "Deal."

"My blood for yours," he vowed.

"My blood for yours," I whispered back.

"What?" Breaker roared, jolting me back to the present. He was facing away from me, the broken picture forgotten. His hands gripped the dresser until his fingertips turned white. "What do you want to talk about? Because the way I see it, you're leaving. No arguments because Violet Abandonato doesn't argue, she doesn't fight, she just does as she's told like a good little girl—"

I threw a heel at his head without warning. It barely glanced off his shoulder and dropped to the floor.

"The hell!

He spun around in time for my follow-up throw and ducked to the side, but this time I'd been aiming for his dick. It narrowly missed his thigh and landed next to its mate.

Why did I have to be the only one who had bad aim in the entire family?

"Missed." He glared. "Unless you were trying to aim for the dresser. Then—just kidding, you missed that too."

"Ugh!" I stomped my foot. "Why can't you just… I don't know, talk to me! You never talk to me anymore!"

"Because!" he roared. "I can't even *look* at you right now! Is that what you want me to say? That I'm pissed, fucking heartbroken? That I'm terrified and that as much as I want to keep you here, I have no choice but to let you go? What the hell do you want me to say, Vi? That I love you? That I can't live without you? I don't think I'm capable of saying it, because then it's true, then I have to believe it, and then there will be nothing fucking *left* of me!"

Tears slid down my cheeks. "Y-yes. I want you to say all those things, and then I want you to kiss me and tell me everything's going to be okay when we both know it will never be the same."

It took two large strides, and then he was pulling me into his arms, kissing my cheeks, healing my tears.

I pressed my hand against his chest. His heart was racing almost as fast as mine was, and then his mouth was moving down my neck. "I lost you before I even had you."

"You'll always have me, Breaker," I vowed.

He stilled. "No, you belong to another, meaning this will never be the same between us."

"I'll cheat," I whispered against his mouth. "I'll come back to you. I'll never be his."

"Don't." He stopped kissing me and stepped away, his green eyes bright with rage. "Cheating gets you killed."

"Then…" I licked my lips. "Have me one last time. Give me at least that."

His eyes lowered to the tattoo on my left ring finger. "You were his the minute that tattoo was drawn on. Had I known this was going to happen tonight, I would have kicked out the driver, then driven in the opposite direction, maybe even off a cliff, but never toward your house, not with you in the SUV, not with my heart cracking with each breath I take."

"Breaker." I sobbed against his chest. "Please, just one last time, please!"

"You made a vow," he said in a dead voice. "Besides, there's someone else."

"Wh-what?" I jerked back. "You started dating someone in the last week? We've been in Seattle, you jackass! What do you mean there's someone else?"

His eyes were dead. "It was fun, Vi. But we both need to move on."

I reared back and slapped him so hard my palm stung. He didn't react just let me hit him over and over again, and each time he squeezed his eyes shut like he deserved it.

"Enough," he finally said. "You know this is for the best. A clean cut always is; the knife hurts too bad when it's dull, Vi. I don't think I could bear it."

I stumbled away from him, my tears falling in rapid succession as he walked back to my dresser and continued pulling clothes out.

And then, after a few minutes of silently crying, I went to my closet and did exactly as he said.

Maybe it was good I didn't have one last moment in his arms.

Because one moment reminded me of the moments taken from me, a lifetime of smiles from Breaker, a lifetime of kisses.

Stolen by a man I barely knew.

One I hated.

And one... I would try to kill.

Because I wanted Breaker.

And if he wouldn't fight for us. I would.

I'd crawl back to him, not the pure Violet Abandonato he was used to.

I'd come back on my knees in my husband's blood—let *him* be the sacrificial lamb.

It was time for me to be the one holding the knife.

It was time to be made.

CHAPTER
Six

Was there even a cause too lost,
Ever a cause that was lost too long,
Or that showed with the lapse of time to vain
For the generous tears of youth and song?
—Robert Frost

Breaker

I was cheerfully drunk last night, everyone thought it was because of the goodbye party, but it was because I had to say goodbye to my soul.

And now I was nursing the hangover from hell.

Something kicked me… or someone.

"Go away!" I shouted then realized I was literally spooning a bottle of gin in my right hand with a bottle of empty tonic in the other. The hell? Was I just mixing the drink in my mouth all at once?

"Get up." The dark voice of my nightmares wasn't helping.

I opened up one eye then two; Chase was towering over me, looking absolutely terrifying.

I had a nightmare like this once.

It ended with my death.

Huh, how very prophetic of me.

I let out a little laugh then winced as hammers went off in my temples like a friggin' high school marching band drumline.

Good movie, solid drumming.

"Are you seriously still drunk?" Chase asked in an irritated gruff voice that had me wanting to cover my ears with those cute earmuffs Violet wore to New Years two years ago, they were pink, and I remember thinking her cheeks matched the hue and made her look so damn cute I wanted to kiss her nose.

Holy hell.

Yeah, still drunk.

I held up my fingers and made a small motion. "Bit."

He leaned down on his haunches, possibly wrinkling that expensive-looking three-piece suit. Damn… dude even had a pocket kerchief or whatever the hell those were called.

I tugged at the silk kerchief. "Are those red polka dots?"

"Father's Day gift." He gritted his teeth when I burst out laughing.

And then I was getting jerked up by my T-shirt, a rip sounded. "Hey, that's my favorite shirt!"

"Oh, I'm sorry let me give you a minute to take it off before I shove you in the shower."

"Really? That's actually super—"

Chase shoved me into the guest room shower after dragging my ass a few feet down the hall of Nixon's house. An icy deluge struck my face and quickly saturated my clothes.

"Aghhhh, son of a bitch, that's cold!"

"Oh, is it? I couldn't tell." Chase held my body under the freezing spray until I started choking.

"I'm sober, I'm sober!" I yelled, shoving him away from me and leaning my heavy body against the cool tile. "Why the hell are you torturing me?"

"I'm bored." He sighed in agitation.

"You've got to be shitting me." I slumped against the tile even more and blinked up at him. "You're bored, so you want to kill me?"

"Correction, if I wanted to kill you, I'd count to three, watch you run, then fire a few rounds." He shrugged like it was normal to hunt humans and then tossed a towel at me. "Go pack."

I sobered. "Do you know something I don't?"

"She's on a plane right now without your protection. Go pack your shit. I know you were sputtering something about Fall break early last night. Junior, Serena, and Ash are gonna take a later flight out tomorrow; God knows they need a break after everything. You'll stay at one of my guest houses for a few days. Just make sure she's safe, report to me, nobody else, got it?"

"Have you... talked to Phoenix?"

"Yeah, why?" Chase frowned.

Shit on a stick.

"No reason." I sighed. "I'll just be packing then..."

"Glad we have an understanding." He grabbed my shoulder and then whispered, "Hurt one hair on her head or make her cry, and I'm going to rip out your spleen through your tiny dick and feed it to the cows."

"The hell is wrong with everyone feeding things to cows?" I muttered. "You know pigs leave less of a mess, right?"

Chase's face freaking lit up like a Christmas tree. "What a wonderful idea, thanks for the suggestion. Looks like we're buying pigs!"

"We aren't pig people."

"We aren't cow people either," he pointed out, then grabbed his cell and started dialing. "Yeah, Nixon, how do you feel about pigs?"

I was clearly dismissed.

I stumbled down the hall and made my way into the kitchen. Phoenix was sitting there, sipping coffee with Andrei.

What the hell were they now?

A mafia version of Supernatural gone horribly wrong?

"Gentleman," I rasped as I grabbed my keys then thought better of it. "Anyone feel generous enough to give me a ride to my house and sneak me in the back door, so my mom doesn't beat me senseless?"

Phoenix slowly took another sip, making a slurping noise that had me wanting to throw something while Andrei just grabbed a newspaper and opened it.

I sighed. "Look, I'm slightly drunk from last night, and I'd rather not get hit by a road raged soccer mom in her minivan while she belts Post Malone like she too knows pain."

"Love that Post Malone," Phoenix said and then slowly, literally slower than an old man getting out of his seat for Bingo night, he rose to his feet, stretched his arms over his head, and said, "I'll take you. We need to talk anyway."

"Figured that's why you were here in the first place," I grumbled.

"We just like Nixon's coffee best." Andrei shrugged. "Hey, since you're taking him can I have the—"

"Here you go." Phoenix read his mind like a good 1950's wife and handed him the business section. "I'll be back soon."

"I'll be waiting."

"So fucking weird." I shook my head at them. "I don't like you two being friends."

"We aren't friends," they said in unison.

And holy shit! I squinted and scrunched up my nose. Were they wearing the same shirt in different colors?

Before I could comment on it, I was getting shoved—again—toward the door and outside.

My poor shirt wouldn't survive the day if the bosses kept grabbing the top of it and pulling.

Somehow, I made it into the SUV without falling on my face.

And somehow, I didn't puke all over Phoenix's shoes when he started the car and said, "This is what you're going to do…"

CHAPTER
Seven

…Has given my heart
A change of mood
And saved some part
Of a day I had rued.
—Robert Frost

Violet

The plane ride was a blur, as was the weirdly boring experience of watching arms dealers unload the plane and shake Nikolai's hand like it was just a Tuesday.

They didn't even spare me a glance.

Probably because they had no desire to purchase a girl who looked like she'd cried herself to sleep and forgot how to brush her own hair.

I was a mess.

And of course, Seattle decided that rain would only make my misery better. The minute I heard the thunder, I wanted to crawl under the SUV and let it run me over.

I checked my phone again.

Breaker had been a miserable bastard yesterday. He'd broken me in a way only he could—by claiming to love someone else when we both knew it was a lie.

To push me away?

Protect me?

Make this easier on me when we both knew I needed my best friend more than ever?

I swallowed, wishing I could get past the knot of emotion in my throat, and then I sent another text.

> Me: I'm in Seattle. Safe. Also, I saw an arms deal go down and lived to tell about it, figured you'd be proud.

He messaged back right away.

> Breaker of Hearts: Um, Nikolai let you watch? IS HE CRAZY?

"Yes, he is," Nikolai said after looking over at my screen with a grin before going back to whoever he was texting.

> Me: We both know the answer to that question.

I almost typed, I miss you.

But I was too afraid of what he would say back if he even responded.

> Breaker of Hearts: I miss you.

Tears filled my eyes.

> Me: I miss you too. You know I'll be back soon...
>
> Breaker of Hearts: With a ring on your left hand.
>
> Me: It means nothing.
>
> Breaker of Hearts: It will mean everything.

I shook my head.

Me: I'll never love him.

Breaker of Hearts: What if he needs your love more than I do? What would you say to that?

My hands shook.

Me: Impossible. He'll have to find it elsewhere.

Breaker of Hearts: Promise me you'll try. We both know deep, deep, deep, deep, so deep down in the smallest crevice of your soul that you care about things that are broken.

I sighed. He wasn't wrong, but still, this guy was the guy that had taken everything from me and clearly didn't know how to stop taking.

Me: I'll slit his throat before I let him hurt me.

Breaker of Hearts: Killing is harder than you think, Vi, especially your own husband. Maybe watch some Dateline first, yeah?

Me: You could always do it for me?

Breaker of Hearts: You have no idea how much I want to.

I stared down at my phone as the little dots popped up, and then, like a knife getting shoved into my chest only to end with a twist, he typed.

Breaker of Hearts: My blood for yours.

With shaking hands, I typed back.

Breaker of Hearts: My blood for yours.

Why did it feel like the end? I swiped the tears from my cheeks and adjusted my sunglasses.

The SUV pulled up to a gorgeous black iron gate; it opened up toward a sprawling property in front of a huge lake.

The house itself was three stories and reminded me of

something that might be seen in a fairy tale book, with moss and ivy intertwined around white pillars that framed the entrance.

The door was black with iron gated windows.

It was both fairy tale.

And prison.

Two men stood at the entrance, both of them in black suits, both of them wearing nearly identical sunglasses. It was a look I knew well with my dad and his minions.

At least that was familiar.

"Sancto will show you to your room; he takes care of the house and is Valerian's personal assistant."

My mouth dried as an attractive man in his forties skipped down the cement stairs and opened the SUV door.

"Sancto." Nikolai greeted him with a grin. "We were just talking about you."

"All good things, I hope." His smile was wide, white, and he had a small dimple in his chin. His hair was a dark brown and a bit wild, his eyes matched, but they seemed to have flecks of gold in them.

For some reason, I felt immediately safe.

"Ignore him. He's a terrible flirt." Nikolai cleared his throat. "This is Violet Abandonato, soon to be Petrov."

I held out my hand.

He took it and flipped it over, kissing the back side with a warm caress that had me staring at him a bit too long. "I'm your humble servant. It's not every day we meet mafia royalty."

"Oh, no, I'm not—"

"You are," they said in unison.

"Now…" Sancto helped me out of the car. I turned around to see Nikolai staying inside. "Let's get you settled.

Don't worry, he'll be back for the ceremony. By the way, your dress is absolutely stunning. We had it flown in from Russia last night."

"My dress?" Tears burned the back of my eyes when I realized I wouldn't even get to do that, go dress shopping with my mom, invite my friends, not that I really had any outside of the Family, but still. "Th-thank you for doing that."

He snapped his fingers, and one of the men in suits came running, grabbing my bags from the back before I could even say please or thank you.

"Shall we?" Sancto held out his arm.

I looped mine in his and let him walk me toward my future, all thoughts of my past burning in my brain.

Remember Breaker.

Remember him.

Not this new man.

Not this house.

Remember.

The doors opened.

And with dread, I watched as Sancto held his arms out wide and said, "Welcome home."

I nearly passed out when a staff of twenty servants bowed in unison.

And when I looked up, a huge family portrait that had to be decades old was draped in gold in the main room.

It looked familiar.

The man in the picture.

Beneath it, in plated gold, it read, "The Petrov Dynasty."

"You will continue that dynasty," Sancto said with pride. "You will bear children under this name, and we'll once again be proud to be Petrov."

"You aren't proud now?"

His eyes died a bit as he looked down, a muscle twitched in his jaw as he clenched his teeth. "We have much to atone for."

"Like what?"

A clock chimed.

"No time." His easy smile was back as he grabbed my arm again. "Let me show you your room; the stylists are already on their way!"

"Stylists?"

"Of course! Your ceremony is in four hours! Let's go!"

He didn't see the tear that escaped and dripped onto the first stair as he led me up, and he didn't hear my heart scream for Breaker with each step I took away from him.

Nobody heard me.

Not even God.

The only thing I could do was put one foot in front of the other as I nodded when I was supposed to and smiled when it was expected.

I spent my whole life faking that smile.

I just never thought that I would have to use my dad's political training on my wedding day—without him.

Without my cousins.

Without my dad walking me down the aisle, kissing me on the cheek, and threatening the man who put a ring on my finger within an inch of his life.

Missing all of these things didn't just make my stomach hurt, it made me want to hurt whoever was causing this hurt.

But you can't hurt destiny, can you?

Wrong place, wrong time.

That was what had gotten me here, counting each step to my bedroom as Sancto went on and on about the ball.

Wait, the ball?

"Sancto, back up. You said *ball?*"

He stopped and grinned down at me, all white teeth oozing confidence. "Of course, it's tradition. At least we wanted to start one without so much bloodshed, and Valerian is appreciative of his Russian history. He wants to do an old-fashioned, traditional masquerade ball. It also helps that... well..." He looked away. "It's not my story to tell but, know that it helps."

"What does?"

He was silent and then. "A mask... sometimes a mask hides more on the inside than it does on the outside." He cleared his throat. "And here we are!"

Finally.

"Finally!" He echoed my mental sentiment as he rubbed his tanned hands together. "Now, if you need me, I'll be downstairs. I'm sending up champagne—" The doorbell rang so loud I almost covered my ears. "Oh, that's them! Let's get the bride ready!"

He left me standing in an ornate room with a full fireplace on one side, my own deck overlooking whatever lake we were next to, and a bed that could fit a harem.

I gripped my phone in my hand and squeezed. Maybe if I texted Breaker and squeezed hard enough, it would be like holding his hand, maybe if I closed my eyes and imagined his face, it would be his mouth that held mine.

"You broke me first," I whispered into the crisp Seattle air.

Because he had.

And for some strange reason, I wanted the universe to know it.

I would have fought for us.

I would have clawed toward him, covered in my own blood, broken bones protruding from my body, voice gone because it had been screaming for him unceasingly until he came.

But one thing I learned about Breaker. His duty was everything, and he measured things by the worst-case scenario and the best. He must have thought this was the best, even though all I could see was the unhappy ending.

Disney truly had not prepared me for this.

I let out a snort.

Hell, Disney was the opposite of my life.

I gripped one of the bedposts and leaned against it, then looked at the screen on my phone.

I clicked through my pictures until there was one of me and Breaker at New Year's two years ago. He was smiling so big, and he was also trying to steal my earmuffs.

He said we shouldn't have evidence of our kissing because Dante, the Alfero boss, could hack our phones in our sleep, but I hadn't cared.

"Kiss me," I taunted, holding the phone up in selfie mode. "And make it good."

Breaker tugged me against his chest. He brushed my face with one finger, running it from my forehead down to my chin, then tilting my face toward his.

"I'm always good."

"And arrogant. You're always that too."

He bit down on his bottom lip then grazed mine with his teeth. "You like the arrogance, admit it, it gets you off."

I gave him a shove, but he hauled me back into his arms and kissed me senseless until I thought I might actually die with the need to rip his clothes off.

And then when he was done, he grabbed my phone and snapped a photo.

His eyes were closed.

He was kissing my forehead with such tenderness that I had a hard time even looking at the picture without wanting to burst into angry sobs.

"Where are you when I need you most?" I whispered into the silent room. "I would have given you everything…"

"Ready?" A chipper Sancto popped his head in the room. "Because I have an army here." He held out a flute of champagne. "Congratulations are in order, to the future Mrs. Valerian Petrov."

With trembling fingers, I grabbed the glass and held it high with my perfect politician's smile, the one that stole pieces of my soul each time I used it, and said, "Cheers, to my future husband. Valerian. Petrov."

CHAPTER
Eight

He gives his harness bells a shake
To ask if there is some mistake.
The only other sound's the sweep
Of easy wind and downy flake.
—Robert Frost

Breaker

I was too sober.
> And she was a vision.

My eyes burned.

My heart thudded its final beats in my chest as if to say I'm sorry, but we can't take it—it burns.

Fire twisted inside my veins, altering every part of me, creating a monster I hadn't even known was still present after all this time.

It became my worst nightmare as I watched.

I couldn't look away.

Save me, my pulse beat.

Kill me. My heart died.

I'm all that's left... my soul bled.

And nobody was there to pick up the pieces.

Nobody was there to hear my scream.

Nobody was there.

Nobody.

Nobody.

I put my fist in my mouth to keep from losing my sanity from hearing my own perilous scream.

"Take it back," I whispered. "Take it back."

And as she smiled her fake smile at her new kingdom.

I experienced true death.

Because the Violet Abandonato I had sworn to protect—wasn't attending her wedding, but her funeral, because her old self was already dead.

And I was the only one she could blame.

"Forgive me—" I whispered into the cool night air "—for showing you the knight, when the whole time, I was the wolf. Forgive me, God. Forgive me. Amen."

CHAPTE
Nine

Three times I had the lust to kill,
To clutch a throat so young and fair,
And squeeze with all my might until
No breath of being lingered there.
—Robert W. Service

Valerian

I adjusted the red and black mask across my face. It covered everything but the lower part of my mouth and chin. My reflection seemed to stare back at me in a way that made me want to immediately look away. A black hooded robe was pulled up over my head to symbolize the respect and humility I would need to show during the ceremony—after all, it wasn't just a wedding—it was a coronation.

One I had never expected.

At least the robe hid the scars.

Inside and out.

"She's ready," Sancto said, knocking on the door even

though he'd been told numerous times he didn't need to. "And might I say, she's a vision."

"Even if she wasn't…" I whispered to my own reflection. "My love would make it so."

Sancto put a hand across his chest. "See? I always knew you were a romantic, even after that one time where you slit that guy's throat for—"

I shot him a glare through the mirror.

He held up his hands. "Yup, message received, let's head downstairs. The music has started, and Nikolai wants a word."

I kept the bitter laugh in. Of course, Nikolai wanted a word. I was just curious if it was with actual words or knives and his own special shot of drugs that stopped your heart before you even felt the prick of the needle.

This was happening, I thought, as I followed Sancto out of the master bedroom, and then I was counting the slow thuds of my heart as the music filled the massive living room, spilling into the ballroom usually reserved for holidays.

There was a mass of at least a hundred people, mostly mine, dressed in flowing gowns of black and masks of white.

It was their job to look like my servants.

And it was my job to wear the only mask that could be picked out amongst the crowd, all but one.

Violet Abandonato.

Hers was a simple red.

It symbolized her blood joining with mine.

A twinge of horror washed over me as I gripped the stairwell the way I'd done so many times when I was young, when I had zero cares, when I had no idea what this life was and why I was raised like a bastard for a few years and then later, like untouchable royalty.

I could still see the smoke stains on the marble even though they were long gone. I could still hear my mom's screams even though she was buried in the cold hard ground.

And my own screams?

I heard them too.

Over and over on endless repeat, right along with my confessions.

Because, of course, this had to be my fault.

Everything else was.

Glinka, one of my favorite composers, filled the room as I descended.

As they watched in awe.

Because their king was finally returning to his throne.

I held my head high as I walked.

And protected my heart from the curious stares like daggers to my soul. I was not safe here. Then again, with me in the room, neither were they.

"This way…" Sancto took me to the ballroom. I walked down the aisle, my legs filled with lead as people lowered their heads in respect.

And when I reached the Orthodox Priest, he gave me a smile that was so sad, I almost lost my nerve.

Instead, I turned, and I waited for my bride.

Abandonato today and tonight a Petrov.

Forever.

Yet again, ruling both families in a way that was more pure than Andrei himself.

Moonlight flickered into the room as candles seemed to pick up wind that didn't exist inside the house. Typically, the *venchanie* or the crowning wedding took place in the morning, but nobody wanted us to wait. I think they were more afraid we would talk and run in the opposite direction of each other.

Whispers picked up around the room.

And then, there she was.

A strong, unwavering flower holding her head high despite the storm threatening to sink her to the depths of Hell.

We locked eyes, though she could barely see mine as she made her way down the aisle by herself.

My fingers itched to stop the ceremony.

To meet her halfway.

To tell her how damn sorry I was—about everything.

And all the things left unsaid that still needed to be discussed but would forever be a black spot on my heart, my soul.

Her dress was blood-red, with a cape that fell like a veil past her a few feet. Her creamy skin was heaven brought down to earth as her chest rose and fell like the wings of a mockingbird or a maybe a butterfly. Her breathing was erratic, but then again, so was mine.

I held out my hand when she reached me.

And I took it with pride as the Petrov ring pressed against her knuckle, as we knelt in front of the priest and said our vows.

"I, Valerian Petrov," I said in a slight accent that I couldn't help even if I tried out of nerves. "Take Violet Abandonato as my now, my forever, my future, my eternity. With this ring, I thee wed." I slid the heirloom ring onto her left third finger, three karats of blood-red ruby that had been in my family for generations.

"Violet," said the priest, switching to English. "Do you take Valerian Petrov to be your wedded husband…"

I lost all focus when she squeezed my hand, her crystal blue eyes were clear as glass, she shuddered and lowered her head.

I reached my free hand out, palm up, and caught the tear that fell. My heart shook as her lips trembled like she wasn't sure she could say the words, let alone go through with it.

"Be strong," I encouraged in a barely-there whisper.

She swallowed and then looked at me and said, "Yes."

It was all that mattered, her yes.

Because she was mine.

And I was not giving her back.

Not after all this time.

Never.

Mine.

A part of me died while another part was somehow reborn with that stare she gave me.

Slowly she pulled out my ring, it was a simple silver, she slid it past my knuckle onto my finger.

And then it was done, wasn't it?

We were both handed gold wine goblets, and even though she had no idea what was going on, I did.

I wrapped my arm around hers as we did a small circle around the large table in front of the priest, and then I repeated the words that would alter us forever.

"I, Valerian Petrov, take the position as head. I am no longer the tail. I will lead this Family into prosperity with my bride by my side." Cheers erupted as we finished the circle and drank from our goblets.

And without warning, an old gold crown encrusted in rubies was placed on my head, and a smaller version placed on hers.

It was heavier than I remembered.

Older.

"I now pronounce you, man and wife, king and queen!" the priest shouted as everyone shouted back in Russian that I knew Violet wouldn't understand.

"Kiss the bride!" The shouts got louder and louder, some in English most in Russian.

I turned her terrified body toward me and pressed a chaste kiss to her mouth even though I wanted to do more.

My heart fell when she didn't respond.

Then again, what did I expect?

To her, I was a monster.

A liar.

Her husband.

And inside, I was broken beyond repair because, in my heart of hearts, I doubted her kiss would fix this. Instead, the touch of her mouth just reminded me of everything I'd lost over the years.

Including a chance at winning her love.

CHAPTER
Ten

Emotional pain, walks with me through the day, and sleeps with me through the night, leaving me depleted with no strength to fight. Anger for not having the courage to turn things around, keeping me anchored to this remorse, not able to untie the chains and change my course. False pride rules supreme,
always there to whisper in my ear.
Time, wasted and badly spent, lots of hurt, lots to repent.
Solace, please come and calm my soul, for this is what I need to make me whole.
Empathy, what I need is for someone to see, someone to see the real me.
Love with no strings, just giving generously amongst other things.
Words, when used as a weapon can cut like a knife, capable of doing so much damage and take the joy out of life, but softly spoken and softly expressed can bring so much happiness.
—Charlene Valladares

Violet

I never imagined my wedding going this way, holding a rough warm hand while I sipped a shot of vodka and watched people dance in front of us like entertainment in an old royal court.

"You're tired," Valerian said to my right without even turning to look at me and gauge if it was even true.

I swallowed more gross vodka and winced. "I'm fine."

"You hate vodka."

He said it like he was amused.

I sighed. "I prefer wine."

"Italians." He smirked. "Though I tend to agree… vodka seems…" His voice had a small Russian lilt to it, and he only seemed to slip into it when he was amused or emotional. "It seems harsh."

"True." I examined him while he watched everyone dance, sipping his own glass of Vodka like it was water. He was constantly alert, and always in shadows, from his hood to the nearly full mask, all I could see was his mouth. I desperately wanted to see more, to ask all the questions, to demand an apology even though he technically had saved me in the only way he knew how.

By taking me as his own.

"Come on." He stood and helped me from my chair; my dress was so heavy I imagined my neck would be sore from pulling the giant cape and train behind me. "Let's go to bed."

I didn't mean to freeze.

"Not here, *moya lyubov*."

I hesitated then locked onto his vivid green eyes. "What does that mean?"

He hesitated at first and then whispered in a gruff voice, "Mine. My love."

I gulped and reached for his mask. Moving so fast he was a blur, he grabbed my wrists and pulled my hands down to my sides, pinning them there. "Don't you want to get comfortable? Besides, you've hardly eaten a thing. I'll order food up once we're settled in our room."

Had I been walking, I would have tripped.

Our room?

So that wasn't my room?

But ours?

Panic seized my lungs as I walked arm and arm with him, past Nikolai and his wife as they raised their wine glasses to us and smiled like everything had worked out perfectly when clearly it hadn't.

I was the princess, promised the perfect ending only to end up with the wrong person, in the wrong city, in the wrong story altogether!

And now, the man who had taken it all from me would take it again, and again, demand it of his queen as was his right.

I was dying for my phone.

To update Breaker.

To ask why he wasn't here objecting.

To demand he say something—anything.

I even hoped at one point one of the bosses, my dad especially, would barge in and put a stop to it.

But it was hopeless.

Because they had no clue, I was up here getting freaking married instead of studying under Nikolai.

It was a good opportunity, according to my dad, and kept me safe from the De Lange Family, who was still lurking in Chicago with the need for all our heads.

He had no idea that I had exchanged danger for a pit of serpents our family mildly tolerated on a good day.

Valerian led me back into our shared room. I let out a gasp right away. There were candles everywhere; the lights were off so I could barely see anything other than the small flames of all sizes that lined the dresser, the fireplace mantle, and the large framed windows to the west. Even the bathroom had them, all shapes and sizes, several smells that reminded me of the woods and being by a campfire.

Suddenly his hands were on my shoulders as he slowly undid the clasp that held my cape in place. Immediate relief hit me when it dropped to a heavy pool at my feet. Followed by terror and guilt.

Guilt that this was him.

Guilt that he would never have all of me.

And resentment that he'd already taken most.

And finally, terror, that he would take it again and again and again while my heart yearned for someone else.

I inhaled roughly when his hands moved to my shoulders and stayed there, and then he was coming around to face me, his mask still on, as was mine. He tilted my chin up toward him, and then he slowly moved to his knees and held out his arms. "I surrender."

"Wh-what?"

"To my queen," he rasped, his eyes sharp, his breathing labored. "I took what wasn't mine last December. The ending doesn't justify the means, and if I knew this would—" He stopped short. "—It doesn't matter now, but I'm sorry, I'm so fucking sorry that you had to go through that with a stranger." He spat the word like he hated himself. "My only wish is for you to live." His eyes locked onto mine with a laser-like intensity that kept me rooted in place. "I need you to live, and one day, hopefully soon, I want a real smile, one that tells me it's going to be okay, one that says we'll make it through together, hand in hand, side by side. Tell me—" He grabbed my hands and held them firm. "Tell me I'm not too late to ask you this, to give you my soul, to tell you from day one it's always been yours and always will be."

I couldn't breathe.

I couldn't look away either.

His mouth was so full and inviting, and my heart was so confused, so out of place in this foreign house without my friends, cousins, or family around me.

My first instinct was to text Breaker and say help, I had no clue what I was doing, and suddenly all his well-placed insults about being innocent and knowing nothing came flying back into my psyche full force.

I was innocent,

I knew nothing.

He was right.

I was a little girl with matches trying to find out how to stop the blaze I'd started with one fatal blow.

And Valerian Petrov was the fire that continued to burn despite the buckets of tears I cried in a vain attempt to put out the flames.

"Don't cry, not for me." His voice was hoarse as he reached

into his pocket and handed me a silk handkerchief that had a white horse embroidered on it.

I almost dropped it.

"It has no meaning except… a reminder for me, for the rest of the families who align with the Italians, how easy you lose when you look at yourself instead of others."

Wordlessly, I nodded and patted under both my eyes; I should want to ruin my makeup and throw the silk right back at him. Instead, it felt precious, like a gift I didn't deserve, which confused me even more.

Finally, I handed it back to him with trembling hands.

He took it and then very slowly stood and moved to my back where he slowly and what felt like deliberately unbuttoned my dress, his fingers shaking too, each time he grazed my skin.

His knuckles dug into my lower back as he unfastened the final button right where my thong met my corset. And then his fingers lingered there as he shakily drew small circles with one hand near the exposed skin between the two pieces of lingerie.

I stood completely still as he continued to explore, unable to understand my own body's reaction. My head screamed it wasn't Breaker, but my body wanted to be loved, and my heart, as bruised as it was, said, *what could be worse than what we've suffered? Let him heal us. Let him hold us. Let him kiss the tears away.*

God, please, let him kiss the pain away along with the slow burn that was beginning to build between my thighs even though I fought it with every synapse still firing in my head.

My dress suddenly dropped to my feet, nearly coming up to my waist with how stiff it still was.

Valerian held out his hand. I took it and stepped over it, unsure what he was going to do to me next.

I was shocked silent when he brought me over to the bed, opened the giant duvet, and tucked me in. Finally, he removed my mask and set it on the nightstand, touching it with his fingertips like it was precious, all before turning to leave.

"Wait!" I grabbed his wrist, nearly pulling him on top of me. "I thought—that is, I mean I wasn't ready but—"

"You might never be ready," he said simply. "Besides, don't they already have their proof from that night? You're mine. You've been mine for months. Let them talk because right now, my bride needs to sleep. And I think, maybe, she needs to shed a few tears for what could have been."

"I'm not…" My voice wobbled. "I'm not sure what to feel." And then without any warning, I burst into gut-wrenching sobs while he watched.

Without any more words, Valerian sat on the bed, pulled me into his lap, and let me cry, and with each tear shed, I found my old life floating down the river of my grief, going, going, going… gone.

I wasn't her anymore.

I was his.

I was Violet Petrov.

As long as I lived.

This was my life.

I watched in utter sadness as the old me floated away and left me with nothing but the last remnants of my shaky heart, and the grip I had on Valerian's hands as he told me it would be okay.

I just wished I wasn't in love with someone else.

Even then I wished, I had something, anything left, not to give my husband, but to keep me sane.

But Breaker had it all.

And now? I had nothing but a masked man holding me close, telling me lies, and a soul that was crushed beneath the weight of responsibility I had never wanted.

I smiled in the darkness because I had no other choice but to play the part I was born to play.

Happy.

Perfect.

Suffering.

Laughing while I danced with the devil in Hell.

Saving my tears for the shadows.

And praying that whatever came for me—came quick.

CHAPTER
Eleven

War is coming, I can hear it in my heart. Blood will
flow along the grounds of the innocent.
I can't deceive the darkness anymore… I'm letting go,
I'm losing control of myself…
—Author Unknown

Breaker

I'd only ever visited the creepy empty lake house mansion
once, and it was with Junior. We'd played hide and seek
and then told ghost stories. Then again, I had been young and
impressionable—so I believed every word he said.

Which led me to sleep with the lights on when he told me
that ghosts would come out of the fireplace and hover over you
if you snored. He then proceeded to tell me I was a chronic
snoring monster.

Ask me if I slept at all that night.

In the morning, I'd looked so shitty that my mom finally
asked what was wrong, and my only answer was "Junior,"

which just made her nod her head and then pull me in for a hug while Junior smirked over his Cheerios.

I got him back by putting a snake in his bed.

He grabbed a frog.

Suffice it to say, the moms decided they'd finally had enough and forced us to make up. I had a bit of hero worship since he was older, and I'd been so new to the family. But after that day, it was like my initiation was done, and I was part of them, part of something that wasn't a nightmare.

I went out to the balcony and watched as the sun started to rise. The house across the way was massive. I wondered how long it would take me to take the boat across the lake, throw a rock up at her window and beg for her to stay. Creepy enough that I was willing her to just come out of the house and wave.

I took a sip of coffee.

"Found him!" Serena yelled, making me nearly drop my entire cup off the ledge into the fire pit.

"Why are you so loud?" I winced and continued my staring across the way.

"You look like shit." Serena pulled her blond hair back into a ponytail and snapped her bubble gum dangerously close to my face as she examined me from head to toe, her light blue eyes missing nothing. "What aren't you telling us?"

Only everything.

I ignored her and took another sip of coffee. In a leisurely move, she stole the mug right out of my hands and walked off, yelling, "Family meeting!"

I squeezed my eyes shut as footsteps neared.

It was like they had brought everyone from Chicago here to witness my pain, my sadness, the death of my heart.

Ash walked out, stole the mug from Serena, and sipped then spit it out. "Are you trying to poison people?"

"First, that's mine," I hissed. "Second, I like it strong."

He moved to hand it back to me, but Junior grabbed it with a wince. I wasn't the only one who looked like shit; he'd been on the receiving end of Nixon's fists a day ago, his face was one giant bruise.

"Great, now that you've all infected my coffee, is there something you needed?"

They had landed last night, so by the time I was done with my midnight walk, feeling sorry for myself, and trying to figure out what to do next, they were already making noise and asking why I was going to bed when we were actually given a bit of freedom and a nice little vacation away from the parents.

I had nothing to say to that.

"Something's wrong with him." Junior squinted his teal eyes at me while Serena wrapped an arm around him; at least it looked like he squinted, kinda hard to tell what with all the bruising.

They were happy.

They were together.

Which just reminded me that I was alone.

Sipping crap coffee.

Staring.

"That's what I said," Serena agreed.

King strolled out to join us, followed by Maksim and Izzy; I was surprised the bosses let Maksim come since he was double majoring as a sophomore.

"Young one, don't you have homework?" I pointed out, earning a middle finger from Maksim, who pulled out a chair, lay back, and sighed while Izzy handed him a bottle of water like she was his servant.

I snorted.

Ash stared right through me then suddenly spoke up. "Let's go for a drive."

"I don't want to go for a drive."

He grinned. "Sure, you do. Did I forget to mention that wasn't a request?"

"Remind me again why we voted you for our leader?"

Junior stood next to him. "He has dark circles under his eyes."

"And he's not smiling. He's always smiling, even when he's in trouble, he's smiling," Ash agreed.

"Why does this feel like an intervention?" I wanted to kick something, shoot something, do anything except for talk about my feelings.

"It's about Violet." Izzy perked up. "She was upset too before she came up here. It doesn't make sense, she doesn't even like Seattle."

I flinched.

Ash caught it.

"Car. Now." He shoved me toward the sliding glass door.

Just. Great.

I stomped through the house toward the garage, and since he didn't specify what car, I decided that I needed fast. I climbed into the Lamborghini. If he wanted us to go for a drive, I was going to be the one behind the wheel.

He got in the passenger's seat.

I hit the button for the garage door.

And then we were off.

I didn't remember stoplights.

I didn't remember even getting on the freeway.

And I sure as hell didn't remember driving toward Alki Beach. Once we were parked, I got out of the car, slammed the door, and walked.

I walked until my feet nearly met the edge of the ocean. Then and only then did I inhale and collapse to my knees.

The world could have burned around me.

I would have let it.

And Ash said nothing, maybe because he didn't need to ask about my pain; he recognized it too well. Sometimes words can't describe what we're feeling; sometimes all we have is silence.

And the slow roll of the waves promising that life continued to go on even when you feel like you're standing still.

"Have you seen her?" Ash sat down next to me. Just his presence had me ready to sob like a child. He and Junior had been everything to me.

And now.

Now I would betray them.

At least they would see it like that.

I just hoped to God they would understand why.

I looked down. "I've seen her."

"Was she okay?"

Emotion clogged my throat. "She was breathtaking."

He exhaled like he was relieved. "What did you say to her to make her so upset, Breaker? What did you really do?"

I let out a humorless laugh. "We don't have the years of therapy needed for me to even start to answer that question, man."

"Can you try without a doctor present, or should we go get Nikolai to inject some truth serum into you?"

My head shot up as I gave him a fake look of horror. "That's real?"

He snickered. "Oh, the things I could tell you about that man. You know he's related to Jack the Ripper, right?"

"THE HELL?" I roared, completely distracted, and trying to pretend like it was new news. "The *real* Jack the Ripper?"

"Yup, creepy, I know. Ask him to tell you how he and Maya met. It's some messed up shit. He can also brainwash you to the point where you forget everything or remember it all. He did it to her when she was sixteen. Why else would the Russian Mafia call him The Doctor?" He shuddered. "Thank God he's on our side."

"Yeah…" My stomach rolled. "Good thing…"

"So, Violet… is she really here studying under him?"

I snorted out a laugh. "What do you think?"

"I think you know more than you're saying. I think you slept with my sister and didn't tell me. I think you guys have been acting weird since last Christmas, and I think you're heartbroken."

I was paralyzed in place. "Is this the part where you pull out the needle, inject me with some crazy shit that stops my heart, and say, if I ever touch your sister again, you're going to rip my dick off?"

Ash barked out a laugh. "I'm not my dad."

My eyes narrowed up at him. "No, sometimes I think you're worse."

"Aw…" He put his hand on his chest. "That came from the heart, man, thanks."

Shit, he really was going to kill me. "Seriously, Ash—"

"Do you love her?"

"Does it matter anymore?"

"It does to me. Maybe I can talk to them—"

"She belongs to someone else, Ash. Someone, I don't think you or any of the Family would actually approve of."

He shot to his feet. "Then let's kill the bastard! Problem solved!"

I smiled. "Yeah, that's the problem... we can't."

"Why the hell not? We'll go grab the guys. Hell, we can even grab Serena. God knows she's been itching for a fight ever since Junior told her she had to start being nicer to people during class—long story—even longer plane ride—she made a professor cry. Come on, let's go."

"No, when I say we can't kill him, I mean we can't because, shit, I don't even know how to say this... fuck." I ran my hands through my hair and tugged. "Something happened to her, man, something... bad. That's why she's been different since last Christmas, and because of that, Andrei and Phoenix, they had to honor a blood oath, and it includes her, so no, we can't kill him because killing him would mean war."

Ash paled a bit, then crossed his arms over his chest. His black shirt pulled tight enough that I knew he'd been trying to suppress all his sadness in the weight room for the last two weeks, which only meant he'd gotten more lethal and less emotionally stable.

That made two of us.

"Who else knows about this?" he finally asked. I could tell he was trying to calculate his next move—our next move. But he didn't know. We were already out of time.

At least I was.

"Me." I licked my lips. "Violet, obviously. And them."

"We can fix this." He looked away. "I know we can."

"No, we can't—"

His fist came flying out of nowhere, sending me stumbling into the sand. Another fist hit my stomach.

I shoved him off me and jumped up. "What the hell, Ash!"

"That's for sleeping with my sister!"

"I didn't even confirm it!"

"You didn't deny it either!" He tried hitting me again.

I ducked.

And then we were in an all-out war.

Him, because he needed someone to hit, and he couldn't hit the guy married to Violet.

Me, because I couldn't do anything to stop the tidal wave.

And then him again because you can't keep sadness locked away forever, it's bound to trickle out, demanding to be experienced, demanding to be acknowledged, and Ash hadn't done that.

For the record, neither had I.

So that left us with anger.

Anger was so much easier.

I kicked him in the stomach, sending him sailing back, and grinned when he nearly hit his head on the park bench. "Losing your touch, Ash?"

"Son of a bitch that hurt, you never used to know how to—" His eyes narrowed. "Breaker, where did you learn how to fight like that?"

"Like what?" Anger coursed through my veins. I seethed with the need to see him bleed. It felt good to feel, so damn good. "Like this?" I came at him again, and he managed to block my next few blows.

He spat out blood and tackled me to the ground. I threw him off me with another kick and then winked. "I'm just getting started."

He wiped the blood from his mouth and then made a face. "Yeah, maybe we should finish this at the house before we end up on the news."

Several people were standing on the boardwalk, mouths gaping, eyes wide with shock, phones filming every little thing we did.

My white shirt was torn on the sleeve, and blood trickled from my mouth, probably not the time to call out, *Don't panic, we do this all the time. Oh, and PS, I fucked his sister, so... carry on!*

Ash gave me one more shove. "This isn't done. We're sparring at home; I've never lost a fight to you, not about to start now. Oh also, you slept with my sister. I'm driving."

"Shit, how long are you going to hold this over my head?"

He shot me a bloody grin. "Oh, probably forever."

He wasn't lying.

We stopped by the grocery store.

I paid because I had slept with his sister.

And at Starbucks? I swiped my card because, again, I'd slept with his sister.

When we got back to the house, I wasn't allowed to bandage up because... exactly, I had slept with his sister.

"FAMILY MEETING!" Ash roared once we made it back.

I groaned into my hands.

"No Advil for you." He jabbed a finger in my direction. "Because you—"

"SLEPT WITH YOUR SISTER. I KNOW!" I roared just as everyone came trickling into the living room.

Junior and Serena high fived.

While King gave me a stunned look that silently told me,

That was a horrible idea, do you know how violent Ash is right now?

I held out my bloody hands; CLEARLY, message received.

A fruit roll-up fell from Maksim's mouth as he grinned. "You must have balls of steel to think that was a good idea. So, when's he killing you? I don't want to miss it, and we're out of popcorn."

"I second this." Izzy smiled. "And then it's my turn. How dare you break her heart!"

Oh, innocent little Izzy.

I tilted my head to the side. "For the record, she seduced me."

Ash growled.

"Keep talking. I want to see him take off your head." Maksim literally looked ready to break out into song and dance while King looked worried that I'd actually be headless the rest of my short life.

"Told you he'd freak out when he found out." Serena sighed while Junior looked ready to play referee. I just wasn't sure if it was the kind that would step between us or just blow the whistle and say round two!

"He's still alive." Ash waved me off. "You're welcome, but I need to see something. Junior, hit him."

"The fuck!" I yelled. "What's wrong with you?"

"YOU SLEPT WITH MY SISTER!" he roared. "You get no vote!"

"He's dying today." King made a crossing motion over his chest like he was saying a prayer for my dark soul.

"Definitely," Maksim and Izzy said at the same time.

Junior dropped Serena's hand and approached me.

"Should we at least move the living room table?" I wondered as he stalked toward me.

"No, I vote it stays." Serena grinned at me. "Imagine the slo-mo angle I'll get on the camera when he picks you up and slams you into it."

"Oooooo!" King rubbed his hands together. "Yes, that, do that, Junior!"

"Some brother you are," I grumbled as Junior continued stalking his prey.

Me.

Which meant I actually had to fight.

I was more lover than fighter.

It was all smokescreens.

A part we have to play.

That had been mine.

Until now.

I'd never been interested in fighting the guys, so when we fought, I typically just let them get a few hits in, jabbed, ducked, and then went on my day. Because I was afraid if they saw this, they'd see too much, and if they did...

I'd be a dead man.

Liar.

The voice whispered in my head as Junior lunged for me.

I side-stepped out of his way, letting his momentum take him next to me as I shoved him down and then kneed him in the stomach, before driving my elbow into his back and driving him into the ground.

"Ouch." Serena winced. "Get up, Junior, you're fine. Nice moves, Breaker. Someone drop you in a tank of superhero? Or have you just been holding out on us?"

"Shit." Junior winced from the floor; my hit had opened up a cut on his chin, whoops. "Didn't see that coming."

"Right?" Ash's eyes narrowed as he helped Junior to his feet. "Why hide the fact that you can actually win fights, Breaker?"

I gulped; I hated lying. I hated it. "Because I'd rather make out with your sister than spend all day getting the shit beat out of me?"

"Not good enough," he snapped. "And mention her and you doing anything physical again, and I'm going to pin you under the table and sit on it until I hear each rib crack, mmkay?"

Serena snorted out a laugh. "I always appreciate Ash's imagination."

"Look, I'm telling the truth." Kind of. "Now, I'm starving, and I'm tired of bleeding everywhere. Can we just—"

"It's Violet!" Izzy jumped off the couch. "She's coming over! I told her we were visiting! She's already on her way."

Panic like I'd never known seized my lungs. My muscles locked up, rooting me to the floor.

She frowned.

"What's wrong?" Ash asked.

"Nothing, she just said she has a curfew?"

Paralyzed, I watched them and tried not to give anything away when Ash's gaze fell to me. "You know about this?"

"I know nothing." I held up my hands. "Remember, I'm the heartbroken one."

His gaze flickered away. "Yeah…"

"She's a few minutes out. She has a driver, that's weird." Izzy just kept talking, and I kept drinking in every piece of information like a starved man. Maybe this would work. Maybe it would be okay.

Maybe, just maybe, we could salvage how messed up this had gotten.

Minutes later, Violet was walking into the living room.

And I still hadn't moved from my spot.

I took one look at her smooth skin and haunting eyes.

Maybe not.

Not a chance in hell.

She moved toward me.

Ash stepped in front, blocking her, and then said, "He looks like shit because we fought because you guys slept together. True or false, you seduced him?"

She peered around her brother, sending me a look that made me almost terrified to breathe. "Technically, I seduced him. And…" She faced Ash again. "I'm not sorry."

"No!" He put his hands on her shoulders. "No sex! Ever."

"Holy shit, he sounds like Chase." Junior burst out laughing. "This is the best; he's turning into a dad right in front of us. Quick, man, grab a tie to hang yourself with because bro, you're done for."

Ash ran his hands through his head. "Just—not with him."

I was the him apparently.

"Okay," she whispered. "Deal."

Why did it feel like she just punched me in the gut all over again? This was for the best, remember? She was married, remember? She doesn't belong to Breaker, remember?

It still hurt like hell.

It hurt to breathe.

Being in the same room with her but not able to hold her hand or tell her that I would figure a way to make this right when I couldn't even get myself out of the mess I was in.

"Ordered pizza!" Izzy called out. "Come on, Vi, tell me all about how terrifying it is to study under Nikolai."

"Did you know he's related to Jack the Ripper?" King offered up.

"How was I the only one who didn't know this?" I threw my hands up in the air and nearly took Ash out even though I'd known for years, we all had to keep our secrets.

"Because you slept with my sister," Ash said simply.

"Yeah, he's not letting that go anytime soon," I grumbled. "I'm just gonna go clean up."

I didn't give Violet a second glance when I ran up the stairs and turned on the shower.

Slowly, I peeled my shirt from my body and tossed it in the trash. What was with Abandonatos ruining my shirts lately?

I was already bruising a bit on my right cheek, and my left brow had a cut on it.

I stared at my reflection.

They were right, I really did—

"You look like shit," came her soft voice.

I hung my head as I braced my body against the sink. "You shouldn't be in here."

"I know." Her soft hands came around my stomach as she rested her head against my back. "But I missed you."

I squeezed my eyes shut, barely able to grate out the words, "I missed you more."

I don't know how long we stayed like that, long enough for steam to fill the room, long enough for me to turn her in my arms and press a chaste kiss to each of her eyelids before kissing each cheek and then her nose. "You were beautiful last night."

She gasped. "What?"

"Creepy stalker, party of one." I grinned.

She gave me a little shove as her cheeks went red. "It was… different."

"Promise me something?" I licked my lips, wishing I was licking hers.

"Anything." Her eyes darted from my mouth, locking on mine.

"Forgive me," I whispered. "Promise me you'll forgive me."

"What are you going to do?"

"It's already done," I said. "And one day soon, it will probably come out, and you won't look at me like this anymore, but know that everything I've done, my reason for living, has always been to keep you safe, first and foremost. I would never do something to put you in danger, and confessing it all right now would make you a target. So just… forgive me."

"I forgive you." She said it so innocently, so simply. I wished it was that easy that it erased the darkest parts of my soul.

It didn't.

"You're easy to love, Violet, remember that, remember that tonight." I removed the rest of my clothes and walked into the shower.

She was still standing there when I was finished.

She handed me a towel.

And then she whispered, "Was there really someone else?"

"That you would even believe that…" I sighed. "There will never be anyone else… for as long as I have breath, Violet Abandonato will forever own my soul."

A tear slid down her cheek.

"Give him a chance, Violet. Get to know him, and maybe you'll figure out this mess all on your own."

Her eyes narrowed. "What aren't you saying?"

"You love me?"

"Yes."

"Then, you'll figure it out." I kissed her forehead one last time, feeling the loss in my chest like I just got ran over by a freight train. "Now leave so I can pee in peace; it would ruin our moment."

She rolled her eyes and let out a small laugh. "Pretty sure I've seen all there is to see, Breaker."

"Mmmmm…" I grinned. "Pretty sure you haven't, virgin eyes."

She gave me a shove, and then she was gone.

I slumped against the countertop again and breathed a sigh of relief. I couldn't tell her my secrets.

That didn't mean she couldn't figure them out on her own.

Hopeful for the first time in days, I smiled at my reflection.

It could work.

It had to.

Because she was mine.

CHAPTER
Twelve

I stalk the desolate streets of night, wondering how to turn wrong to right, knowing that I was the one who made the choice doesn't lessen the darkness that hides my voice. I am the demon you know my name, say it three times, then say it again.

—Valerian Petrov

Violet

I had no idea why Sancto had said I had a curfew. It was weird, to say the least. Valerian was gone all day, according to the staff, and I'd been so on edge that when Izzy texted and said they were in Seattle, I'd nearly sprinted out of the house.

Except.

I was a Petrov now.

I had a driver now.

I wasn't allowed anywhere without security.

Valerian's rules.

The only reason they even let me go was because they knew that my family would protect me till the death.

Now that I had returned, the loneliness crept back in. Was this my life now? Just waiting for my husband to come home?

Waiting for him to sleep with me?

I swallowed a gulp of wine and stared at my half-eaten food. I was surrounded by a staff of people, and yet, I'd never felt so alone.

"You should eat," came Valerian's dark voice.

I sighed and looked up, but nobody was there.

And then a hand pressed against my shoulders, I was just about to turn around.

"Don't." He hissed like he was in pain. "Not unless you're ready."

"Ready?" I winced. "For what?"

"Your wedding night."

"So, I can't see your face until I'm completely naked in front of you? Doesn't seem very fair." None of this made sense.

"What if I'm horribly scarred?"

"Are you?"

"Yes."

I sucked in a breath. "I'm so sorry, what happened? And if you don't want me to see you, you could always put on your mask from last night until you think I'm ready.

"Hmmm, beautiful, and smart." His voice was laced with humor. "I'll be right back, eat your vegetables first, and maybe I'll give you more wine."

"Ooo, high-handed, and mysterious."

His laughter had me suddenly relaxing as I turned around to watch his retreating form.

"Knew you'd do that," he called as he took the stairs one at a time.

He was lethal.

And familiar.

He walked like he was a king.

His pants were black, his shirt matching; he clearly had a thing for black. His hair was blonder than I remembered from last night.

So he was blond.

Why did that disappoint me?

I sighed and started eating a few vegetables. By the time he was back, he was still dressed like a king, but this time the top button of his shirt was undone, and he was wearing his mask.

It should look absolutely ridiculous.

But he was so beautiful it didn't.

His eyes were a striking green, brighter than Breaker's in a way that was hard to explain.

Why was I comparing him to Breaker? It was almost unfair. Breaker wasn't scarred, Valerian was.

Valerian had taken something from me.

Something I chose to give to Breaker.

They couldn't be more different.

I sighed in frustration as Valerian rounded the table and grabbed my glass of wine, taking a sip from it before setting it back down with a smirk. "Sorry, I was greedy for your taste and figured it was still on the glass."

"And was it?" I cleared my throat nervously.

"Not enough." His eyes flashed.

I stared at his mouth; I could almost imagine those lips were someone else's… almost.

"You're thinking of him." He said it like a statement.

"No."

"Don't." He reached out and grabbed my hand. He had a sickle tattoo on his left ring finger like I did, only his was larger, more intricate. I wondered why I didn't notice it last night. "Don't lie to me, please."

"Sorry," I whispered and lowered my head.

"Another rule." He tugged me out of my seat and sat then pulled me onto his lap. "This is your kingdom; this is where you rule. You never lower your head to your prince. You are and will always be better than me, understand?"

His fingers trembled as he cupped my chin and then inhaled like he missed my smell when he barely knew me.

"I understand."

"Did you eat your vegetables?" His grin was killing every wall I erected; it was both playful and confident, and sad. Why was he so sad?

I gave my head a shake. "Yeah, I ate some of them. Did you eat?"

"Are we making small talk?" he teased.

I laughed. "The worst small talk ever. Should we move on to the weather?"

"It's sunny," he deadpanned. "And your day, how was that?"

"Lonely," I answered honestly. "And then it got better. My brother and a few cousins are here for a small vacation."

"Ah spies, how nice." He released a soft chuckle.

I rolled my eyes. "They have no need to spy when the Russians are already on our side."

He stilled. "About that…"

"What?" I narrowed my eyes. "Are you about to tell me bad news?"

"Nikolai and Andrei can only keep them in check for

so long, living in Chicago, Violet. I hope you know that, especially with the core of them living here in Seattle."

"I never thought about that, I guess, because Andrei's so terrifying." Had that been the plan all along? Send me here? Pray I fall in love with him? Make me stay?

"I can see the wheels turning," he said with a tender smile. "Let's not solve world hunger right now. Let's just get to know each other. Do you like games?"

"Games? Like board games?"

"No, sexual games where you get tied up and have safe words..." His gentle laugh made my skin tingle. "Yes, board games."

Why did the other games suddenly sound so much better? "Umm."

"That is unless you want me to take off this mask and let me kiss you from head to toe? Because that's my vote. Every second of every day since laying eyes on you."

I frowned. "Even that day?"

He stilled. "Even that day, Violet. I wanted to save you. But I can't lie and say I didn't want you. I wanted you with every cell in my body."

"Did you know this would happen?"

"No." He didn't even hesitate. "Not that it matters, Violet, because it did happen, we saved lives without realizing we were damning our futures."

"I like board games." I changed the subject. "Winner gets to ask twenty questions?"

"Steep." He played with my hair, wrapping it around his right hand the way Breaker used to, then as if realizing he was touching me again, he stopped. "I'll agree to your terms, if and only if I can pick the game."

"Trickery." I pointed at him. "But I accept, as long as I know how to play."

"All right," He helped me off his lap but didn't let go of my hand. I felt my ring press against his fingers and liked it. I liked it a lot but couldn't figure out why.

He led me past the living room and into a large office that I imagined was his. There were no windows, only a huge fireplace on one wall, and another family portrait hanging on the other.

There were burn marks around the picture like the flames had tried to destroy it but couldn't.

"Must have been some fire."

"It would have to be to cause my scarring…" And then he changed the subject. "There it is, the old checkerboard. My mom used to play with me in here before…"

"Before what?" I sat down on the plush brown leather couch while he pulled the table over to us and set the game on top.

"Red or black?"

"Red."

He seemed to like that answer as he gave me the red checkers and took the black.

The fireplace gave us enough heat that I didn't need to scoot closer to him, but I wanted to, so I'd use being cold as an excuse, plus something about the room creeped me out.

"Are you going to ignore my question?" I asked.

"Do you have a right to ask since you haven't even won the game yet?" He shot right back.

I straightened. "Fine, I'll ask after I kick your ass."

"I've never lost."

"Then, I'll try to make the pain quick." I winked.

He stared at me for a few seconds. "You have no idea how beautiful you are."

"And innocent," I grumbled.

"Something tells me my princess knows how to get dirty if she wants to."

The compliment made me blush.

"Ladies first." He nodded toward me, the mask did a good job hiding his face, all red and black, intimidating as hell, but necessary, apparently, until I was ready.

The game was quick.

And as predicted, I won.

Minutes later, he was still staring at the board in disbelief. "But—"

"Aw, better luck next time, husband."

His head shot up. "Say it again."

"Husband," I whispered.

He squeezed his eyes shut. "You have no idea how nice that sounds, especially in this room."

"Twenty questions." I grinned and rubbed my hands together. "Anything off-limits?"

"I'll let you know." The corners of his mouth ticked up in a small smile that gave me the impression he was thinking about kissing me. He reached across the table, grabbed a crystal decanter, and poured each of us two small glasses of something that looked like brandy or whiskey.

"Sip slow." He winked. "It's Russian."

"It's not vodka. Are you even allowed to have other alcohols?" I teased.

"Great fist question, yes, actually we are."

"Not fair."

"I never play fair." He licked his full bottom lip, drawing

my attention to it before I could look away. "Keep looking at me like that, and I'm throwing this mask off, apologizing for the shock, and taking you against this couch."

"Why would I be shocked?"

"We don't have enough time to even begin that conversation, princess. Just know, things aren't always what they seem. We see, a lot of times, what we're told to see."

"Vague." I sipped the whiskey and made a face. "Wow, now I know why you said sip."

"Next question." He leaned back against the couch, crossing one of his legs over his knee.

Why did I want to sit in his lap again?

What was wrong with me?

I gave my head a shake. "The fire, what happened?"

He sighed and leaned forward again, clasping his hands in front of him. "Another long story, I was young, really young. My mom and I were living together, my dad was… killed when I was even younger. I barely remember him, and his dad, my grandpa, was also killed. He was bad, though, so…" He shrugged. "I was hidden here. Only one person knew I existed, and he wanted me dead."

I covered my mouth with my hands.

"People often do, when they see a throne they want to sit on," he continued. "The fire was too hot. My mom got me out, but I was upset." His voice started to shake. "I slept with this stupid blanket ever since I was a kid. It had a white horse on it, and I pretended—" His voice cracked. "I pretended that one day, my dad would come through that door and save me, claim me, that my life wouldn't always be about death and secrets. You know what's really stupid? I just wanted to go to a theme park with him, spend the day with him, hear him say he was proud of me. Every little boy needs to hear those words from his father, and I imagined if I had that blanket, one day, it would just… happen, like the magic my mom convinced me existed once I realized that I wasn't a bastard but actually loved."

A tear slid down my cheek, followed by another. They were hot; they burned my eyes as he spoke.

"My mom never came back out." Slowly he got up and walked over to the desk and pulled out a black blanket with a white horse sewn onto it.

And next to the horse were the initials VP.

He was so young. So brave despite being afraid. My heart broke for him. The blanket was tarnished, half-burnt.

"I was broken that day, like glass shards that refuse to fit after being dropped over and over against the concrete." He sighed and tucked the blanket back inside the desk and made his way back over to me. "And now, here we are."

"Did you have any family left?"

"Only the man who tried to kill me," he whispered.

"Who's that?"

"Andrei Sinacore-Petrov."

I covered my mouth with my hands. "God, you must hate him."

"I tolerate him," he said through clenched teeth. "Mainly because now that I'm older, I know he'd been given misinformation by someone."

"Who?"

"You want to know all my secrets then?"

"You're my husband."

"Yes." He smiled sadly. "I am."

"Who was it?"

"It was old information, from an old source, one he had at one point trusted. All of the Russian mafia did. You know her as Mil De Lange. Your father, however—"

"—won't even mention her name in front of me," I finished.

"Yes."

"Did Andrei take you in then?"

He snorted out a laugh. "Hell, no. And since then, he has apologized, but it was my fault. I shouldn't have made my mom cry, I shouldn't have made her go back and get a stupid bl—"

My kiss silenced whatever else he was about to say.

His lips were plump, smooth, as they slid against mine. I moved to straddle him, and he let me, and everything about it felt familiar.

Maybe because we'd kissed last year.

Maybe because even then, he was mine.

His hands ran down my back, holding me prisoner as he deepened the kiss, tasting my tongue with his in a way that drew me closer to him, made me want more as I dug my fingers into his hair.

It was so soft.

My fingers found the edge of his mask, but he jerked back, chest heaving. "Let me be selfish for two more days before you do that."

"Because everything changes when the masks are gone," I said softly.

"Everything." His throat moved. "Because it has to."

"Okay, Valerian," I whispered. "The mask stays on for two more days, and then no more hiding."

"Is that what you think I've been doing?" he rasped, his eyes searching mine.

"You tell me."

"I wish I could." He looked away. "It's getting late, I have a busy day tomorrow, and I know you'll want to visit your family again."

"Take it off," I found myself saying before I knew what was happening.

He went still. "What do you mean take it off?"

"At least the evening, I want to do something. This is the part where I ask for your credit card and make sure that you really are rich enough to have one without a limit."

He snorted out a laugh. "Are you buying a country?"

"Could I?"

"The Petrov accounts have been unfrozen for two weeks—last I checked we were at seven billion, so yeah, you probably could."

"Two billion," I repeated. "Wow, and I thought my dad was rich."

"He is." He chuckled. "Then again, when you deal drugs…"

"Dad doesn't deal drugs."

"Okay, not hard drugs, but he does own at least a dozen dispensaries."

"That's what I call smart investing." She winked. "Credit card."

He reached into his pocket and pulled out a wallet that looked new, not worn, which was weird.

He slid a black AMEX card from the inside and handed it to me. "Try not to bleed the Family dry, all right?"

"Trust me." I smiled.

"I do." He pressed a kiss to my mouth. "I have no choice."

"We always have a choice." I shrugged.

"No." His eyes were haunted. "We really don't."

I was about to ask another question, but he pressed a finger to my lips. "You should sleep."

"Are you sleeping with me?"

"Do you want me to?"

"Yes." I started fidgeting immediately.

He shook his head. "How about I lay with you until you fall asleep?"

"I would like that."

"If you're really good, I'll even read you a story."

"Which one?" I grinned as I hopped off his lap. He grabbed my fingertips and kissed them.

I swayed toward him.

"The Polar Bear King, it's a Nordic fairy tale about a king who's trapped as a bear during the day, but every night during a certain time of the year, he can visit his bride as a man, as the man he truly is."

"Do you imagine yourself as the polar bear?"

"No." He sighed like he was disappointed. "I've always been and always will be, the wolf."

CHAPTER
Thirteen

Reflection shows me lies—but truth is no better because those words will burn, will scar forever. Reflection shows me what must be done—but the strength to grab the knife hasn't been won. Blood drips from the tip as I watch him die, and a cruel smile passes my lips because I'm the reason why.

—Valerian Petrov

Breaker

I wasn't the best at writing letters.

I was more of a one-word texter or meme sender.

So, this felt foreign.

The pen strange in my hand as I gripped it tight, my conversation with Phoenix washed over me in a fit of rage that somehow descended into peace.

I hated that he was right.

Not just about this, but about everything.

I had always looked to Junior as the one who would rise

out of the ashes. After all, he was Phoenix's son, but now I wondered if that wasn't the idea for every one of the heirs.

The ashes of those killed cried out for justice, didn't they? Their souls didn't sleep, and it was our job to rise up and fight for the good as much as we fought against the bad.

There was an inequality in the way our dads had served, a blind need to protect us at all costs without thinking about how it would affect us in the future, and that was what made these crowns so fucking heavy.

The knowledge that they were the reason they felt that way.

That Tex Campisi, in all his greatness, thought he knew best.

That Phoenix Nicolasi, in all his wisdom and secrets, could not prevent even this from happening.

That Nixon Abandonato, in all his arrogance, didn't even see it coming.

Dante Alfero, the one closest to us in age next to Dom, didn't see it.

They were too consumed with their wives, their need to be with them, that they had missed us, hadn't they? They'd missed the clues.

Even Chase, in all his suspicions, with all his secrets, thought he knew what was best when he threw me in the shower that day, not realizing that he was playing perfectly into a plan that had been ordained the day I came screaming into this world.

God, my chest hurt.

I rubbed the middle of it with my right hand.

It was early in the morning. They would be up soon, and they'd wonder where I was, and I wouldn't be here to tell them.

"Do you think we have a chance to go to Heaven?" I asked Phoenix as we'd driven around while he told me what I needed to do.

His sigh was heavy as he pulled the car over to the side of the road and gripped the steering wheel until his hands turned white. "Nobody deserves Heaven, Breaker, not even the best of us and definitely not the worst, but I don't think a truly loving God would keep you out just because you made an impossible choice. I used to think the opposite; I used to think a lot of shit until I had Junior and realized that it is, in fact, possible to have your heart walk outside your body and run into oncoming traffic, then wonder why you suddenly sprout a gray hair." He didn't laugh, he rarely did unless something was really funny, but he was smiling over at me, another rarity that almost shocked me speechless. "When you're a parent, suddenly everything that used to matter doesn't. And everything that used to be so simple becomes so fucking complicated. But one thing I can promise you, my son. No matter how many times he screams at me, fights, makes me bleed, tells me he hates me, says he wants nothing to do with me, there will never be a day in my fucking life where I won't wait for him with open arms to come back to me. There isn't one hair on his head I don't pray for, there isn't one second of the day that I don't think of him, even if he hates me, even if he comes back to me a murderer, blood staining his hands, demons in his mind, soulless— He is mine. Do you understand? He is mine." He pounded the steering wheel with his hand. "So, do I think God would kick out his children? Not anymore. No. I think he's used to people walking into his arms with blood staining their souls, I think he's used to darkness as much as he is the light."

His words hit home, and then he reached over and put a hand

on my arm. "You know, I loved you like my own the minute I found you, Breaker."

"When I chose my name," I whispered.

"When you looked up at me with tears in your eyes, screaming that you broke her, so that's the only name you deserve. You screamed it again and again like you'd never stop. Until I pulled you into my arms."

"And said it wasn't my fault." My voice shook. "You told me I was brave."

"Because you are," Phoenix rasped. "And I'm proud of the man you've become. If you hear nothing else, hear this. You, Breaker Campisi, make me proud to call you family, and even if you are under Tex's protection, I'll always think of you more as my son."

I didn't want to cry.

I didn't want to tell him I didn't deserve his words even though I needed them so badly my body physically hurt with it.

"I can do this," I whispered.

"Son, this is what you were born to do. There's only one person standing in the way."

"Yeah," I croaked. "Stupid bastard."

He sighed. "We're all stupid bastards."

"That's true."

He gave me a bit of a shove. "Tell anyone this conversation happened, and I'll shove you over a cliff."

"Good pep talk."

"I'm shockingly better at them than everyone else."

I shuddered. "Tell me about it. When I asked Dad for encouragement during a test, he literally patted me on the head and called me slugger."

Phoenix burst out laughing. "Oh, I'm using that next time I see him."

"He hates the reminder."

"Even better. He used to want to kill me. This brings me more joy than I've had in a week." He winked. "Thanks."

"Yeah, yeah."

"Be safe, Breaker."

"Be safe, Phoenix."

I leaned back in my chair. The paper in front of me was still empty. I needed to finish this before I lost the nerve, didn't I?

Plus, it wasn't forever.

Right?

I quickly jotted down the name Junior and kept writing.

But I couldn't bring myself to write her name down.

I wanted to.

But I couldn't.

So, I didn't.

God forgive me, but I couldn't do it, couldn't say goodbye. Hell, I'd had a hard time saying hello to her the first time I met her.

"Dipshit." King snickered as he ran down the stairs like they were on fire.

I quickly shoved the notes into the black briefcase and then watched in amusement as Maksim chased him, holding his cell phone high. "Dude, you slept with her best friend?"

I winced. "King…"

"What?" He frowned. "She was hot!"

"Wow." Maksim tossed him back his phone. "Never mind, you deserve everything that's happening," He looked over at me. "The friend found out. They told their dads."

I burst out laughing and then slow clapped. "This is

turning out to be a glorious day. Please tell me their dads are terrifying."

"You do realize who we live with, right?" King snorted. "Though one did send me a threatening text. Numerous body parts were involved, lots of blood, burying, skinning."

"Hey," I pointed out. "That's a new one, skinning, I like it."

"Very well done," Maksim agreed, leaning against the leather chair. "I think I saw that in a movie once. They use that skin graft thing and just glide it over like a razor— Hey, here's a thought, we can make them a skin hat to remember you by!"

King narrowed his eyes. "Yes, because that's what says, take me back, I'm an idiot, skin from my own body made into a hat."

"Just a thought." Maksim shrugged.

Junior and Serena slowly came down the stairs then, followed by Izzy, who seemed to skip around like she had endless amounts of energy. Naturally, she made a beeline for Maksim, who seemed only too happy to entertain her as they ducked their heads together and started talking.

Most likely about science, because it was them.

"Why's King so upset?" Junior jerked out a chair next to me.

"Oh, that." I leaned back and crossed my arms. "His dick got him in trouble—again, and now we're talking about skinning him and selling hats."

King just groaned into his hands and plopped down onto the chair.

"Hey." I nodded to Junior. "You and Ash got a minute?"

"Who's skinning King?" Ash took the stairs two at a time and made it to the bottom, his eyes darting between all of us.

Serena patted him on the back. "I'm not sure, but I imagine it's either an angry ex or a father."

"Ding, ding, ding, you win today's prize." I winked at her.

Serena stuck her tongue out and then made her way toward the kitchen, "Speaking of skinning and prizes, I'm going to make some eggs, you guys want?"

"Damn, man, you got her trained to make you breakfast?" I chuckled under my breath, earning a *don't say one more word* glare from Junior.

Serena stomped over to me, smacked me in the head, and then Junior for good measure. Ash ducked away, smart man.

"I hate it when ma does that." Junior rubbed the back of his head. "And Serena's very sensitive this early without her coffee."

I snorted. "When is she not sensitive? She yelled at me one time for standing too close to her breathing bubble, and I was literally trying to help her get an eyelash out of her eye."

"Women." Junior shuddered.

"Heard that!" Serena yelled.

"Sometimes…" Junior whispered. "She terrifies me."

"That too!"

He pounded his fists onto the table, causing it to shake. "GO MAKE EGGS WOMAN!"

Serena came flying around the corner, knife in hand, stomping toward Junior in a way that meant blood.

"Fifty says she gets him first." Ash pulled out a seat.

"Eh, he's feisty this morning, I say he draws first blood. A hundred?"

"Deal." He yawned.

With a face-splitting grin, Junior hopped to his feet. "What, woman? Where's your apron? Shouldn't you be vacuuming—"

With a roar, she charged him, knife pointed directly at his chest.

He kicked it out of her hands, and then they were on the floor grappling.

Ash and I peered over the table as she elbowed Junior in the face. He bested her with a sucker punch to the gut, sending her sailing backward.

She was on her feet again.

Bleeding from her lip.

"Winner!" Ash yelled.

She still wasn't done, though. She bared her teeth at Junior and then flashed him what looked like a pink lacy bra.

His eyes immediately dropped.

And then so did he.

"Son of a bitch, Serena!" Junior cupped his balls. "Are you kidding me right now?"

"Ha-ha," She swiped the blood from her lip. "Oh, and PS I'm buying you an apron for Christmas now instead of that Rolex. You're welcome."

"Crawl, man." I shook my head. "Just crawl right back to her, say you're sorry, and give her a pony."

Ash chuckled into his bottled water as Junior did just that, and then the kitchen was silent.

When they came back about a half-hour later, he had lipstick on his neck, and she was flushed.

"You got a little something." I pointed to his everything. "Like everywhere, and probably places I don't even want to know."

"She likes marking her territory with bright things." He winked.

Ash stood. "Yup, could have gone my whole life without

that mental picture. Thank you for officially ruining red lipstick for me, man. Really, I appreciate it."

"Anytime." Junior shrugged, and then his eyes fell to me. "You said you needed a minute. It's been nearly forty-five. Is this conversation private, or—"

"Kind of, yeah, it's personal. Let's go out on the balcony, it's a nice day."

"I'll bring you guys a pot of coffee," Serena said cheerfully, earning a weird glance from Junior. "What? I just don't like being told what to do."

Junior wiped down his face with his hands.

Ash snorted. "Don't look so grumpy. You at least get sex out of this... with my cousin." And then, as if remembering his gaze shot to mine. "And you with my *sister*."

"Really, really not ever letting it go, are you?" I groaned.

"Never. It's going to be on my gravestone." He grinned.

"That's... weird." I pointed to the sliding glass doors. "Let's go, I've got an appointment."

Once we were nearly outside, Ash looked over his shoulder. "Should I be concerned that Maksim and Izzy haven't even looked up from his phone?"

He glanced ahead again just as Maksim grabbed her hand and kissed her fingertips.

Junior and I both shared a look, then we both spoke at once.

"Nah man, he's harmless."

"Total science nerd, probably can't even you, know... sex."

I mouthed "sex?" at him.

Junior winced

Ash visibly relaxed. "Good, because I don't want to kill one

159

of her best friends. He's the only one who will help her with her science homework."

"That would be because he's a genius." Everything that seemed hard in school for any of us was like breathing to Maksim, and sometimes it made him an idiot when it came to all the other things like the fact that Izzy had been in love with him since he sat down next to her one day, pointed at her textbook and said, "Osmosis."

As we all stood on that balcony, the breeze picked up, and suddenly I was pushed into the past, when I'd first met Junior, here at this house, when we'd finally become something more than friends—brothers.

"I have to do something hard today." I licked my dry lips. "I just want you guys to know I don't want to, and if something goes wrong..."

Junior's head turned, his teal eyes narrowing. "If there's potential for something to go wrong, then maybe we should come with you?"

"You can't go where I'm going." I looked down. "Not this time, man."

Ash leaned up, crossing his arms. "Now you're starting to freak me out. Did one of the bosses give you a job or something while you were here?"

"Yeah. And I can't exactly say no because a lot of people will die if I do."

"Shit, man, how deep are you right now?" Junior lowered his voice. "You know we got you, right?"

He was like a brother, the concern in his face was real, but that was the hard part; it had to be real, didn't it?

And I'd sworn an oath I would do anything to keep her safe.

From them.

Wow, a year ago, I would have never thought it would come to this.

And now that it had?

I didn't feel like me; I felt like someone else watching it take place, like a bad movie you can't look away from.

"When do you take off?" Ash asked.

"Now." My voice shook. "Look, if something goes… sideways, I'm leaving the briefcase on the table for you, call Phoenix, and make sure that you burn it all."

"What the fuck, man?" Ash shoved me. "You can't just say shit like this to us, not after Cl—" A spasm of pain claimed his face. He still couldn't bring himself to say her name, and now he would hate me more than he hated himself for not protecting her—the hate that my brothers would have for me.

Forgiveness wasn't in my future, at least not that I could see.

It all went back to that day.

"It's not your fault," he said, pulling me into a hug. "We'll fix this."

You tried, Phoenix, in the only way you knew how.

And now it was my turn to do the fixing.

"I don't like this," Ash said again.

"Well." I patted him on the shoulder then squeezed. "Welcome to the mafia, right?"

"Damn mafia." Junior sighed. "Just give us a call when you're safe."

"Yup." I gave him a quick hug and then Ash.

They didn't see my hands shake with bitter anger.

Could they sense the loss of this clinging in the air? The

loss of us? Could they tell that I was walking out of here, but I would never be walking back in.

I poked my head in the kitchen. "Hey, Serena, I'm gonna take off."

Her eyes narrowed. "You're pale."

"Thank you?"

Something changed in her stance, and then she was walking over to me and pulling me into her arms. "Violet's gonna be okay, I promise."

I sighed; she had no idea how badly I needed to hear that. "Thanks, Serena, you'll always be my favorite."

"Back at ya." She winked.

King was back downstairs with Maksim and Izzy. I gave them both side hugs, probably freaking them out, and then I met King's eyes, and I knew he knew.

He fucking knew.

"No." He shook his head. "No."

"King—"

"You promised me!"

Tears filled my eyes. "I've been given no choice."

"You promised!" he roared.

And then he was throwing punches, and I was holding him in my arms, keeping him close even as he beat me and sobbed against my chest.

Because he knew.

Because he was the only one I had confided in other than the other two people who knew.

Because he was the brother I'd always wanted.

The one I'd been given.

"It's going to be okay." My voice cracked.

"It's the end." He shoved me away. "It's the end."

"All things end, King. Just because this one came sooner than we thought—doesn't mean we can't—"

"Go."

"King."

"Go!" he thundered.

So, I went.

I walked with heavy footsteps toward the red corvette I'd parked outside. The papers were in the glovebox, my name on the title.

My clothes were in the trunk. All of them.

I started the engine and sped off before I lost my nerve.

CHAPTER
Fourteen

Glass shattered across the stone as the prince rose from the grave and walked, muddy, shattered, toward his broken throne. The crown was heavy, the cost too steep, someone kill me before I'm in too deep.
—Valerian Petrov

Ash

"That wasn't normal behavior," I said, more to myself than to Junior. He eyed me and then the briefcase. "Screw it." It wasn't locked.

I quickly opened it and peeked inside.

All I saw was a black folder, which was, I guess, semi-normal for our family, and beneath it, a fucking white horse.

I dropped it like it was possessed. Ignoring my freak-out, Junior shakily picked up an envelope that said his name.

He ripped it open.

"Fuck!" he bellowed. "Get the keys NOW!"

Numb, I reached for the keys on the table as my eyes fell to the other picture in the briefcase.

Of Claire and me.

Smiling. Happy. Together.

"Ash!" Junior shook me with his hands. "We need to get the hell out of here now!"

"What?"

He shoved me toward the door. "I'm driving. Turn on your Find My Friend and ping his location."

I shook out of the sickening daze of anguish and quickly found him. "He's going north?"

"SHIT!" Junior hit the accelerator, passing cars in a blur as we made it on the freeway. "I can't go any faster!"

"Why do we need to catch him?" I asked, trying to understand the situation without thinking about her. Thinking about her last breaths nearly took all the energy I had.

"Read." He slammed some white papers against my chest. "It's a goodbye letter. He's saying goodbye like he knows he's going to his death, and we have to stop him before something happens."

I read over the words and suddenly felt like I was going to puke. What was so dangerous that he felt like he had to write us goodbye notes?

"Why the hell didn't he ask for our help?" I slammed the papers down on my thigh with shaking hands, then glanced back down at my phone. "He's taking the exit for Everett."

"How close are we?"

"Maybe five minutes."

They went by slowly as we tried to tail him.

"I see him!" I pointed. "Up ahead on the bridge—he's going into the right lane—" No sooner had the words left my mouth, then that same Corvette drove straight through construction and off the bridge, falling at least sixty feet to the water below.

Cars screeched to a stop.

Junior was screaming.

So was I.

But I heard nothing.

Nothing but the sound of metal twisting metal.

No sound but the slow beat of my heart as it came up to speed with what my eyes were seeing.

The car started sinking, and somehow caught fire, which seemed impossible as it continued to sink.

Junior pulled over to the side. I backed up to run and jump in, but he grabbed me before I could go over the edge.

People took pictures with their phones like my brother wasn't drowning.

They gasped and stared and pointed like it was a TV show and not reality.

And whatever good parts of me that still existed, that still believed that people were inherently good and deserved to live—fell in angry shards and sank to the bottom of the Sound with one of my favorite people.

One who was too young to die.

One who seemed to know he was going to his own funeral.

My brother—who took his last breaths alone.

A car.

Twisting metal.

My knees hit the ground as my legs gave out. The sting of gravel through my jeans barely registered as I leaned over and puked.

I heard Junior yelling into his cell phone.

I heard the sirens.

I felt nothing.

So, I sat on my haunches, and I waited for Junior to do what I couldn't. Make the calls, burn the information, pay off the police.

My phone started ringing. God, not now. Not her.

Violet.

It said, Violet.

I squeezed my eyes shut as tears I didn't even realize I still had flowed down my face.

She just kept calling.

"Yeah." I could barely get the word past my lips.

"Hey! I was thinking about coming over again since—" She stopped. "Ash, talk to me, what's going on? You know you can talk to me about Claire, right?"

I sucked in a shuddering breath. "Not Claire." I clenched my teeth. "Breaker, it's Breaker, I don't think… we couldn't save him, we can't save anyone."

"No." It was such a quiet no; it was worse than the yelling. "I just saw him, he was fine; he—he wouldn't leave me like this. Not like this, Ash, not—tell me—I can't—"

One of the detectives I knew well since we had them placed all over the cities we had dealings in, walked over to us and gave us a sad understanding smile. "It's already been dealt with. You can go back home."

People were still scattered everywhere as sirens went off, alerting everyone to the disaster to the tragedy. My heart thudded to a stop in my chest.

Home? What was that anymore? When everyone you love is constantly taken from you?

Junior looked ready to lunge at him. "What the hell do you mean it's been taken care of?"

He held out his cell.

I put it up to my ear.

"Get back to the house where it's safe," Phoenix said in a cold voice void of emotion. "Burn everything in that briefcase, including the tape."

"Tape?" I repeated my voice sounded foreign to my own ears, hollow like it no longer belonged to me, to this body but someone else, someone else who was going through hell, through unimaginable pain. "I don't understand?"

"Look at it, and it's your ass." He hung up.

I handed the phone back to the detective and shook my head at Junior as we wordlessly got back in our car and drove to the house.

Neither of us spoke.

I was afraid I'd crack.

I needed his anger right now.

Just like he needed mine.

But we had a job to do first.

And blood always came first, even when you wanted to crawl into a ball on the floor and sob your way through life— blood came first.

Violet was at the house when we got there, sobbing on the couch while Izzy and Serena held her.

And King was staring straight at the wall, his jaw clenched as he bounced a ball against it over and over and over on an endlessly repeating cycle until I was afraid I was going to go crazy.

Maksim was pacing.

And I had no purpose other than burning.

Nothing else mattered.

I grabbed the briefcase, pulled out all the letters, and was even more pissed when I realized Violet's was the lightest.

"I'll burn everything." Junior's voice was barely recognizable from the screaming he'd done. "You give them the letters."

With shaking hands, I grabbed the letters and dispersed them to each of my friends, my family. It wasn't supposed to be like this. God, why was this even happening? I couldn't even look at my sister. I could feel her pain like it was my own.

Like being set on fire with no relief, dying of thirst without water, having your soul stolen never to return.

I saved her for last.

Her broken sobs filled the room as she shoved me away, covering her face with her hands. "Y-you read it."

With trembling fingers, I opened the simple white envelope that bore her name and slid out the small crisp piece of paper.

"You have been and will always be my best friend. I love you. I'm yours in life, in death, in sickness and in health, I'm yours. Forever. My blood for yours," I read, my voice heavy with grief.

Why?

WHY!

A scream built up inside my chest like a living breathing monster with teeth as it ripped at my throat over and over again, its nails digging into me from the inside out.

Pain pulsed instead of a heartbeat.

What good parts of me were left?

She pressed her left hand to her face.

And that was when I noticed the monstrosity on her finger.

"What the hell, Violet!" I roared my hands shaking.

Because how dare he!

How *dare* he!

The letter fluttered to the floor, I was ready to bring him back to life just to kill him all over again.

The rage was back.

And so was the disappointment that I knew nothing when I thought I knew everything.

"I'm married," she said quickly.

"He *married* you?" I roared, kicking one of the chairs into the wall, it impaled itself into the side.

A picture fell with a crash, spreading shattered glass all over the hardwood floor. "Then had the fucking audacity to die?"

"Not him." She burst into tears again, her body rocking back and forth. "Not him."

"Ash!" Junior barked my name. "A word real quick."

"This isn't over." I pointed at her while Serena gave me a stop making it worse look. "You will explain to me what the hell is going on!"

I'd lost my ability to stay calm and didn't give two shits if I was making things worse. My sister was somehow married, apparently to a complete stranger from where I was standing, and nothing was what it seemed. Nothing. Why else would they send her here?

It was all a ruse.

A setup.

Had he known?

And why the hell didn't he say something to us?

I followed Junior outside where he'd already tossed in the video and a few other items; the black folder, however, he was holding in his hands made me want to hurl all over again.

Do your job, just do your job.

"It's our names, ages, aliases," I whispered.

"It's our garage codes," he hissed. "Our driver's license numbers. It's not even useful unless they actually get in, whoever they are."

"Oh, that's the weirdest part..." He sighed. "There are records from here to Seattle Penitentiary and back and then back again. Phone conversations about carrying out hits and the contact person is—"

"The guy who cut all our brakes." I grabbed the paper. "I wish I could kill him all over again."

And then I wished I could bring her back, bring him back—all the loss, all the heartache. Maybe it was my penance for killing my own cousin in cold blood because he had the strength to say no to this life.

Maybe God was punishing me, the way I punished them, over and over, for not submitting to the Family, for choosing themselves over blood, however stupid that choice may be.

I bit back a curse. "Who's asking for the intel, and how can we tell who's in on it?"

He looked on the next page and the next.

And at the very bottom of the documents was a contract between Mil De Lange and Victor Petrov—signed in blood, dated a year before Violet was born.

"Russians," I whispered in horror. "It seems like they've gotten tired of Andrei's leadership."

"Because he's half." Junior sneered, looking ready to rip the papers in half. "And they think we're bad when it comes to blood." He kicked a rock and then another. "That means Andrei knows, which means my dad knows, but what the hell does it have to do with Breaker?"

"Collateral damage." I started dropping the pages into the fire one by one, more secrets would die with those I loved, they would burn. "The cost of knowing too much or being in the wrong place at the right time, or maybe a combination of both."

My mind flashed to the last year and how he and Violet had started acting strangely and how he was constantly looking over his shoulder when he was with her.

Now we would never know why.

Because Breaker Campisi was dead.

CHAPTER
Fifteen

A fool with a crown on his head and enemies who lie—I
saved the world, and I didn't even try, to be anything
but what I was born to be, prince of the East—Russian
Royalty.
—Valerian Petrov

Valerian

I got out of the Denali, greeted by Sancto, whose normally
chipper demeanor was as grim on the outside as I felt on
the inside.

"Good day at the office?" He approached, his brown eyes
searching for the answer he'd been waiting for—the answer
they'd all been waiting for since my birth, it seemed.

"Yes." I held my head high. "It seems we've decided that
the merger wasn't entirely working out for us. I've made some
changes I think the men will find... inspiring."

His grin was wide, and then his eyes filled with tears as he
reached out and grabbed my hand in his, pulled me against

his chest, and kissed my forehead. "Mother Russia would be proud; your mother would be proud."

"May God bless her soul," I whispered in Russian.

"We celebrate!" Sancto shouted, earning more shouts of appreciation throughout the yard as men in suits acted more like men who'd been freed from a prison they didn't even realize they'd been in.

For years under a thumb they despised, looking for the long lost boy, the only one who could potentially get them out.

And free them all.

But at what cost?

They were free, and now I was the one behind the bars, the crown heavy on my head as I watched them for the first time in what seemed like days actually smile.

My phone buzzed in my pocket, the readout showing *unknown*. "Yes," I answered.

"It's done." The voice was cold as expected. "I'll contact you depending on how the next few days go. There will be fights. Blood. And there will be retribution, but you must—"

"I know." I interrupted. "I know what I have to do."

"We all have choices."

"Not me." I lowered my voice. "Not me."

"The crown is only heavy because it's new, you'll get used to the ache, and then you'll yearn for its power. Trust me."

"I do." I sighed. "Trust you, that is. Otherwise—"

"—Otherwise, this would have ended badly."

"Yeah."

"She's not herself," he said after a few seconds. "I thought you should know."

I let out a bitter laugh. He was joking, wasn't he? "How the hell would anyone be okay after that news?"

I wasn't okay, and I was used to this.

"It's the mafia." His simple clipped answer as if it made everything better like a Band-Aid you put on a mortal wound and wonder why the person's still bleeding out.

I mentally rolled my eyes as another SUV pulled up. My heart stilled in my chest. "It's her, I'll talk with you later."

I quickly made my way inside so she wouldn't see me. After all, if she was going to be mine, if she wanted to be the princess in the high castle, she had to choose it in her own timing.

And tonight was not the night.

Death and rebirth rarely happen in the same twenty-four hour period.

I waited in the shadows as she attempted to hold her head high upon entering the mansion. Her cheeks were stained with tears, her eyes swollen. Never had I wanted to touch her more, hold her close, kiss away the sadness that I would never be able to fix.

Because this was my fault to begin with.

And if she knew that—she'd reject me—and I wasn't sure I could handle that sort of death, the death of love, the death of hope that she put there when she kissed me last night.

She moved through the house like a ghost, slowly she took the stairs even as Sancto offered her a glass of champagne.

That wasn't going to get her through the night or last longer than two minutes. She was grieving.

And I hurt for her, so far inside my chest that no matter what I did, it burned.

"Sir." Sancto appeared behind me. "Your mask."

"It's only until she trusts me until she sees me and not the scars."

He frowned. "The scars on your thighs?"

"The ones on my soul."

"Ah, those ones, yes, I see those too. They're ugly and beaten to a pulp, those scars, but some might say they made you what you are today." His brown eyes bore into me.

I sighed. "And what's that?"

"A leader." He bowed, and then he was gone, his footsteps light enough to make him more spy than butler.

I donned the red and black mask one more time, hoping it would be my last as I took the stairs, following her familiar scent, the one that haunted my dreams, my nightmares.

She was in our room.

The bathtub was running.

And under the noise of water filling the tub as a toe peeked out from the room, I heard the sobs.

Sobs for a man she'd loved.

Sobs for a chance she would never get again.

Sobs for a life that was forever altered by one choice.

Choices.

I was out of them.

Now I was living through them.

And it hurt like fuck.

Slowly, I rounded the corner. She didn't even see me as I knelt next to the bath, reached for the body wash, pouring it onto the loofah as I slowly washed her.

She said nothing.

She didn't cover herself.

Just stared straight ahead as I washed her back, her neck, between her perfect breasts as water trailed down the middle.

"He's gone," she whispered.

"I know." My voice caught. "I wish I could take this from you…"

But all of us had our burdens, and this, this moment would be hers, and then I would take it from her when I could. But she would need to mourn Breaker Campisi. He at least deserved that much.

My throat threatened to close up as I dipped my hands in the water, cupping it and spreading it all over her smooth skin.

I loved her curves.

Her heavy breasts.

The small mark beneath her chin from fencing class that day I had watched by the tree.

"I will be ready." She finally looked at me, her blue eyes locking with my gaze in precision that I'd only ever seen in my enemies. "I will be ready for you to say yes, to this… to all of this, but I need—I need just one night where you tell me a story, where you let me cry."

I frowned. "One night seems very… little."

Her smile was sad. "He took all the pieces, Valerian, I hope you know that. The one you had was stolen, the ones he had were gifts, and I can't take those gifts back and give them to you. I'm afraid there's nothing left because I'll always belong to him in a way, even though I'm bound to you." A tear slid down her cheek; I caught it with my thumb, swiping it away. "I'm sorry."

"I can think of no better way to leave this earth than with the knowledge that he held something so special in his hands, and he didn't have to steal it, to get it," I finished.

She reached up and touched my hair. "Your accent, it's stronger when you're emotional."

She really had no idea, the restraint. No idea. "I can't seem to help it around you."

"I like it."

I don't.

"What can I do for you right now? What does my princess need?"

She was stoic for a minute and then burst into tears and sobs. "A hug, I just need a hug."

Without saying anything more, I grabbed a towel, then picked her up into my arms and carried her into the bedroom. I dried her off as carefully as I could. Then I moved to her semi-wet hair. I pulled it into a low ponytail, so it was out of her face, and then I drew her into my arms and whispered, "The prince was scared of so many things. Would his princess leave him? After all this time? Was she bored? Did she still love him despite his many sins? And then the day arrived, or the week that is."

"What happened?" Her voice was rough from crying.

"The princess visited her mother and was given a magic candle that would allow her to see the king at night. She was so eager to see his face, to reveal his secrets that she took it. And later that week, a day before he was to be broken of the spell, he visited her, and she used the candle."

Violet turned in my arms and clung to my shirt with her fingertips. "She betrayed him."

"No." I cupped her chin. "He failed her."

Her brow furrowed. "How?"

"He should have been honest from the start. He should have found a way to tell her to let her see." I slowly started to twist her hair between my fingertips. It was a bad habit, one I would never quit. "He should have fought, and now that she'd seen him, even though the curse was almost broken, he was summoned by the witch into her realm to serve."

Violet scooted closer, laying her head on my arm. "So, what did she do?"

I smiled. "She fought for him even though some may say he didn't deserve her loyalty, her love—and in the end, the brave princess, saved her prince, her soon to be king."

She licked her lips. "You're eyes…"

"What about them?" I held my breath.

"Against the black, they seem so bright, for a minute, I just…" Her own filled with tears. "Imagined a world where life was fair."

"Life isn't fair, and my eyes only look that bright because of the mask you choose for me to keep on." I leaned forward and pressed a kiss to her nose. "You can always take it off, Violet, when you're ready."

She sucked in her lower lip. "I'm afraid. Not of your scars, but I'm afraid…" Her eyes filled with tears again. "I'm afraid I'll like you, and that feels like betrayal."

My chest cracked. "It's okay to like more than one person, Vi. I promise I won't tell."

"What?" Her eyes narrowed. "What did you just call me?"

"Vi." I smiled. "It works, right? I mean, we are married…" I took her left hand in mine and kissed the back of it.

"Right." She clutched my hand and then looked down at the small sickle tattoo on my left ring finger, the one given to me as a child—marking me. "Do you think you could kiss away some of the sadness?"

I thought back to all the times I was forced to hide that tattoo.

"Only if we play another game to distract you from your broken heart."

She looked away. "I had a thing planned for us today, you know, I moved it to tomorrow, after everything… I don't know if I could even play a game right now."

"We'll play it in bed," I suggested.

She frowned. "What sort of game?"

"Sadly, not the kind I want," I teased, hoping to earn a smile from her, and failing miserably as her eyes once again filled with tears. "How about a rematch?"

Violet shrugged. "I mean, if you think your pride can take another loss, then sure, we can have a rematch."

I crossed my arms and grinned. "I think I can handle another blow. Besides, I never lose twice."

"We'll see." She chewed her lower lip. Her voice was small as she sat up on the bed, covering herself with the towel. "But first, I need clothes."

"Do you really need them?" I said in a dark whisper.

She pulled the towel tighter around her like I hadn't already seen what was underneath.

"Fine." I went to my dresser and grabbed a white shirt and a pair of Nike sweatpants, and tossed them onto the bed. "Dress."

"Turn." Her eyebrows arched.

I grinned and held up my left hand. "Married."

"Cute." She crossed her arms over the towel. "Turn or no game."

I adjusted my mask with irritation. "Didn't know the Italians taught you torture."

"They taught me everything." She lifted her chin in pride. Good for her.

It was on the tip of my tongue, my response.

Instead, I said nothing.

I held back.

And then I turned.

After a few seconds, I heard her plop on the bed; the casualness of it made me smile beneath my mask. "Ready."

She was devastating, even in sweats with wet hair and tear-stained cheeks. Then again, she would be, she'd always been that way, all classical beauty that demanded to be seen. Hell, she was a weakness I hadn't seen coming because I would do anything to keep her safe, and it bothered me that I'd done the exact opposite.

I'd married her.

Securing a cellmate.

She didn't understand.

But she would.

And then I would have her hate.

I grabbed another checkers set from the dresser and brought it over to the bed.

She frowned. "Do you really have a checkers set in every room?"

"Actually, yes." I shrugged and started setting out the pieces. "It calms me, and it makes sense. It's rational, it's win or lose, strategy, it's concentration. And it's always the same."

"I take it you enjoy consistency and a challenge?" One black eyebrow arched up. Her eyes were so damn swollen.

"Yes, a little of both." I looked away from her grief-stricken face. All it did was remind me of things I couldn't change, and a burden so heavy that she was sick with it, one she wouldn't share with a stranger like me, one she would bear on her own while she grieved.

"Ladies first." I cleared my throat.

She made her first calculated move. Her fingers were trembling, maybe this was a bad idea, but I knew her—I knew if she went to bed right now, she'd just think about Breaker, she'd blame herself, she'd dream of him.

Was it so selfish to want her to dream of me instead?

To want her to lean on me?

Hug me?

Let me take away the pain?

The room was thick with it; a heaviness descended over us as we played, and no matter how many times I tried to ask questions and get her distracted, her chin wobbled like she was just barely holding it in.

"What did you love about him?" I finally asked as we started our second game; she lost, then again, it wasn't fair she was barely concentrating.

A tear spilled from her cheek to the checkerboard, and I was instantly angry I'd missed the chance to wipe it away.

"Everything." She wiped her cheeks with the back of her hands. "I loved everything about him. He was…" She locked eyes with me. "…mine. The one thing that I had in the Family that I claimed when I first saw him was Breaker himself. He was so… broken when he came to us. He smiled, and he fit in perfectly, but at night he cried."

"Did he ever tell you why he cried?" My body tensed.

"He said he was broken." Violet reached for another checker and clutched it in her hand. "And I told him it was okay to be broken because when you're broken, all you need is a best friend to help you find the pieces and put them back together again. And I promised him I would."

"He was lucky to have you as a best friend, Violet, and more…"

"He was mine," she said again, this time louder. "My dad has politics, my mom has my dad, Ash has his rage, Izzy has Maksim. Everyone has someone or something that they're good at. He was my one thing; don't you get it? He was it; he was mine! And he was stolen from me!"

A mixture of a scream and a sob pierced the room as Violet threw the checkerboard against the dresser. The red and black pieces clattered to the floor, almost in slow motion.

I didn't move.

She shoved at me.

And I let her.

She pounded her fists into my chest.

I welcomed the pain.

And then she was sobbing against my chest again. I pulled her into my arms; I wondered if she knew I mourned him too?

The way she saw him was more than he deserved.

"I'm so angry…" Her body shook against mine.

"Then be angry, Violet. Bruise me, beat me, scar me—you have to let it out, or it will destroy you."

"It's not fair!"

"It's not."

"I don't want you, Valerian. I want him!" She shoved me again.

I squeezed my eyes shut. "You'll always have him, Violet, always."

And I will always be second best.

Or in this case—last.

I let that revelation sink in while I twisted her hair in my hands and kissed the tears on her cheeks.

Twenty minutes later, she fell asleep in my arms. Suddenly I felt very much like the king from the fairy tale as I turned off the lights and finally took the mask away and set it on the dresser.

Only visiting her in the blanket of darkness when it was safe.

I was cursed, just like him.

Did she see the similarity?

I left her then and went into the bathroom to take a shower. If she saw me if she saw it all—I would welcome the final nail in my coffin, because the crown was full of secrets, and secrets were heavier than the truth, they outweighed, outmatched, outsmarted.

And I wanted to be done with them.

All of them.

I stared at my reflection in the mirror: green eyes, light blond hair with threads of gold intertwined like an actual crown on my head. And when I took off my shirt. All I seemed to be able to focus on was the hidden sickle tattoo on my chest.

And the name Petrov etched beneath it.

I squeezed my eyes shut and braced myself against the counter, muscles flexing as I finally turned around and stripped off my pants.

The scars on my thighs were light, hardly noticeable unless you were touching my marred skin, and easily hidden by the necessary tattoo on my right thigh where the scarring was the worst.

People only saw what they wanted to see.

Even people you loved.

With clenched teeth, I went into the shower and let the searing water run over my back, and then I slumped to the tiled floor and sat. Tears of frustration filled my eyes as the water soon turned cold.

"The only way…" he said. "Breaker Campisi must die."

"Why? Why kill him?" I demanded.

"Because…" He sighed. "Valerian Petrov must live, and as long as Breaker's alive, you're in danger—you made your choice then, you must make your choice now."

I swallowed the lump in my throat. "I'll do it. I'll kill him."

He sighed like he was relieved when I felt like puking all over his Armani shoes. "Good choice."

Couldn't he see that I was shaking? Couldn't he see that I'd already done the unthinkable in order to save her? Her eyes had begged me to just get it over with.

I'd thought to prevent the horror.

Instead, I was the one who had delivered it.

And because of that one choice, I'd damned us both without realizing it. I wondered if he had, though. I wondered if it was truly convenient that I was there that night, or if it was something else entirely. And one day, I would ask. One day, I would find out if this was a setup from the very beginning by the very men who had demanded this of me.

The greatest betrayal of all.

I slammed my hands against the shower floor and then rose to my full height, grabbed a towel, and wrapped it around me.

I looked haunted. My cheeks were gaunt and sunken, dark circles were visible under my eyes.

"Breaker Campisi," I whispered. "May he rest in peace. Blood in. No out."

CHAPTER
Sixteen

Her tears were like acid on my tongue, burning my body, seizing my lungs, and still, I held her despite the pain; in fact, I welcomed the feeling as if it were rain.
—Valerian Petrov

Violet

I hated him.

I hated Valerian.

I didn't want him touching me.

I didn't want him consoling me.

I didn't want him trying to cheer me up or even trying to pretend to understand how deep my grief went.

But there was no escaping him.

Or my brother, who wouldn't stop calling or texting. I got it. He was worried, but I couldn't speak, I couldn't let the words out. I was afraid I wouldn't be able to stop crying again.

So I clung to the anger.

Even that next morning as I lay in bed, stayed there and

just stared at the wall, I could smell Valerian, I could feel his presence in that house like I was being haunted by his ghost when he was at the office doing whatever Russian mob bosses did during the day.

I hated him for making me feel bat shit crazy.

Because I did.

Not only was it hard to breathe in and out—but he twisted my hair like Breaker did, his eyes were a more brilliant green than Breaker's, but I'd only ever seen him under the shadow of night.

Our wedding.

And both checker games, he donned a mask that covered most of his face. But his mouth, it was familiar to me.

That mouth was mine.

And I hated him for looking like Breaker even a little bit.

And I hated him for still being alive when Breaker was dead.

I gripped the dagger in my right hand until my fingers went numb, and I stayed that way despite Sancto trying to get me out of bed or trying to get me to eat.

I lay there and waited for my vengeance.

I would kill Valerian Petrov.

This had started with him.

And it would end with me.

A single tear ran down my cheek as footsteps neared. The door opened, and then he was there.

I could feel him, but it wasn't my Breaker. It was Valerian, a man who spoke English with a Russian accent, spoke the Russian language fluently, lived in a castle on the water, and had his own throne, his own people to rule.

I just wanted to go home.

But I couldn't, not if I was still married to him.

So, I would eliminate him.

It would be my first kill.

I would be made after this.

Bloodlust filled my line of vision as the floorboards creaked. He moved over to my side of the bed and sat. "You should eat."

"Déjà vu," I whispered, and then I jerked the knife out from under the pillow aiming for his chest.

The knife missed his heart and embedded a half-inch into his right pectoral.

He stumbled back, his eyes cold as he slowly jerked the knife out of his skin and threw it to the floor. I dove for it, missing it when he shoved me out of the way.

"Violet." He held up his hands while I kept charging toward him.

With a scream, I aimed for him. Even though I no longer had a weapon, I had my fists. Let him feel what it was like to bleed from the inside out, to burn and feel the flames lick your wounds until you were paralyzed with agony so unimaginable it hurt to breathe.

"Stop."

"This is all your fault!" I screamed. "At the club, he could have saved me, I know he could have! Instead, you saved me when I didn't want to be saved! I would rather have been fucked by a complete stranger than be tied to you!"

He flinched, but I couldn't stop talking, couldn't stop trying to attack him. It was like someone else was controlling my body.

"I don't want to hurt you, Violet." His eyes narrowed. "But if a fight's what you want..." He rolled up his shirtsleeves like it was normal for his wife to pull a knife on him, and then he picked it up and handed it back to me. "Have at me."

"You don't even have a weapon," I hissed.

He smiled that perfect smile that reminded me of Breaker, at least the parts I could see. "I don't need a weapon."

"Don't insult me," I said through clenched teeth.

"Fight me." He crooked his fingers at me. "I dare you."

So, I charged again.

This time he hit the knife out of my hand before I could get close enough, and then he was dodging each punch and kick, protecting himself, but refusing to hit me.

Why did I want to be hit?

To feel the pain?

I'd never been that person.

I always watched in the background while Serena lost her mind when Junior or my brother taunted her.

I knew how to fight, but I'd never needed to—because I'd had him, Breaker, my own personal weapon.

Now I had nothing.

I was naked without him.

Defenseless.

Pain that was somehow both searing and icy surged, filling the Breaker-sized void in my soul.

Swirling black mists of emptiness.

He left me.

"Fight me back!" I yelled, landing a punch to his solar plexus.

His nostrils flared. "You want pain, or do you want pleasure? Either way, you will learn your lesson. Nobody pulls a knife on me in my own home, not even my grief-stricken wife."

"Stop calling me your wife." I went to kick with my right leg. He grabbed it and then threw my body onto the ground, stealing my breath completely from my lungs as I gasped for air.

"Pleasure or pain?" he demanded through clenched teeth.

I squirmed beneath him. "Get any closer, and I'm biting your ear off."

He laughed. The bastard laughed like he was entertained! "You're more than welcome to try."

And then he pinned my arms above my head. "Hmmm, this might be difficult with a mask on…"

"Take it off, and I'm closing my eyes." I squeezed them shut.

I didn't want to see his face.

I didn't want to see how human he was.

Right now, he was a faceless man who had tricked me.

A man in a mask who'd married me under the cover of night.

If he took off the mask, it would be real.

All of this.

"It's off," he whispered.

The clunk of it landing and the hiss as it slid across the floor attested to the truth of his words.

"So, if you're still afraid to stare at your future head-on, by all means, keep your eyes closed…"

I kicked under him.

He had me pinned and completely at his mercy. "You want a do-over, Violet? Is that it? You want to go back to that night and take everything back?"

Memories washed over me.

Of his taste.

Of how tender he was.

How he had tried to trick them.

And how he'd failed miserably.

"I'm not having sex with you." I gritted my teeth. "So get that idea out of your head."

"I never asked." His voice was hoarse and yet tender. "You're upset, you're grieving, you want to pick a fight, you want to blame someone. You have to; otherwise, it doesn't make sense, and if that needs to be me, then so be it, but killing me isn't going to bring Breaker back from the dead, Violet. Killing only takes more of your soul away from this earth. Believe me, I know."

"*How* do you know?"

He ignored my question. "Let me fix that night. Give me a do-over, and I'll tell you."

"Sex isn't going to fix us. It isn't going to bring him back either," I whispered as his mouth came down on my neck.

His tongue was like velvet.

And then his teeth grazed my neck where his tongue had been, a small bite followed by another sent pain zinging all over my body.

Breathless, I craved more.

"I won't make you beg," he hissed. "But you need it. Pain cancels out pain, so let me give you both."

"I don't trust you." I swallowed the lump of grief that refused to go away, heartache that just permanently set up residence in my throat. "I will never trust you."

And as he held me there, the haze of hatred slowly lifted, the haze of confusion dissipated. Only his warm hard body pressing me into the floor existed.

And then it occurred to me why he didn't need a weapon,

his body was the weapon, and it was cutting like a just-sharpened ax as I tried to ignore my own response.

I was disgusted with myself.

What the hell was wrong with me?

Minutes ago, I had been going to kill him, and now just the feeling of him on top of me sent my body into overdrive.

The memory of his kiss.

My chest heaved as his mouth very gently met mine in a soft kiss that had me reaching for him, eyes still closed, my hands came into contact with smooth skin on his cheeks.

No scars.

And yet I still couldn't open my eyes.

I was a coward.

Afraid to look at my future.

Afraid of the empty spot where Breaker should have been standing, afraid to admit it, to look at it.

"Violet." His voice was deep, his accent thick. "If you need to keep fighting, I'll be here to fight back. If rage is how you want to grieve, then rage it is—but promise me one thing."

I trembled as one finger traced my jawline so tenderly that I wanted to cry. "What is it?"

"Give me four nights before you make any decisions, and at the end of those four nights—if you want to go back to Chicago and stay… I'll let you."

"Oh, you'll let me?" I snorted, jerking my head away from him.

"Violet, we're married, there is no getting out of that, but if you need to go, and you need me to stay… I'll make that sacrifice."

"What's the catch?"

"Like I said," he whispered in my ear, his lips tickling the flesh there. "Four nights—four nights where I'll try my hardest to win your body and your soul as Valerian Petrov."

I frowned. Why was he saying it like that?

He was waiting for my answer, but all I kept focusing on was the fact that I could go home. Back to what was familiar, back to the way things had been before they were broken.

"Just four nights," I repeated. "What about the days?"

"Yours to do with as you please as long as you get out of bed, eat some food, and stop hiding weapons under your pillow."

"You have a gun under yours." I jutted my chin out.

"Touché," he whispered. "But it's not because I'm planning on going Dateline on your ass. It's to protect you from my enemies."

"Got a lot of those? Shocker," I snapped.

"Well, apparently, I need to add wife to that list since she just tried to stab me in the heart. Your aim was off, by the way."

"I still drew blood," I pointed out.

"That you did." He sighed. "So, do we have a deal?"

I gulped. Was I really willing to give him four nights? Four nights really wasn't anything… And then I could go home.

Four nights, and I'd return to my family.

And bury my best friend.

"Deal, but—"

His mouth devoured my sentence, his hands dug into my hair, his tongue invaded, dominating—both promising and threatening.

And then his heat was gone.

His mouth.

His body.

"Open your eyes," he ordered in a stern voice.

And when I did, the mask was back as if it had never come off, and his eyes were lingering on my mouth like he wanted to kiss me again.

I fought to keep my hate in place, along with my grief. I needed someone to blame; that was the only capacity in which I needed Valerian Petrov.

I stared straight ahead at his chest, then frowned; a button was undone so I could see the top of a massive chest tattoo or what appeared like one.

I reached out. He jerked and stepped back, holding up a hand as though to ward me off. "If the shirt comes off, so does the mask."

"Which one?" I challenged. "I'm sure you have several metaphorical masks, right? As a boss, you'd have to."

He flinched and then started twisting the giant ring on his finger, the one that showed the world who ruled it.

Him.

"You know, if you could just stop being so fucking stubborn for one second…" His accent thickened. "…you'd realize you need me, Violet."

"Need you?" I scoffed. "For what?"

He twirled my hair with one of his fingers and then twirled again, jerking me toward him until we were chest to chest. "Be smarter, Vi."

"Be crueler, Valerian."

"Don't tempt me to fuck some sense into you. At least maybe then you'd stop crying, stop feeling sorry for yourself. This is a tough world, Vi, and I need you to be the person that—" He stopped himself and looked away. "I need you to be Chase Abandonato's daughter, not Breaker Campisi's ex-lover, do you understand me? You have a job now, and that doesn't disappear just because he's dead, just like the danger you're in even now doesn't disappear because you need a minute to grieve." He stepped toward the door. "Dry your eyes. I'll give you five minutes before I come back. Our first night starts now."

Leaving me with a mouth that had gone dry as a freaking desert.

CHAPTER
Seventeen

In all my nightmares, I never imagined this outcome, in all my days living, I never understood the true meaning of hell—until she said his name.
—Valerian Petrov

Valerian

"She fucking stabbed me," I hissed into the phone. "So don't tell me to calm down and that everything's going to work out."

"You took a blood oath, Valerian." He sighed. "One you can't get out of. At least the evidence was destroyed. Imagine if Chase got his hands on that video? Do you realize how reckless that was? How damning?"

"No," I said sarcastically. "Please tell me while I clean up the flesh wound delivered by the woman sleeping next to me at night. By all means, continue your lecture."

He chuckled. "At least she's not boring."

"She's never been boring," I said defensively. "Look, I

asked her for a few more days. I'll personally deliver her for the funeral, and then she can make her choice."

"So, until then, you're just going to what? Play fucking house?" He wasn't amused by my need for more time.

"I need more time before I tell her." I rested my forehead against the wall while he sighed heavily on the other end. "I need more time before I tell her I killed Breaker. Please."

"You have your four days. Bring her for the funeral, maybe they'll let you give the eulogy."

"Very funny."

"I thought so." He always did find himself hilarious when he was the exact opposite of funny—bastard was too terrifying to be anything but a monster.

I checked my watch. Five minutes had passed, and at least now, I wasn't bleeding. Damn that dagger had aimed true, hadn't it? Truer than I'd wanted to admit to her.

I didn't think Violet had it in her. Ever.

That was why you never trusted women in the mafia. They were scrappy, beautiful, cunning black widows that would sink their poison into you the minute you orgasm, bringing you to the brink of death while you begged them for it.

I walked back up the stairs, blindfold in hand, my mask firmly in place, because even I wasn't dumb enough to think she'd accept this life, accept me just yet.

Violet was standing in the middle of the room, close to where I had left her. She had a pair of black silk sleep shorts on and a matching cami. Her hair was pulled away from her face, and she had her hands on her hips like she was lecturing the air in front of her.

"Knock, knock…" I grinned.

She scowled.

Well, they didn't say it would be easy.

"Done crying?" I asked.

"Done being a monster?" she fired back sweetly.

"Not yet, actually, thanks for asking." I approached. "Close your eyes."

She squinted and then closed her eyes. She immediately tensed when I tied the black blindfold around her eyes. "Is this necessary?"

"I stole something," I whispered from behind her. "I intend to give it back."

"You can't give someone back their virginity."

"No, but I can give back her dignity, her trust. I can give back those tiny moments."

"Nothing will erase that moment, Valerian."

"No, but hopefully, I can do something to give you a new memory, a new story, a new ending…"

"What did you say?" she whispered, her lower lip trembling.

"Maybe…" I shrugged, even though she couldn't see me. "Maybe instead of me, you met someone else at that club, maybe it was Breaker—did he take care of you that night?"

"He took care of me every night, every day, it's what he did." She held her head high.

"Would you still love him if he betrayed you?" I circled her trembling body as she fisted her hands at her sides. "If he slept with countless women while you pined for him from afar…"

She moved from one foot to another. "Breaker didn't—we didn't. It only happened once between us."

"How fortunate then." I sighed. "That all I have to do is outperform a distant memory, and that one time you and he were together…"

"I'm going to imagine it's him," she taunted.

I grinned, tossed my mask onto the bed, leaned in, and whispered in her ear, "Good."

Goosebumps flared and ran down her arms.

She started rubbing them away.

I inched my fingers across her shoulders and down her arms, and then I pulled her back against me; she let out a gasp as my hands found her hips.

It felt like I'd been walking around hard as a rock, unable to touch, unable to bring myself to do something that would so completely alter what we could have if she would just accept it.

Because I had sworn my silence.

Not that it mattered because eventually… she would know.

Whose blood was on my hands.

And why.

"I'm going to kiss you." I turned her toward me, and then my mouth was on hers, my tongue sliding past her lips despite her attempt not to kiss me back. "Open, Violet, let me taste you. You promised you'd try, you said four nights, this is the price…"

"You're expensive."

"I wondered if your sense of humor died with him—good to see it's alive and well." I kissed her again and again until finally, she kissed me back, I coaxed her with my tongue, I held her tenderly with my hands, and then I nipped at her lips and sucked them with mine.

She released a small whimper.

"There she is," I encouraged. "Forget about everything, but this moment, this kiss. This… should have been our very first… this…" I grazed her nipples with my thumbs. Her body jerked in response. Her mouth parted even more as I deepened the kiss, ready to rip the blindfold completely off.

A promise is a promise.

Figure it out, Vi.

Figure it the fuck out.

"For us to be together…" I said against her lips. "He had to die."

She stiffened, but I kept talking.

"The price I paid last year…" I sighed, resting my forehead against hers. "Was coming back from the grave to save the one girl who could put me in it with just one seething glare…"

"I didn't know you then…" She tilted her head. "I mean, I just—I was drugged and blindfolded, remember? And they kept yelling 'proof, proof, proof.'"

"Russians are ruthless like that, princess." I lifted her into my arms and gently laid her down on the bed. She was like a feast.

I gripped her thighs and then slowly tugged down her silk shorts.

"You're naked underneath." I could barely speak.

"I figured the sooner we get this over with, the sooner I can go back to plotting your death." She grinned.

I burst out laughing. "See, this is why I like you… always so honest, unlike some people…" I threw off the silk shorts, letting them fall gracefully to the floor.

She let out a little sigh. "Are you calling yourself a liar?"

"I'm the worst of them, I'm afraid," I admitted. "But lying to save someone you love—that will always be worth it, even if they hate you in the end."

"If you lie to save someone…" She arched her back as

I spread her legs wide, then started drawing small circles followed by light pinches. "…then how could they hate you?"

"Love and hate are cousins, didn't you know?" I chuckled. "Best friends, brother and sister, however you look at it, they're so closely blurred that sometimes extreme hate is truly fear that you'll lose the love, and extreme love is obsession bordering on hate."

She stiffened and sucked in a hard breath. I gave a harder pinch, followed by a sweep of my thumb.

"Valerian!" She yelled my name, not his. Pride swelled as I made her pant, as I made her body buck against my hand, and then my palm. "That feels… nice."

If she could see my face. "Nice? It feels nice?"

I pulled my hand away immediately. "What? Where did you go?" She sat up on her elbows.

"Oh, I'm still here, but the hand was too insulted to stay, so it tapped in my mouth…"

"Wh—" She clutched the sheets with her fingertips and squeezed, pulling them up with each stroke of my tongue as I worked her into a feverish state.

She was mine.

Mine.

She had always been mine.

From the day I first saw her.

"Violet…" I wanted to worship between her thighs, lick my fill, and come back for seconds as she coated my tongue. "Let go."

"No." Her body shook.

"Of everything…" I whispered, gripping her ass with my hands. "Let it all go."

"I can't." She heaved a sob.

I moved to stand, then slowly freed myself and slid my cock between her thighs.

Shit, she was so wet.

"Are you going to—" She squeezed me between her thighs, and it took every single restraint I had to keep from thrusting instead of teasing her, instead of rubbing my length against her.

"Let go," I said it softer this time.

She reached up and clung to my arms, then came apart all over me, exactly how she should have the first time. Had things been different, I would have taken my time like this, I would have tortured her in the best and worst ways until she felt no pain.

She was silent and then. "I imagined it was him."

I stilled and whispered back into the darkness, "Until tomorrow night, Violet, I'm sorry for breaking you first..."

"Let me go home."

"Three more nights." I sighed. "And at the end, you will see my face."

"Will I hate you?"

"More than you will ever know." I taunted her because I knew she wouldn't commit to me, and I knew once this was done, once she knew.

She would be lost to me forever.

For how could the pure princess, white as snow—end up with the man who took everything from her and then took some more?

"Did you have anything to do with his death?" she asked just as I reached the door, my hand on the handle.

I sighed and looked back; she lay there like the queen she was, fully exposed, chest still rising and falling like she'd run a marathon when I was the one who was hard enough to roof an entire house with only the nails. "You know the answer to that. Don't ask questions you don't want the answer to. Until tomorrow, Violet."

"Until tomorrow," she whispered back.

CHAPTER
Eighteen

Torture wasn't dying—torture was living.
—Valerian Petrov

Ash

I paced the room, back and forth, back and forth. We'd all returned home the night of the accident—all of us but Violet.

I went to my dad first. He had to know what was going on. Only I was waylaid by Phoenix, who gave me a cruel smile and shook his head.

"How are you even still alive after all the shit you've pulled?" Not my finest moment, but I was hurting, and I was pissed, and I had nothing fucking left, so why not let the sick bastard kill me?

I was ready for it.

I welcomed it.

Breaker was fucking gone.

Junior and I didn't talk about it.

Serena was a ghost of herself.

And Violet was somehow married.

This wouldn't happen unless one of the bosses knew, and I suddenly realized with glaring clarity that Phoenix was most likely that boss.

"You know." I crossed my arms.

"You should show more respect." He shrugged and then put a bulky arm around me and led me away from my dad's office and down the hall.

"How the hell did you even get in?" I said more to myself than anything.

"Oh, I'm the one that saved whatever the hell your mom calls dinner—it had Kale in it. Just call me a pizza delivery boy now." He grinned.

"You're not funny, and I hate you at least ninety percent of the time."

He just nodded. "Honestly, I would be concerned if you didn't."

"Well, at least you know."

"I always knew." He led me outside, and when we were out of earshot of the house and the dozen suits that guarded it, he spoke. "Violet has a different life now."

I was quiet and then. "Did she have a choice."

"No," he whispered into the darkness. "She didn't. I guess she could have said no, but at the end of the day, she was owned by the Petrovs the minute she put her life on the line for her family, and there is no getting out of that sort of pact."

Blood roared in my ears. "The Petrovs!"

"Valerian Petrov, to be exact." Phoenix sighed. "She's his now, and once we make it official, of course, he will be the new boss to the Petrov Family, leaving Andrei less stressed about getting killed all the time, and more focused on the Italians as it should be."

I frowned. "What could she have possibly offered up to the Petrovs of all—" I stared at him, hard. "No, don't tell me she sold herself to them. Don't tell me she gave herself over to one of those bastards that are twice her age, ugly as hell, and reek of vodka."

"He's not ugly."

"That's what you focus on? That he's not ugly but could be her dad's age? This is Violet we're talking about. When she was little, she told her teacher she wanted to be a ladybug when she grew up! The hell, Phoenix!"

He smirked. "Your dad really did sew a fantastic costume that Halloween."

"Phoenix!" I clenched my fists, ready to punch him regardless of the fact that he would kick my ass later for touching him.

He was untouchable.

He was Nicolasi.

And me? I was only an heir.

So, punching him would mean minutes in the ring and possibly another missing tooth. Not that it mattered anymore, because nothing mattered, did it? I'd lost Claire, and I'd lost Violet without even realizing it.

I was used to losing.

Everything that mattered.

Even my sanity.

So why not a molar?

They could add it to the collection.

I definitely wanted to punch something, but there was nothing nearby, only him. Shit, I would kill for a tree to shoot.

"So, that's it?" I threw my hands up in the air. "I just keep this secret from my entire family."

"They'll know soon," he said. "But I think we need to focus on the funeral before we try to solve the problem that is Violet Petrov."

My fingers curled into fists. The name alone had me seeing red.

She was married.

To a monster probably.

To someone who didn't know what she needed and how she needed it.

"It should have been Breaker," I said in a harsh whisper. "As much shit as I gave him for sleeping with her—"

Phoenix's eyebrows shot up. "Oh, keep going. I'm curious how he imagined they could get out of the whole, we will kill you for hooking up rule..."

I gulped. "She loved him."

"Her love wasn't enough," Phoenix said gruffly. "Not so soon after Serena and Junior, not with Chase. No, their love, it would not have been enough, Ash, you need to know that."

"My dad can be... complicated," I admitted.

"Ash, your dad would have killed him in cold blood for touching her after being her personal guard for that long. Everything we do in this Family, the secrets we deal in, the lies, the end goal is always to protect you, and sometimes that means even from yourselves." He patted me on the shoulder and looked up at the stars. "Make a wish, Ash, Violet will need you when she comes back. She'll need all of us."

"Because of the monster she married?"

He shot me an unreadable look. "Because of the person the

monster had to become in order to keep her love, in order to be worthy of it."

And with that cryptic message, he left.

I dragged my ass back to the pool house, grabbed a bottle of Jack, and did what I did every night.

I grabbed my favorite picture of Claire, and I talked to her until I passed out.

On some nights, she talked back.

Tonight.

She was silent.

And all I heard in my nightmares were the sounds of screeching tires, metal on metal. All I saw was Breaker's face.

And all I felt was numb.

CHAPTER
Nineteen

I would take the lies from her lips, would die for that final kiss, I would lose again so that the love of my life could finally win. —Valerian Petrov

Violet

I slept the day away—but I did eat.

And I stared down the clock like it was going to explode when it finally struck ten. When my villain would once again visit.

It was day two.

Day one had left me in a confused haze of aftershocks that had my body primed and ready even though my heart and head were one hundred percent against it.

He made me feel.

He took his time.

My brain told me that we should at least give him points for trying, for not just taking me, but trying to give something back.

My heart beat for Breaker, though.

My body, however, was starting to warm toward Valerian.

I still didn't want to face him, to take off the mask, both of our masks. I was so thankful for the blindfold that I'd willingly put it on the minute the clock struck ten.

My door creaked open.

"Say something, so I don't think I'm about to get murdered," I blurted.

His laugh was deep, sexy. "Look at you, already sitting on the bed, ready for me to torture you in the best sort of way."

"How are you going to win me over tonight, husband?" I taunted him and liked the tension that spiked in the room.

"Hmmmm…" He was walking toward me, and while my heart was bruised and broken, I found the darkness lifting a bit as his hands found my shoulders.

He leaned over and kissed each of my cheeks. "I brought you food."

"I've been eating."

"Not this, you haven't…" He was close.

I could almost taste his lips, the familiar full lips that felt so much like Breaker's, and to an insane person like myself, I could almost believe it was Breaker. And like someone who'd finally lost it—I did. I pretended it was him, I pretended he was back, he was holding the blindfold, giving me pleasure.

"Open."

I frowned but did as he said, parting my lips slightly as he put something inside my mouth.

It tasted like spiced chocolate and melted instantly on my tongue. "That's good."

"It really is," was all he said before kissing the crap out of me and running his hands over my body like he wanted to worship me. "It tastes better from your lips, wife."

He laid me back against the soft mattress nudging my legs apart with his knee and then sliding it up.

"Only two more nights after tonight."

"You can count," he teased, with a soft laugh. "I'm so proud, my wife, the genius."

"My husband, the sarcastic cruel man who wears a mask to hide from the world…"

"Not the world," he said. "Just you, and only that first day, so you'd understand what you're getting into. I had other reasons…"

"Did you kill him?" I couldn't believe I was asking what I already suspected, that in order for me to be loyal to Valerian— he had killed Breaker.

Because what sort of accident has a person going nose-first off of a bridge?

"I can hear your mind trying to figure out the pieces, just the wrong ones, not the ones I want you focusing on, not that it matters now, I guess…" He sighed like he was disappointed.

"Why doesn't it matter?"

"Because I'm out of time. I was out of time the day he died, wasn't I?"

His tongue licked at the corner of my mouth.

I didn't moan.

But my body trembled beneath his touch. "Tell me more about you."

I was trying to put off the inevitable. Where I would fall apart in his arms and feel guilty later for giving in when I just wanted to leave.

"Well…" He drew small circles on my chest with his fingertip. "I went to university."

"What did you study?"

"Sex," he said in a teasing tone. "Or as my friends would have said, I was too focused on girls to really take a major and was extremely frustrated when I found out that wasn't a thing."

"It's definitely not a thing."

"Most disappointing day of my life. I nearly cried."

"Somehow, I doubt that." I found myself smiling.

"Yes, well… my heart and my head were in different places than my cock at the time."

"What do you mean?" I suddenly wished I could see his face.

"Oh well, my cock just screamed, 'girl, girl, girl,' but my heart said, 'we're already spoken for,' and my head said, 'don't be an idiot.' So, I'd like to think I came out of it with a moral compass that didn't completely point down and stay there, if you get my meaning." His accent somehow seemed lighter, or maybe it was the story—how easy he told it.

"Nice double entendre there." I smiled at his easy tone, and then the smile fell away as Breaker's face lit up in my head like a Christmas tree. He'd been such a player.

I was always afraid to ask how many girls he slept with at Eagle Elite. But this wasn't Breaker, was it?

"So, Mr. Moral Compass…" I leaned in until I could feel his face with my hands. "How many girls did you end up sleeping with?"

"Actual sex?" He was quiet for a few seconds. "That's a trick question. You see, before college, there were quite a few, and then something happened… and after that, there was only one, and I told myself that they didn't count anymore, only her."

My heart squeezed in my chest. "What happened to her?"

"She got married to a total tool."

I burst out laughing. "So, I'm basically her?"

"Basically." His mouth found mine.

And for some reason, it felt right.

I let him kiss me.

Seduce me.

I let him put his hands on my hips, and then I let him pull my shirt over my head as his palms cupped my breasts.

His kisses moved down my neck until he stopped at one breast, took the nipple between his teeth, and sucked, sending a shot of pleasure all the way down my legs.

"Do you think—" I licked my dry lips as he continued sucking on my breasts, distracting me from my own breathing. "Do you think she's happy?"

"Without me? Highly doubtful, princess, highly doubtful."

"Arrogant."

"Reason to be." He chuckled. "Shall I prove it to you again why I'm arrogant, or can you even take it?"

"I can take whatever you have, Valerian."

A shiver rippled through him, so slight I might have imagined it, then he released a long sigh. "Say it again," he whispered, his head resting between my breasts as I started massaging his scalp, tugging at his hair.

"Say what again?"

"My name." He sounded like he was in pain, so I brought his head up, cupped either side of his face, and spoke his name across his lips. "Valerian."

I barely got the name out when he slammed his mouth against mine like I'd just validated him in some way.

His kiss was destructive to what remaining sanity I had left. His lips were almost too hot, his tongue seducing mine in a cadence that reminded me of sex, of him, of him between my thighs.

I moaned in his mouth.

His hands moved to my ass, and then he was tugging my silk shorts down to my ankles again, and I was helping him.

Because for the first time since Breaker's death, I didn't feel like I was dying inside. I felt like Valerian was giving me something.

I had no idea what.

But it felt good.

For a few brief moments, the numbness and rage subsided—all I had was pleasure, his, mine, and as selfish as it was to just take—I did exactly that. I did what Valerian had done a year ago.

He offered.

And I took.

And I felt zero guilt as I blindly reached for his pants. He was wearing dress slacks again—probably black. He always dressed so perfectly, so professionally, that it was maddening.

I flicked open the button and then needed two hands as I slid down the zipper and gripped his length in one hand. He was rock hard, pulsing in my palm.

"Fuck." The word exploded from him as he pulled his mouth away from mine. "I can't decide if I'm terrified you're going to pull a knife on me again or actually do what I've been dreaming of for weeks."

"Weeks?" I deadpanned.

"Weeks." He confirmed. "Trust me when I say in my mind it's been weeks since I've had this touch, weeks since I've smelled this skin, years since I've felt this. Damn, you drive me insane."

There was something very powerful about holding him prisoner, about the way his body responded.

I wanted a moment.

Just one moment of pure bliss with no sadness.

He hovered over me while I kicked down his pants, and then he was taking off his shirt. I raked my nails down his chest feeling a massive tattoo there.

"What am I touching?" I asked as he jerked me against him, his cock between my thighs so close my body wept.

"A tattoo," he finally said. "My lie."

"Your lie," I repeated. "Will your lie ruin me?"

"Without a doubt." He was out of breath. "It's why I need you now."

"Ask."

I couldn't see him, but I could almost imagine his stupefied look as he stared down at me.

"Ask me for it."

"You." His voice shook. "Please, Violet, can I have you? Don't promise me forever, just promise me now, and I swear I'll give you everything I have right now. It's your turn to take, Violet, so take."

I gripped him and led him to where I wanted him most. And as he slid home, I shut down all thoughts of death and only focused on his slow thrust inside my body, followed by another and then stillness as he circled his hips, hitting me exactly where I needed him.

A small cry slipped out as a tear trailed down my cheek.

Not Breaker, remember it's not Breaker.

"Violet…" He growled my name, his mouth on mine, our breathing in sync as we moved together. "Mine."

He slid a hand between us, I cried out in pure pleasure as he deepened his thrusts, and then I was flying.

I was in heaven.

I was with Breaker.

My eyes flashed open, but all I saw was black because of the damn blindfold. I went completely still as he rolled over and lay down next to me.

"How old are you?" I asked.

"Old enough." His answer.

"The girl… what was her name?"

"So, I don't get to catch my breath? All right," he said, more to himself. "And I can't remember."

"Are you a liar?"

"Yes."

I rolled my eyes, and then I reached for him again, my hands running over his face, digging into his hair. It wasn't him, but for a minute, I just—my soul recognized something.

My heart was screaming in my chest, beating against my body.

My pulse was erratic, I could feel my sanity slipping again.

"Did you have anything to do with his death?" I asked a second time like I had the night before.

"Don't ask questions you don't want the answer to, Violet." He sighed and pulled away from me. "Until tomorrow."

"Until tomorrow," I said back.

The minute the door clicked shut, I pulled off my blindfold and searched the room, not certain what it was I sought. My sanity maybe, but something was off, right? Something wasn't right, I could have sworn in those few moments, I could have sworn he was here with me.

I'd felt him.

Tears filled my eyes. I had fucking *felt* him!

Sleep didn't come, and I knew it would be a long time before it did as I stared at the picture on my cell phone.

Green eyes.

Reddish-brown hair with shots of gold.

Perfect smile.

Strong jaw.

Something wasn't right, but it wasn't wrong either. Was I just in another stage of grief, imagining him when he was gone?

I was literally going to attend his funeral in a few days.

With a last shake of my head, I tossed my phone away, then thought again, grabbed it, and sent a text.

Violet: I will miss you forever. I love you.

Nothing happened.

I hated that I had gotten my hopes up.

I clutched the cell to my chest and fell asleep, my dreams filled with visions of Breaker's taunting smile as he twirled my hair between his fingers.

CHAPTER
Twenty

I should have said something, but the deeper I fell, the more I resolved, I would have her before my descent into hell.

—Valerian Petrov

Valerian

I'd slept with her.

My body was sated.

My heart and soul were disappointed; in me, in my tactics, in my seduction. Who the hell had I become?

He'd said it would be hard.

But the deeper in I got, the worse I became until it was the parts of me I hated most that seemed to be ruling all logic.

Two more nights.

The funeral was tomorrow.

I would be there with her.

I would hold her hand.

If she let me.

"Fuck." I kicked the barstool over and grabbed the decanter of whiskey and the two glasses.

I'd spent the entire day both dreading and looking forward to tonight in a way that had me distracted at the office to the point of everyone asking who pissed me off and who died.

Apparently, owning several shipping companies and being the boss to over a thousand employees all of a sudden wasn't what was getting to me—it was a girl, one simple woman, one complicated woman. One woman who I had given up everything for.

One who would not keep me once she saw me.

I grabbed the bar stool, bent it over my knees, and cracked the wood into kindling. You'd think I'd feel better.

I didn't.

"Sir?" Sancto hurried around the corner. "Everything all right?"

"Great," I huffed, tossing the wood pieces to the floor. "Sorry about the broken barstool."

"Er, it put up a good fight," he teased, then grabbed what was now firewood and started piling it up on the table. "So, how is our princess this evening?"

Beautiful.

Mine.

His.

Confused.

Sad.

"She's... it's complicated," I finally said.

"Well, then uncomplicate it." He made it seem so easy when it was anything but that.

"Good idea," I said mockingly. "I'll just head over to

Chicago real quick, admit everything, get shot in the head, and be right back."

He stared me down with a smirk. "Don't be dramatic, you have a few on your side. You'd be fine."

"A few against Chase Abandonato? Do you even know who you're talking about? His rage is legendary."

"He's just a man." Sancto gave me a serious look. "And so are you."

"Yeah." Just a man who would do anything for his daughter. Just a man who you didn't double-cross. Just a man who would rip me apart with his bare hands.

The clock struck ten.

Night three was ahead of us.

I took the stairs two at a time until I finally reached the top and the master bedroom. I had my mask in place just in case.

After knocking twice, I let myself in and nearly dropped the crystal glasses.

She was naked.

One hundred percent naked..

In the middle of the bed.

"Am I hallucinating?" I gasped.

She turned her blindfolded head toward me. "Do I have clothes on?"

"Hell no."

"Then you're not hallucinating. Congratulations, I'm naked."

"Thank God." I rushed over to her, hands shaking, firewood forgotten.

And Chase Abandonato a distant memory.

She sat up and looked in my general direction. "One question before you touch me."

Shit.

Damn it!

Shit.

"What?" My body trembled.

I burned for her in a way that was otherworldly.

"Did you have anything to do with his death? Answer me even if I hate the answer, and then you can have this."

Manipulation. I should have known. I was the king of it, wasn't I?

I said nothing and then, "Even if you hate the answer, Violet? Even then?" I shook my head. It was time, wasn't it? Maybe that's why I'd been anxious all day. I'd known I was on borrowed time. I'd known the minute she gave herself to me.

It wasn't free.

I had thought—hoped I could buy the days from her.

I'd just wanted… more than what I had been given.

But I would always want more, wouldn't I?

Two more nights would never be enough.

I pulled the mask from my face and tossed it on the floor. It mocked me from where it lay, staring with vacant eyes.

It was over.

"Yes." I squeezed my eyes shut. "Because I'm the one who killed him."

CHAPTER
Twenty-One

Drown me, take me, torture me, steal me, use me, words etched on my soul, would that she could make me whole.

—Valerian Petrov

Violet

I had the blindfold on.

I was naked.

But I was in control.

That was what I kept telling myself as my body buzzed with the awareness that he saw everything, that he was drinking his fill, that he wanted.

I had no idea where I got the nerve to even do this, but I was tired of his games, tired of the lies, and tired of not sleeping, wondering what could be so horrible that I would hate him for the rest of my life.

And my answer was always the same.

What could possibly gain my hatred so much?

The death of the man I loved.

And those hands, the hands that had loved me last night, seduced me, made promises—those hands were the ones that did it.

"Because I'm the one who killed him." The words felt like a bomb as my entire body tensed, ready to fight, ready to avenge the death of the man who promised to never let me go.

And in that same breath, did exactly that.

"Does that mean…" I whispered, every muscle on alert, every synapse ready to snap me into action to avenge him, to kill this man, my husband. "…that I get to avenge him?"

"Killing me won't bring him back, we've been over this," he said. "But one thing that does kill me over and over again is how beautiful you are, and how badly I want to touch you, how desperately I want one more night—no, not one more, a dozen more, a hundred, knowing that you'll deny me that one thing because you know how desperately I want it."

My next breath stalled momentarily. His words affected me in ways I wasn't prepared for. He made me feel bold, this killer in front of me, with his lies and his wicked mouth.

My body was at war with my heart because even now, I was yearning for him in a way that was sick and twisted.

"You can't have me," I lied.

"You promised two more nights. You took an oath, did you not?" He was closer now, though I hadn't heard him moving. "Or are you too innocent to imagine what it would feel like to have the hands of a killer mar your perfect skin?"

It triggered me.

I hated being called innocent.

It reminded me of being powerless.

Being weak.

I sat up and stared in his general direction, my vision completely black, and then I spread my legs over the bed and lifted my chin. "A promise is a promise even with a killer like you."

"A killer like me," he rasped. "Funny, I imagine you prefer the monster even though you want to deny it. He wasn't like me, you know. He wasn't like this. He was hiding from who he was." His hands gripped my thighs, keeping my legs apart, and then one hand gripped my chin painfully, forcing me to look up at him even though I couldn't see anything. "He would never have done this."

I was ready to ask what, and then he picked me up and flipped me over onto my stomach. My breasts rubbed against the sheets, and my nipples hardened to taut peaks. I let out a moan at the sound of clothes rustling, and then a rough palm was grazing my ass.

"Innocent." His hand descended, slapping my sensitive skin so hard my eyes watered. "Little." His hand hit again. "Violet." Another slap sent my body arching off the bed. "Petrov."

The final slap had me ready to commit murder, to turn around and kick him in the face, then pull him close and beg him for more.

"Pleasure and pain," he said in a low voice. "I told you I would give you both. They go hand in hand, something you would know about me, Violet. I will give you everything you need, and that includes the pain that you don't even realize your body begs for, so the numbness goes away, so the fight returns." He rubbed his hand where he'd hit, and then he was gripping my thighs, pulling me back.

With one violent thrust, he was inside me.

I cried out with pleasure, hating myself for loving what he was doing, hating him for the blood on his hands, mourning Breaker in a way I'd never understood I needed.

"I'll never be able to quit you." He swore violently and pumped into me, both hands holding tightly to my hips and keeping me in place. It didn't matter. I didn't want to go anywhere. The pressure building inside was making me weak. If he hadn't been gripping me, I would have sagged to the mattress. Heat surged through me, radiating from the point where we connected and washed over my face and neck, reaching to my fingers and toes.

I clung to the sheets as my back arched. I saw him then, Breaker, I saw his smile, his protective stance, and then he was gone.

He was gone.

Gone.

I cried out.

And then I was in Valerian's arms as I clung to him, to the only real thing right in front of me.

"No matter what happens right now," Valerian whispered, his breath hot on my ear. "Remember, he's gone, and he's not coming back."

"You think I don't know that?" My lower lip trembled, but I would not cry, not now, not naked in the arms of my husband, my enemy, his killer.

Gently, Valerian set me down on the bed and then pulled a soft blanket over my naked body.

What was he doing?

"You promised me one more night, Violet." His accent had somehow… faded.

My heart pounded in my chest.

"And…" He sighed. "…I know how you hate it when your makeup gets ruined, so don't cry anymore, I don't think I can bear it."

A buzzing sounded in my ears as I lay there, nearly paralyzed with confusion and desperation.

"Your accent, it's gone." My voice trembled.

"Oh, it comes and goes." The accent was back.

"What's going on?" I reached for him.

"I wanted one more day to lie, Violet, one more day just for me, one more day just for us, because I know how this ends, and it's with me taking you back to Chicago and you hating me forever."

"What?" I frowned. "I haven't made that choice yet."

"You will." With the accent gone, he sounded like Breaker, identical to Breaker. "Trust me on this, I've known you ever since you promised to put those pieces back together—I wanted to thank you for trying. I also wanted to let you know that I prefer to stay broken. After all, you can't become whole without your other half, and right now she's wondering if she's crazy, wondering if I somehow drugged her, wondering why I lied all this time, wondering why I broke her in the first place that night at the club, wondering all the things that started this slow descent into hell, and I doubt she'll ever look back and offer forgiveness. Her hate, you see, will outweigh her grief, and I, Valerian Petrov, will deserve it."

Tears leaked from my eyes, soaked the blindfold, streamed down my cheeks.

What he was saying was impossible.

My stomach lurched.

My heart pounded.

With trembling hands, I reached for my blindfold, but he beat me to it and very slowly tugged it down to my chin.

And there he was.

My best friend, but different.

His eyes brighter.

His hair lighter.

His demeanor more haunted than I'd ever seen.

And I knew, in my soul, he was right, whatever I would have hoped would be left of Breaker had died that day... and had been replaced with this.

CHAPTER
Twenty-Two

A truth and a lie, I knew she'd ask me why, but we all have our orders, our emotions a tangled flood; in the end, all that mattered was blood.
—Valerian Petrov

Valerian

She was staring at me like I wasn't real, and then her gaze fell like she was mourning me all over again.

"Why?" Her eyes filled with tears. "Why would you—" She put her shaking hands in her lap and squeezed her eyes shut. "It was you that night, wasn't it?"

I swallowed the lump in my throat. "There is nothing I would not do for you, Violet. Nothing." Anger coursed through me then, anger at our situation, anger at myself, at Phoenix, Andrei. "They were going to rape you, and I couldn't just stand by and watch—" My voice cracked. "I had one choice, and I made it."

She looked away from me. "That choice, it caused a ripple effect, didn't it?"

"It brought Valerian Petrov back from the dead and made Breaker and you a target," I admitted. "The minute those thugs reported back rumors of my existence, well let's just say I should have known that day, that I would be forced out of hiding, and then not only did they demand me, but the Italian princess, pure of blood." I stood and gave her my back, fists still clenched. "I broke you, and then I damned you—you had to believe it was real, you all had to mourn. Phoenix and Andrei helped me set it up—I couldn't exist in both worlds, and the Russians needed their heir."

"Their heir," Violet repeated, her voice hollow. "I take it you and Andrei are related then?"

"His dad, the old boss, he had an estranged brother who married my mom—"

"Making Andrei the bastard and you the royal blood," she finished.

I turned back around.

Slowly she stood and walked over to me. I didn't know what to expect, but her expression was destroying me bit by bit as she slowly, finally made eye contact and whispered, "You're right, Breaker Campisi is dead."

"Violet—"

"Breaker Campisi would never mess with my heart. Breaker Campisi would never—" Her voice broke as tears streamed down her cheeks. "Never do this to me. He was my best friend."

My heart cracked in my chest.

"He was everything, and I'll never forgive you for killing him."

"Violet, you have to know—"

"Take me home now."

"You are home." I swallowed. "I will always be your home despite his death. You married me, and you promised me one more night." I locked eyes with her. "So, you either give it to me here or in Chicago, but you will give it to me."

Again, she approached, lifting her hand and slapping me across the face so hard my skin burned. "I. Hate. You."

"I know." I squeezed my eyes shut. "I hate me too."

I walked into the closet and grabbed a bag.

"Pack, I'll have the jet fueled to take us back for the funeral."

"You're unbelievable!" she roared. "You can't just show up to your own funeral!"

"Oh, trust me, I don't want to, but now that you know, they deserve to know too, and Phoenix refuses to tell them. Andrei says I'm all out of favors, and I owe it to my old Family."

She smiled at me sweetly.

I frowned. "Why are you suddenly smiling?" Was she going to forgive me? Tell me I was a jackass, but at least run into my arms and say she had missed me.

"Oh, nothing," Her grin widened. "I just can't wait for my dad to slit your throat."

I gulped. "He won't kill another boss."

"He just might… for his favorite, innocent little daughter, whose virginity got taken by Valerian Petrov."

And just like that, that tiny glimmer of hope flickering in my chest died a quick death.

Because if she wanted her dad to kill me, I might just let him, so I didn't have to remember what it used to be like to hold Violet Abandonato in my arms and hear her say my name.

Not Breaker.

But my true name.

Valerian.

No matter what, I was hers for a few days, and she was mine, and even death would not take that away from me.

And then I smiled too and left her to pack. The smile fell when the sound of things breaking against the wall hit my ears, and then a muffled sob followed by a scream.

I broke her first.

I broke her last.

So even though Breaker was dead—it seemed I kept all those tendencies to hurt and break those I loved the most.

CHAPTER
Twenty-Three

My truth was out in the open, but my battle had just begun because what was broken would make them come, weapons in hand, poison raised, the people I once called family to end my days.

—Valerian Petrov

Ash

"Another funeral." Junior handed me the flask.

It used to be Breaker's. We'd filled it with gin, so each gulp made me want to hurl, but it was Breaker, and it felt like the world was ending or was about to.

"I don't want to go," I admitted. "I don't know how to put one foot in front of the other."

My dad poked his head in the kitchen. We were all at Nixon's waiting to go to the funeral together. The mood was somber. Tex had been drunk all day yesterday only to finally crumble at his wife's feet.

The toughest of them all, sobbing like a baby in his wife's lap.

I had shed too many tears this year for people who had left.

Everyone left eventually.

I took another swig.

Junior hung his head as Serena came over and sat between us on the couch. "Gin?"

"Yup." Junior handed it to her.

She just shook her head as a tear slid down her cheek.

The only person who wasn't drunk, drinking, or trying not to cry was King.

No, King was just pissed.

So angry that he'd gotten into a fight with every single boss and member of the Family, including Dom, who was the silent, deadly type one did not pick a fight with.

He got a few hits in on him before Dom slammed him against the ground and told him to control his rage before he tied him up and put him in the closet.

King just sneered at him.

And we all knew what Tex was thinking.

He had lost two sons that day.

Because King would never be the same. He was… altered, so when I caught him smoking pot, I said nothing.

He thought it would help.

It wouldn't.

It just made you more numb; I'd gone down that road and came back even more depressed than before.

"Sister's almost here," my dad finally said after taking in the mood in the room. All the bosses were there.

Phoenix and Andrei were the only alert ones. What the hell kind of monsters counted weapons on the kitchen table before a funeral?

Those guys.

Phoenix started strapping a few guns to his chest.

Andrei did the same.

What the fuck? Did they think we were going to get attacked at the funeral of all places?

Good, let them shoot at me. At least I'd see Claire again.

Our baby.

I squeezed my eyes shut. "Do you know if Violet's staying?"

My dad offered a sad smile. "All I know is she's really enjoying studying with Nikolai. He checks in every day."

I snorted. Dad was going to shit a brick when he saw her ring. That was if she was going to tell him that she was currently sharing a bed with some psychopath Russian who, according to Phoenix, wasn't ugly, so yay for her.

"Hey." Serena nudged me. "You already drunk, cousin, or are you just being your normal grumpy self?"

"Normal grumpy self," Junior answered for me. "And for a second, I thought you said elf and started to laugh then realized I should probably stop drinking if I thought you calling Ash an elf was funny."

Serena snorted out a laugh at that.

It was crazy to me that they even knew how to still laugh.

Mine was fucking broken as hell.

Why him?

No offense to my other cousins, but I would have preferred any of them die over this. Breaker was just too... happy.

The rest of us had darkness.

We had pain.

When death came calling, we yelled right back, flipped it off, and then pulled out a gun. He made jokes, then zig-zagged in the opposite direction in hopes of finding a girl he could make-out with.

I leaned back, tipping the last bits of gin down my throat as Phoenix grabbed a knife and handed it to Andrei.

"Something's up." I eyed them suspiciously. "And that's not the alcohol talking."

"They've been literally suiting up for the past half hour," Serena agreed.

"Guys, that's just them." Junior stood and then grabbed the flask from me. "I'm going to go refill this."

"Okay, elf." Serena teased. "I'm coming with. You're not even walking in a straight line."

"This is straight." He was literally walking a diagonal path toward the kitchen.

"Sure." She patted him on the back and then shoved him in a more straight line toward the bar while I continued to watch Andrei and Phoenix act like we were about to go kill some people.

Maksim plopped down next to me. "Dad's acting weird."

"Weirder than normal," I agreed.

"He was counting bullets," Maksim said under his breath. "And then he asked me to come sit by you and hold you down just in case."

"I'm sorry, what?"

"I think he was kidding? Maybe?" Maksim frowned. "Sometimes I don't get his humor, though. It's very…"

The door opened.

"Russian," I finished for him and stood, ready for trouble, only to get knocked down the minute I set my eyes on the "Russian" and my sister.

And then all hell fucking broke loose.

CHAPTER
Twenty-Four

Deadman walking had a new meaning as their love twisted into hate and descended upon me as I accepted my fate.
—Valerian Petrov

Valerian

When I was little, I imagined this moment. I tried running away a dozen times, convinced that if I could just get back to Seattle, back to my old house, that Mom would be there waiting.

And then I would come back with the force of a hundred years of Russian prosperity and men at my side and prove that I had left as a prince and returned as a king.

Funny how in your ten-year-old head, things were wrapped up into perfect packages with neat tiny bows, whereas now all I saw was blood.

All I felt was betrayal trickle through the air.

And when I locked eyes with King first, he just shook his head like I should have figured out a way to do better.

He had found me that last night I ran.

And that was when I told him who I was.

We became brothers that night.

We became enemies this morning.

Because I did what I had sworn to him, I would never do—abandon him.

I wanted to reach for Violet's hand.

Instead, I stood, head high, eyes sharp as both Phoenix and Andrei moved to stand in front of me, fully armed, offering their protection.

Violet went stock-still next to me.

"What. The. Fuck." Tex ground out, his eyes on me, then back to Phoenix, over to Andrei, and one by one, the bosses and made men faced us.

Dante Alfero.

Nixon Abandonato.

Dom Abandonato.

Tex Campisi.

Chase Abandonato.

They faced us down like a bad western, each of them with weapons pulled, and then Junior grabbed a lunging Serena shoving her behind him, then literally tackling her to the floor and sitting on her while she screamed for my blood.

Literally, screamed for it.

The wives who were present gave no more than cold expressions. My adopted mom, however, Mo rushed to my side and pulled me in for a hug.

"You're alive, you're alive, you're alive." Kisses rained down on my face as I hugged her back.

And it killed my soul to have to whisper, "Breaker's dead."

How many times would I have to utter those words?

How many times would it take for it to finally not hurt?

Slowly she pulled away from me, leaving her scent clinging to me. She always smelled like vanilla and cinnamon. Her blue eyes filled with tears as she shook her head and then turned her rage toward Phoenix.

He was prepared for the knife.

And the kick as he caught her by the ankle and shoved her toward my adopted dad.

Our Capo.

"You dare go against me?" He sneered at Phoenix and then rolled his eyes at Andrei. "I expect this of *him*, not of you."

"We're kind of a package deal now," Phoenix said it like it annoyed him while Andrei grinned like it was the best day of his life. I half expected him to burst out laughing and go. "Gotcha!"

"Move." He took a step toward Phoenix. "Now."

"I can't." Phoenix had his Glock in one hand and a knife in the other. He would protect me to his death.

I saw the flicker of movement in his right hand.

And I couldn't let him be the guilty party.

In a flash, I grabbed the gun from Phoenix's hand, pointed it at my dad and shot him in the foot, then held it to Phoenix's head while I trained my own gun on Andrei. "We should probably all sit down before someone gets hurt." My dad screamed in rage from the floor. "Or more hurt, and it went straight through, so get up and stop yelling. You're making Mom sad."

"I'M GOING TO KILL YOU!" Dad bellowed.

I sighed. "To be fair, I did already die, and you'll be late for my funeral, or worse covered in my blood, which really doesn't look all that great to all the families we swore to protect."

"Violet." Chase held out his hand. "Walk toward me."

She stood still and then gave me a syrupy smile. "No, I think we should all talk, get things off our chest, I'll go first—"

"Fuck." I didn't lower the guns, but the bosses did stop moving, and Andrei looked proud that I was holding my gun to his head. It was the only thing I could think of that would make them not attack all of us in their hurt and their rage.

And now I was a dead man.

"Vi?" Chase frowned. "Honey, why is—" His brain worked. I could practically hear it. His eyes widened, and with a yell that sounded like it came from the pits of hell, he charged us.

All to get to Violet.

As if I would hurt her.

I tossed the gun back to Phoenix and spun around, grabbing Violet by the arm and pulling her against me, protecting her against whatever Chase was going to do and taking whatever anger he had for her.

I was dead already.

Why not be a human shield?

She stumbled back against the wall, my body covering her.

"My dad would never hurt me." She shoved at me.

"No offense." I gritted my teeth as Chase drove a knife directly into my back, poetic, really. "But he's fucking crazy!"

"Get." Stab. "Away." Stab. "From." Stab. "My." That one went deep. "DAUGHTER!"

I dropped to the floor in a heap of burning pain from the short stab wounds in my back, and the entire room fell quiet until someone muttered, "Was that a steak knife?"

Welcome to the mafia.

I groaned and pushed to my feet, but I'd barely found any balance when Chase kicked me in the stomach and sent me sailing to my ass again.

Rolling to the side, I reached out and grabbed his ankle, then spun around and kicked him in the shin. A crunching sound filled the kitchen as he fell backward and then wobbled toward me.

I jumped up, even wounded. I'd been training for this since I was three. My mom had demanded it. I knew how to fight; I'd just always chosen not to.

I dodged a punch and then landed one to his jaw while everyone watched in horror, unable to move.

Blood trickled down my back as he tackled me to the ground, straddling me, ready to beat my entire face in.

I smiled when Phoenix held a gun to Chase's head, followed by Andrei. "He's already dead, don't kill him again."

"I told you." Chase sneered. "What would happen if you touched her!"

"You did." My smile was probably bloody. He'd gotten a few good blows in there. "But it's not illegal to touch my wife, is it?"

"Before you pull the trigger." Chase's voice was a deathly whisper. "I'm going to kill him, then do whatever the hell you want to me. Phoenix, he dies first, then kill me, but I get to send him to Hell!"

"I wouldn't." Phoenix sighed like he was bored. "Since he saved her life and died in order to do it."

Chase's fist didn't come flying. He held it over my head then slowly turned toward Violet. "Is that true?"

"Yes." She didn't look happy about it, though. What did I expect? "But because I think you actually might kill him, and

I think Ash and Junior deserve that honor—I'm going to wait until you're not on top of him to tell you why."

That's when I saw it.

The pain in Junior's gaze as he walked over to us.

And the absolute rage in Ash's. "Dad, I'm their king, remember? I get to decide what happens and who dies, and in this case, it will be my fucking pleasure to continue what you started—" He narrowed his eyes. "Also, you slept with my sister so…" He kicked me in the side and then pulled out a chair and sat. "Let's talk. I have a funeral to go to and a person to kill."

"Savage." Maksim grinned at the spectacle and pulled out a chair while the bosses all set their weapons down on the table and sat.

My mom went and sat on my dad's lap, waiting, her expression hurt, he was bleeding all over the floor from the gunshot wound in his foot, but he didn't even seem to care.

I had put those tears there.

I had done all of this.

None of my cousins would look me in the eyes, and the worst of it, Violet went and sat next to Chase.

On the opposite end of the table like she'd already made her choice despite the ring on her finger.

Despite the hole in my heart.

I winced when Phoenix grabbed a towel and held it to my back. "Superficial, you'll live."

"Unfortunately." Nixon finally spoke. "Someone talk now."

Dante still had his gun ready to shoot, so clearly, nobody trusted me anymore, and he'd always been one of my favorites, closest to us in age, fun.

Now he looked lethal.

Great.

"Before we talk..." Andrei stood and then walked over to me; he knelt in front of my chair then pulled out his knife; it had the Petrov crest on it. I knew it well. He undid the buttons of his shirt.

I didn't know he was going to do this here.

For all of them to see.

But I knew what he wanted me to do.

So, I too slowly unbuttoned my shirt, revealing the Campisi crest that had been tattooed there, right along with the Russian symbol beneath it, hidden in the ink.

"Blood of my blood." Andrei's voice shook. "Nephew." His eyes bore into me. "True heir to the Petrov line." He sliced across his hand and then brought the blade across his heart, doing the same then handed it to me.

I made the same cuts and then put my hand across his heart while he put his across mine.

"Blood over life, the prince... has returned as king, protect the Family, thrive, love, dance, drink... live." He slid the crest off his finger.

I held out my left hand, the sickle tattoo seemed to glow to life as he slid the ring onto my finger.

And crowned me, king.

Boss of the Petrov crime Family.

And the Petrov Family line finally set to rights.

A weight seemed to lift off his shoulders as he kissed my right cheek, then wrapped an arm around me and pulled me against his chest.

"Regardless—" He stood and faced everyone. "—of what's said today, he is the Petrov boss—and you owe him your allegiance the same you did me. We are thankful that I'm no longer divided between two families, now we can truly be one." He said that last part with his eyes on Violet.

She held her head high and then lifted her left hand, heavy with my mom's old ring. "One Family."

Andrei nodded to her.

Gasps were heard all around the room.

I expected Chase to launch himself across the table and kill me.

Instead, he looked between us with a frown. "Not training under Nikolai, are you?"

"She's training under someone…" Maksim joked, earning a seething glare from Dad and choked out. "Too soon?"

By the looks of Chase's white fingertips, as he squeezed the knife in his hand, I would definitely say it would always be too soon to have that discussion.

"We're going to need more wine…" Andrei went over to the bar, grabbed seven bottles, and put them on the table.

Once everyone had a glass or a bottle to chug from if you were Chase, Andrei sat and started talking.

"Last Christmas, Violet was kidnapped."

Violet's mom Luc gasped and reached for her daughter. Chase looked ready to break someone's neck.

Phoenix continued. "She was dancing at the club. Tank was taken down, a few rogue Russian associates were there to kill Andrei."

"Because everyone wants to kill Andrei," Andrei said, making a face as he tossed back a gulp of wine in the most un-Italian way. "Good thing I am not easy to kill."

"I wouldn't go that far…" Chase smiled a cruel smile.

And I was back to wondering if I would live through the night.

Phoenix rolled his eyes. "You're lucky I tolerate you—"

"I tolerate you too. I think this is what you call friendship?"

"Could you guys table the bromance for like five seconds?" Junior snapped. "What happened after that?"

Andrei sighed and shared a look with me that basically said I'm so sorry that you're going to die now. Perfect. "Breaker, as you know him, was with me. We were approached by the men, they drugged her and said that I needed to prove that I was still the Russian boss—typically my father would—" He made a face. "—fuck one of the women or take their virginity as a consolation prize for himself, it's a sick tradition, twisted even for my own men, and one of the old ways I've extinguished for obvious reasons. I had to choose between my loyalty to the Sinacore Family, my family, or loyalty to the Russians, and already as you well know, we've had men weekly trying to rise up and take the Family back from my grip because as much as they fear me, they don't want my loyalty split."

Violet locked eyes with me.

"I'm sorry," I mouthed.

"I hate you," she mouthed right back.

Well. It was worth a shot.

Pain pounded in my back, and now my skull felt like it was on fire as Andrei kept talking.

"Breaker has had full knowledge of his destiny since he could walk. You see, I'm the one who tried to kill him all those years ago—" He winked. "So sorry about that, by the way."

"No, you aren't." I rolled my eyes. "You literally set my house on fire, but sure, you're sorry. My mom died. But that's on me," I said gruffly. "Not you."

"Phoenix found out about my plan because he knows too

much and likes to check up on all of us. Trust me, he has trackers on all of you and friends in every high and low place."

"I think that was a compliment." Phoenix clicked his glass against Andrei's. "All I saw was a scared little boy who thought he killed his mom and had nowhere to go, a boy that would be a target until he was able to fight back or take back what was stolen." He eyed Andrei. "I took him in, gave him a new life, and the protection of Tex's Family until it was time. The plan was to wait until he finished college and then let him slowly take the Family back."

"Until I rose from the dead," I whispered, staring into my wine glass. "Until that night when Violet was threatened, when she was going to suffer at the hands—" My voice cracked. "I couldn't do it, I couldn't just stand there and let them hurt her. One of the guys started taking off his jacket, and I just lost it. She's my best friend," I rasped. "Was my best friend. I would do anything for her, and I knew there was a chance that they'd demand this, but I did it anyway." I raised my head and locked eyes with Chase. "I went into that room with her. She was blindfolded, she was so brave. She asked for my name." I swallowed, throat dry. "So, I told her my real name, Valerian Petrov. They were watching on the cameras. They demanded my identity, and after proving it—" I lifted my left hand where the tattoo stained my finger. "I tried to fake it, but one of these assholes came in and showed me his phone. A gun was trained on Chase, Luc, and Ariel at the Christmas party while he danced with Luc, a gun was trained on Andrei, a gun was basically trained on me. I had three minutes left, so once he was out of the room, I panicked. And Violet, perfect Violet, so calm and innocent, told me she forgave me before I even sinned. I took her virginity in a club while my own people watched, and I'll live with that for the rest of my life."

Chase slammed his hands onto the table and stood, his head was lowered. "And now? What are you now?"

"Married," I whispered. "Because word of Valerian Petrov reached Seattle and they said if I didn't take my rightful place and bring my Italian bride with me, the alliance with the Italians, despite what Andrei said, would be null. And Phoenix was right. Breaker had to die so Valerian could live, so all of you could live." I stood. "So, if you want to kill me, kill me, but I would do it again and again, make those choices, even if it means you look at me like I betrayed you. When I was ten, you invited me into your family. Trust me when I say, killing off the son, cousin, friend you loved, was one of the hardest things I've ever had to do, but love sometimes asks us to die." I jerked my head toward the clock. "You're going to be late. Bury me well."

I couldn't take it anymore.

I left the table.

I walked on wooden legs toward the basement door, stripping off my shirt and dropping it on the stairs, then stepped into the middle of the sparring ring, fell to my knees, and screamed.

CHAPTER
Twenty-Five

In sickness and in health, in death and in life, but what about purgatory, darkness as they drive the knife.
—Valerian Petrov

Violet

As far as funerals went, it was uneventful compared to the scene back at the house.

I mourned him while Junior gave the eulogy.

I cried when asked to put a flower on the casket.

I was inconsolable when I looked at the picture of him, so vastly different from how he looked now. I had so many questions, but I was afraid that by asking him, I'd fall in love with him all over again—and he didn't deserve that love.

All of this could have been avoided if he'd just told me.

I would have run away with him.

But deep inside, part of me asked... at what cost? My dad would have killed him, disowned me, we both would have been in constant danger. But our love would have sustained us, right? Was that just my innocence speaking?

"You know..." Phoenix stood next to me while family members said their goodbyes and started shuffling out of the church. "You would have never been able to be together."

I opened my mouth to tell him that wasn't true but found I couldn't lie, not here, not now. "I would have found a way."

"Funny you should say that, because on the outside it appears to me that we did find a way, Violet. When you're young and in love, you tend to get lazy—I saw you in the church that day with him. However stupid it may have been, that choice you made sealed your fate, so when you go home with your hate, remember your love did this—that tattoo is on your finger because you put it there. Not by accident, but by choice."

He left me staring at him wide-eyed, mouth gaping. He didn't even let me deny it because, how could I?

When I seduced Breaker?

When I loved him?

When I was on the verge of losing my mind trying to think of ways to be together?

When I mourned the loss of him?

I denied nothing.

Because Phoenix was right.

I had chosen this too.

And it was time I faced that choice head-on rather than projecting all that hate onto the one man who had saved my life and my dad's, my families.

Valerian. Petrov.

One more night...

I hung my head and sighed.

"We'll find a way out of this," Tex whispered as he put an arm around me. "You were taken advantage of, I won't let him—"

"Tex." I looked up at him. He looked exhausted, dark circles marred his face, and his lips were pulled tight like he was going to growl any second.

"Would you ever have let me marry Breaker, as the Capo?"

He clenched his jaw shut and avoided my eyes. "No."

"Even if I loved him?"

"Oh, if you loved him well…" He said sarcastically. Then he released an exasperated sigh. "Violet, we have rules for a reason. Junior and Serena nearly died because of it, but even I wouldn't have prevented you from someone you truly loved. I would, however, have sent you far, far, far, far away, beat the shit out of him, made him wait seven years for your favor, and then given him someone else."

"Um, isn't that in the Bible?"

"Is it?" His face softened. "When it comes to our children, especially the girls, we get protective, as far as I'm concerned, nobody deserves you."

"Nobody deserves you either." I nudged him.

He barked out a laugh. "Vi, you are everything to me, you're more daughter than niece, I guess now you really are in a roundabout way my daughter," He gave his head a shake. "How could you ever think that there would be a man worthy of the love you give us? It doesn't exist; everything is secondhand. My love for you, however, is so vast, so wide, so insurmountable that if you came to me, truly came to me and told me you loved him—I would have found a way for you to be together even if it meant going to war with my own family, just maybe don't tell the others that, we don't want mutiny."

"Good thing, then," I whispered, "that you didn't have to."

He stopped walking. "You love him."

He didn't ask it, he declared it.

"I loved Breaker," I admitted. "I kind of hate Valerian."

"Love doesn't change just because a name is different, Vi. You either love him for who he is and has always been—or you let him go." He kissed me on the cheek and walked off to shake hands with someone who looked like he killed people for breakfast and sprinkled their blood on his cereal.

Tex always did like the scary ones.

I thought about his words the entire ride home. It felt like a lifetime ago when I had come home from another funeral when I'd mourned the loss of Claire and the loss of the old life I thought I wanted.

The SUV pulled up to Nixon's.

Food would be prepared.

Wine would be guzzled, not sipped.

And I would have a choice to make.

My chest hurt from all the breaking, and I wondered if I even knew how to forgive him after everything.

A small part of me understood the secrecy—but what really hurt the most was that he was my best friend.

And he never trusted me with the truth.

I loved him.

And he had kept this from me for all those years. Then, when finally given the opportunity, he had decided I couldn't handle it, had decided I wasn't strong enough. And he'd kept it from me.

He was wrong.

I wasn't innocent, Violet Abandonato.

I was brave, Violet Petrov.

His wife.

The more I thought about it, the angrier I got until I walked into that house, stormed past my mom, and yelled at Junior. "Where is he?"

"Oh shit," Maksim muttered.

"Downstairs, probably beating the shit out of Ash because he said please." Junior smirked.

Serena and I made eye contact, Izzy walked up sandwich in hand, Maksim took it, and then we all charged down to the basement.

There would be blood.

And it was going to be his for daring to put me in a corner for my safety.

By the time this was over, he was going to be the one cowering.

Fucking kneeling.

At my feet.

His Russian queen.

CHAPTER
Twenty-Six

Spilled blood, broken heart, she had it first, from the very start.
—Valerian Petrov

Valerian

"Again!" Ash screamed.

His nose was broken. My first hit had been a bit hard, and I wasn't really thinking, and then he hit me back, breaking mine.

So, both of us could barely breathe through all the cartilage and blood loss in our noses, my right eye was bleeding, the wounds on my back had cheerfully opened up, spilling enough blood to make the mat slippery, and Ash was still coming at me.

"Ash." I dodged his punch. "I told you I was sorry!"

"Sorry doesn't cut it!" he roared. "You'll fight me until you pass out, and then you'll do it again and again, and one more time because you SLEPT WITH MY SISTER, fucking faked your own death, and somehow she's still not happy! What the hell did you do?"

A few of the De Lange recruits were currently training over in the corner since Nixon had given them full access to the gym—they all stopped sparring and stared in shock as Ash threw another right hook catching me in the side of the head and making me stumble toward the ropes.

"Nothing to see here," I grumbled as Tank, our FBI recruit, winced in my direction like he knew it hurt too much to talk. "You're going to traumatize all the new blood, Ash."

"Good." He sneered. "Maybe one day they'll help me kill you. We've been busy for the last few days. So much dying does that to people, makes them prepare for war. You did that."

I blocked his next hit with my forearms then kicked him in the stomach, sending me onto my back. I jumped up as fast as I could, and my vision doubled for a second as Violet walked into the basement with Izzy, Junior, Serena, and Maksim. They all looked way too happy to have just attended my funeral.

Son of a bitch, my head hurt.

"Leave," Serena snapped to the De Lange recruits. With a sigh, Tank jerked his head toward the door. All five of them followed, their faces pale.

King had been leaning on the wall, watching us fight for an hour now, and every so often, he'd yell something like, "Kill shot."

And Ash would literally aim for my dick.

It was a bad day. A very bad day.

And now it was worse because Violet was here, and she looked pissed enough to join in on the fun.

"Vi?" I blinked up at her.

"Ash." Violet smiled sweetly at her brother. "It's my turn."

"Oh, shit." Maksim whistled. "I've never seen her fight, but she's probably pissed off enough to kill him. This really turned out to be a way better day than I thought when I woke up this morning."

"Shut up, Maksim," King snapped. "I hope she kills him."

"He can hear you." Everything hurt. It was like my back had a heartbeat as it pulsed with pain every few seconds. I slumped to the mat, my vision still crossing as Ash walked over and offered his hand.

I blinked up at him. "Is this a trick?"

"You're a boss. Technically I can't kill you, and I don't want to make my sister cry—like you've been." He glared. "For days." Just as I reached for his hand, he jerked it away. "On second thought, I can make it look like an accident just like you did, so maybe I will kill you." His blue eyes flashed.

"Nope." Violet hopped into the ring in nothing but spandex shorts, a sports bra, and her hands wrapped. "If anyone kills him, it's going to be me."

"You look really pretty," I murmured. "I like the sports bra—"

Sharp agony exploded in my ribs as Ash kicked me. "Stop looking at her bra."

I couldn't keep the groan from spilling out.

"Um, they are married," Maksim pointed out.

"Thank you." I jabbed my finger in his direction.

Fear that I was going to pass out ripped at me until Violet helped me to my feet.

I offered a shaky smile of hope, and then she gave me a shove backward.

"Fight." Her nostrils flared. "Defend yourself, Valerian."

She said my name like a curse. "Because we all know Breaker was shit at hand-to-hand combat."

"I'm not going to—"

She had aimed a swift foot for my dick and missed only because I bent over and stepped back, but she grazed my hip with bruising intensity.

I roared out a curse and charged her, wrapping my hands around her body, lifting her into the air and slamming her down against the mat. "You wanna fight, princess? Fight!"

Her fist came up, smashing my chin. "I want your blood."

I smirked and pinned her to the floor, straddling her as I leaned down and whispered, "Am I not bleeding enough?"

"You lied to me." She didn't blink, just stared into me like she could see all my darkness, all my truth. "You should have trusted me."

"They were going to kill you!" I thundered, angry at her, angry at myself. "So, don't tell me what the hell I should have done!"

"Not that!" She swallowed and broke eye contact, and her voice grew hollow. "You should have told me you were Valerian. Not last week, not last year, but the day I forced my friendship on you. I wish you would have told me; I wish you would have shared that burden, and that's the problem. You say you love me, but you won't share yourself with me. Your secrets will always be the canyon between our hearts." She shoved at me, then throat punched me.

Coughing and gasping, I sucked in a few short, painful breaths and fell away from her. "Violet..." My voice was hoarse, sore. I coughed again. "Wait..."

"What?" She held up her hands again, fingers curled like talons, as though she was going to go for an eyeball gouge next. Great. "You have more excuses to make? More lies to spew? When you love someone, it's either all or nothing—so I guess *we're* the latter."

"No." My vision blurred as I gasped for more air. "That's not true."

She landed a left hook to my cheek, and because I was struggling for air, her aim was perfect as it sent me to my knees.

"How many more secrets are you keeping?" She yelled. I'd never seen her look so beautiful or terrifying as my blood caked her knuckles, as sweat ran down her perfect chest.

I squeezed my eyes shut and tried to stand only to have her put her foot on my bloody back, shoving me back down.

My fight was gone. If she wanted to kill me, at least she'd feel vindicated.

"In the Russian mafia, after they break you," I flinched past the burning pain in my back and on my cheek. "The boss will typically give that woman to one of his higher-ups."

You could hear a pin drop in the gym.

"So, you're right, I did this to us, without realizing what would happen, by keeping you, I claimed you as mine, by keeping you from them, I damned you to a future with me."

"Did you know?" Her voice shook. "That any of this would happen?"

"Not until it was too late," I admitted, going still beneath her foot.

"Why isn't she killing him?" Maksim whispered loud enough for most of us to hear. If I wasn't bleeding out, I'd probably manage a solid eye-roll, but this moment felt tense, important like Vi was making a life-changing decision, and any movement on my behalf would shatter her resolve.

She started getting out of the ring then looked over her

shoulder. "As Breaker Campisi, would you have married me? Eventually?"

The truth hurt. It burned down to my very soul as I slowly shook my head. "No, Violet. I love you with everything in me, but I took a vow, my blood for yours, remember? I promised your father. I could only give you my body as Breaker—as Valerian, you own my fucking soul."

A tear slid down her cheek; she quickly wiped it away, her anger back.

"Ballsy," Junior muttered. "Telling her the truth and literally pounding that last nail into your coffin—"

"—up top," Maksim held up his hand for a high five, "You know because it's literally his funeral? Too soon?"

I groaned and moved to a sitting position as I watched indecision flash across her face. Sometimes life gives you moments, moments where you see something in someone else, something they're trying to hide, something that bursts through the smokescreens and demands to be noticed. This was our moment. All along, she'd asked me to fight her.

What she really meant was fight for me.

Fight for us.

So, with a cocky grin, I moved to my feet and leaned over the ring. "One more night, Vi." She stilled. "You promised."

She was quiet and then offered a cruel smile that made me want to immediately hide behind something. "Sure, Valerian. You know the garage code, 666. If you can make it into the house without dying, I'll give you one last night and then this?" A solitary tear slid down her cheek. "Is done."

"Fine." I lied.

"Fine." She flipped me off, and then all that was left was

my blood, some of Ash's blood, I think a missing tooth—not mine.

And a very beaten down heart that still refused to stop beating her name

They were silent, all of them, my cousins, my family, as Violet left the basement.

I fell to my knees and watched, wishing she would turn back around and say we could try again, but who was I kidding? I had known this would be the outcome.

I knew it the minute I said my vows.

She would never forgive me.

And I would spend the rest of my life alone in Seattle, praying for the day that she walked back in that door and told me it was worth it—that we were worth trying, that even though Breaker was dead, I was very much alive, that she was what kept me alive.

"I don't suppose…" I found my voice even though it still hurt to breathe. "Any of you know how to get into Chase's house without getting shot on sight?"

Serena snorted. "Yay, another funeral."

"Serena," Junior hissed. "That's not nice—besides, he looks half dead already, he probably can't even get it up, forget trying to sneak into that fortress."

The adrenaline seeped out of my system, leaving weakness in its wake, and I lay back against the cool bloody mat and stared up at the ceiling the fan whipped around once, twice, three times.

I squeezed my eyes shut, and then someone was laying down next to me.

Ash.

"You here to finish me off?" I saw two of him. Damn it.

"Give me one good reason I shouldn't kill you—just one." The entire gym was quiet.

"I love you," I whispered. "That's my reason, and it will always be my reason. I love you. And sometimes love asks us to do the impossible, and all we can do is hope it's strong enough, big enough, to cover a multitude of sins."

With a groan, I relaxed into the mat. Then, with a foul curse, he pushed himself up and then reached down and actually pulled me to my feet. With another curse under his breath, he glared at me. "I'm still pissed you slept with my sister."

I barked out a laugh and winced. "Ouch, it hurts to laugh."

Junior was the first to speak. "Probably not a good sign considering you're going to Chase's tonight. You plan on eating through a straw the rest of your life or what?"

"He won't get caught." Ash assisted me out of the ring, and Junior helped me not fall flat on my face as I got down. King and Maksim must have left when Violet did, leaving only Serena, Ash, and Junior.

"Um…" Serena raised her hand. "Sorry to be the negative one here, but Ash, you got caught at least a dozen times last year sneaking back into your own house; how the hell is he going to sneak in? You know your dad's probably sharpening his knives with a smile on his face in hopes that Brea—Valerian stops by."

I tried not to flinch at the sound of my old name and reached for one of the folded towels to wipe it down my face. "She's right, you know."

When I looked up, Ash was grinning down at me with a knowing look and then nodded to Junior. "The things I do for a dead man…"

"What am I missing?"

Ash sighed. "It's not as if I have a heart anymore anyway, and since Junior has Serena and nobody would believe it, I guess I'm taking one for the team."

"Taking what for the...the—ohhhhhh..." Junior burst out laughing. "Sorry man, at least you know you're going to get caught and then lectured. God, I hate their lectures."

"I'm lost." I shook my head at Serena. "You lost?"

She smirked. "What's the one thing that pisses the dads off more than anything else?"

"Weapons next to the lasagna?" I guessed.

Ash smacked me on the back of the head like I hadn't just gone five rounds with him and one with the devil, aka my wife.

"Outsiders brought inside," Ash said proudly. "And not just any outsiders. They hate it when we bring girls over because, according to them, they gotta be vetted first, just their way to control everything."

"Last time we—" Junior flinched when Serena reached for her knife. "I mean last time Ash brought home girls that weren't even pretty and were... uh... short—" She lowered the knife to his dick as if to say keep talking.

Ash groaned. "Okay, killer." He flicked the knife out of her hands. "It was years ago, and Junior was too heartsick over a psychopath with the last name Abandonato to even touch one of them. The point is, the dads were pissed, so pissed that we would be so irresponsible and also because I may have been slightly intoxicated and half-naked with not one, but two of them splayed across my lap doing... things. Anyway, it might be enough to get Valerian in. We'll have to rely on Dad's tender spot for Violet to get you out, though. But she can handle him, she always does. Plus, we could always tell Mom."

"Bingo!" I snapped my fingers. "Tell her to keep him in bed."

"Don't think that will be a problem." Ash scrunched up his face. "Mom bought bagels so…"

"NOOOOO!" Serena plugged her ears while Junior started gagging.

I rolled my eyes. "Guys, parents have sex. Trust me, I wish I could unsee and unhear about ten years' worth of moans."

Serena shuddered like she needed a shower. "Fine, fine, I'm over it, sort of. So, I guess now all we need to do is go hunting?"

"And the best place to hunt…" Junior grinned.

"Campus." They high fived each other.

Ash's smile was forced.

I put an arm around him. "I know it's soon. You don't have to—"

"Ah, maybe sex will fix my broken heart. God knows the booze, pills, and fighting are doing jack shit." He shrugged. "It's not a big deal." He eyed me up and down. "You need to wear a beanie and sunglasses. You still look too much like your older, weaker self."

"Gee, thanks," I grumbled. "I wasn't weak. I was trying not to draw attention."

"By having sex with everything that walked?" Junior nodded. "Solid plan, really, can't believe you thought of that all on your own."

"Are we doing this, or are we talking about my sex life? Because this one over here still wants to kill me for—"

"*Sleeping* with my *sister*," he said through clenched teeth.

"That." I pointed.

"He'll never let it go, just get used to it." Serena grinned. "And I know exactly where to go. There's a small party later tonight to celebrate the end of the Fall Semester."

"Where at?" Ash asked.

Serena shrugged. "You'll see."

"I have a bad feeling about this," Junior whispered under his breath as we all made our way up the stairs, me hobbling, Ash wincing, and the other two giving us shit for walking so slow.

I had a bad feeling, too, though it had nothing to do with the current situation but what would happen after the fact.

She said, one more night.

I killed Breaker Campisi.

But I wondered if she understood the power she had—to kill Valerian Petrov, to kill the remaining parts that needed her more than she would ever know.

This time my life was in her hands.

And I was so damn terrified that she was going to pull the knife, sink it deep into my back, then make sure I saw her face as I took my last few breaths.

The thought haunted me still, even two hours later, as we drove into downtown. Ash had spent that time bandaging me up, so I wasn't a walking talking bloody wound. My back had been patched up with surgical glue, and once I washed the blood from my face, I actually looked half-human even though I still had bruising on my eye and jaw compliments of Ash's right hook.

I tried talking to him a few times about doing this, being with a girl so soon after Claire, but the minute I said her name, he got this empty look in his eyes and told me to drop it, and

I had to because I knew what it felt like to lose what you loved the most. I couldn't imagine being in his position even though I could imagine loving someone who wanted nothing to do with you, even when you save them.

I sighed and looked out the SUV window. We were a few blocks from campus, and some of the upper-class dorms were moved to that location as the school continued to expand, but I didn't actually know anyone who lived there.

Then again, I'd never really cared, so…

Junior parked in the garage while Serena made a call. "Yeah, we're here, awesome, we won't be long."

"Where are we, exactly?" Ash asked once we went into the apartment building. The lights overhead flickered. "And why does it feel like a horror movie?"

Serena laughed. "Chill cousin, it's an old building, but all the apartments are lofts that have been refurbished. No murderers here except for the ones walking down the creepy hall."

"I prefer the term assassin," Junior grumbled.

I shook my head at him. "You would."

The click of Serena's heels on the hardwood floor echoed off the hallway walls as we walked past doors that had been painted a dark navy blue. The sound of music got louder the farther we went. At the end of the hall, near another set of stairs, Serena stopped in front of the last door.

Room 729.

She knocked twice.

The door flew open, revealing Tank.

He looked so different from the first time we'd met him when he'd been undercover. He was stocky, wearing a black beanie, and had a cocky grin on his face as he crossed his bulky arms over his chest.

"Huh," Serena winked at him. "You're even wearing designer jeans, I'm so proud, I could cry."

He just snorted out a laugh and rolled his eyes, then opened the door wider, turned around, and shouted, "Our king needs a few concubines."

The best part was that he was dead serious, even if it sounded ridiculous. A few gasps were heard as someone turned down the music. I was surprised girls weren't clawing at each other in an effort to get to Ash. He was even more popular now that his eyes were dead—probably because every woman saw him as a project, a man they could fix, a man they could love back to life. But the problem was, every girl thought she was the exception—and none of them would be able to replace Claire.

All in all, there were maybe fifty people scattered around the large loft apartment. One wall was completely brick while the other two were painted a tan color that made the room look more masculine.

Serena was right. The apartments were nice.

I checked my watch and tried not to look like the old Breaker as I stood there, probably unrecognizable anyway, with the bruising on my face compliments of Ash and his fists.

"What's going on?" A girl stepped forward, and I recognized Annie. She was wearing a black cardigan and a khaki skirt. Where the hell did that girl shop? She was dressed like a nineteen-year-old soccer mom. Her eyes glazed over me like she didn't know me. And then her hurt expression fell to Ash.

Yeah, I know how this story ends.

Not well. For her.

My heart clenched as if to remind me how it would end for me after tonight.

Serena gave her a genuine smile. "Hey Annie, I miss you. You should come hang out."

Annie smiled back, the curve of her lips taking her from nice-looking to strikingly pretty. Now, if only she would stop wearing super tight buns. They made me uncomfortable; they looked too perfect, not one piece of dark hair out of place. "I'd like that," she said.

Ash cleared his throat. "No offense, but we aren't here to plan a slumber party. Two girls." He snapped his fingers. "Now."

Two blondes in tight dresses—one red, one black—laughed and walked forward.

I looked the other direction because I was ninety-nine percent sure I'd made out with both of them—at the same time—at a party last year.

But when you're drunk so that you don't think about the girl that you're in love with—you tend to forget the faces and focus only on the feeling.

Ash eyed them up and down for a bit before shrugging. "They'll do."

I was pretty sure Chase would burn his house down before letting those girls get their talons into him.

Hurt flashed across Annie's face. "Wait, I could… I mean," She licked her nude lips. "I mean I don't mind I know your—"

"I'm going to stop you right there." Ash took a predatory step toward her. "I take these girls who, full disclosure, I'll probably call blonde one and blonde two, and my dad thinks I've been spending hours in debauchery." The girls giggled. "I take you," he said, drawing out the word as his eyes went from her head down to her toes and back up again, "and he's going to ask who my new tutor is."

Students around us started laughing to themselves.

Her chin wobbled.

Shit.

"Knew this was a bad idea," Junior said under his breath. "He's not okay and hasn't been okay, just pretending to be okay, and he's mean when he's like this."

"I'll grab him." I moved past Junior and Serena to the scene Ash was making. "Let's go, man, it's late, you're tired, and you have two sluts to please."

"Hey!" One of the girls snapped her gum and then blew a bubble.

I just shuddered. "And I rest my case."

The other girl just smiled like, yup I'm easy, but according to every girl on campus, Ash was the hottest thing to land there since forever.

But he was too mean to be pretty.

I imagined they saw a guy they could tame.

And he saw someone he could control.

Annie still hadn't said anything.

And Ash still wasn't budging.

"Ash," I jerked his arm. "Come on."

"I can be slutty," Annie finally said, and with shaking fingers, she took her hair out of her bun, letting it spill in gorgeous waves past her shoulders.

Ash's eyes flared to life like he'd just been given water after forty nights baking in the desert heat.

"You think having your hair down's going to convince him?" His eyes narrowed. "Hmmm, maybe you do have it in you, Annie…" He reached out and slowly started unbuttoning her cardigan.

I was close enough to notice, though.

His hands had a slight tremble.

The hell.

Did he *like* her?

She stiffened, then whispered. "Not them, please…"

Ash's nostrils flared before he grabbed Annie by the hand and jerked her toward him. "You better be fucking convincing."

She gave him one solid nod.

And then he was practically dragging her toward the door.

"Sorry, girls." Junior shoved past the two girls who looked ready to plot Annie's death, and I followed while Serena said goodbye to Tank.

When we were back in the hall, I gave her hand a tug pulling her back. "Care to fill me in on the drama that I missed while I was away?"

Her shoulders slumped a bit. "She likes him."

"Everyone likes him until they find out he's a jackass most the time," I said. "What makes this different?"

"He pretends he can't stand her," Serena whispered under her breath. "Remind you of another couple?"

"No." I shook my head. "Because Annie is nothing like you or Junior."

"No, but I think she's exactly what my cousin needs."

"Or—" We were catching up with them. "—he's going to eat her alive and ruin her life, but sure, let's be optimistic about this."

Rolling her eyes, she pushed open the door to the garage. "She's tougher than she looks."

Junior was already starting the car.

I got in the front while Serena sat in back with Ash and Annie. Even with Serena's constant advice—I mean, if explaining how slutty she had to act was actual advice—it was tense, really tense.

The closer we got to Ash's house, the more I felt his rising temper and my own panic that I wouldn't make it, that I wouldn't be able to touch her.

Violet.

Mine.

Junior pulled up to the gate and, after waving at one of the security guards, was let in. They'd just assume we were all going to hang out, only I wouldn't be leaving, I would stay.

"Showtime." Serena rubbed her hands together in excitement, and Annie, well Annie looked seconds away from throwing up.

The things we do for family.
The things we do for love.

CHAPTER
Twenty-Seven

My love was still drowning with him in that car—my heart was in pieces—and yet there he stood demanding I hand them over.
—Violet Petrov

Ash

I couldn't look away from her khaki skirt. I mean, khaki? Really? Serena's tight leather leggings and crop top looked absolutely scandalous next to her.

God, even her fingernails were bare.

I shuddered. The last thing I wanted was her blunt nails digging into my skin while she straddled me with a khaki skirt and white Keds on.

Her hair was nice, though.

If you liked naturally bouncy, thick, luscious jet black hair that shined like a conditioner commercial.

We'd been waiting for Serena to "fix" Annie for the last hour; Valerian wouldn't stop pacing a hole in the hardwood.

He was different in so many ways that it really did seem like Breaker had died.

Everyone leaves.

My chest ached at the thought. He was still my best friend, but his hair was different, and I don't know why the hell it bothered me; it just did. He stood taller, looked more mature. It was like he shed his easy-going party boy attitude and came back a man.

And it shamed me to admit that he'd done the right thing and was still fighting when I was constantly contemplating running my own car off a cliff.

My fight had gone.

I looked away toward the house.

Violet was on the second level in the far east bedroom. Getting by the suits was one thing, getting into her actual room without my dad seeing something else entirely.

But as long as Annie was a willing participant, I could make it work. I had a plan that would most definitely make my dad come stomping outside.

Finally, the stairs creaked as Serena and Annie descended.

I saw the khaki skirt first and shook my head then did a double-take when I realized that Serena was the one wearing it. In fact, she was wearing all of Annie's clothes.

Even her hair was in a tight bun.

"Fuck me. I think every single hot librarian fantasy just came to life." Junior shoved me out of the way, reached for Serena, then jerked her into his arms, lifting her by the ass, literally grinding all over her in front of us all before Serena pulled back and bit down on his neck then waved over at Annie as if to say *my job here is done, and now my just reward.*

Junior smacked her on the ass then called over his shoulder, "Be right back, bro."

Valerian smirked over at me. "He's totally going to have sex either in your bed or against one of your walls." Serena let out a little scream. "If they make it that far."

I sighed as jealousy flared to life, not of my own cousin but of all the sex, all the love, the fact that they would get married soon. "I'll bleach the house."

Annie finally appeared.

Her hair was hanging past her shoulders in soft waves that made my hands clench; the white crop top fit her perfectly. I nearly swallowed too much air and choked when I saw how nice Annie's tits looked in it. I always had her pegged as a B cup—not that I often looked or tried to figure it out—but she was all D, and I had a sudden vision of pressing my face between the valley of them.

The rest of her, unbelievable. She was small but packed a punch in a way that had my eyes burning.

"So?" She gave us a shy smile.

Valerian sighed and walked over to her. "You're going to have to let him touch you without flinching, you know that, right?"

She literally flinched as he said it.

He sighed and went over to my kitchen, grabbed a bottle of Jack that I'd been saving for later that night, handed it to her, and said. "Chug your bravery."

After a bit of hesitation, she grabbed it, unscrewed the cap with her perfect little hands, and tilted the bottle back.

A groan made it past my lips before I could stop myself. Her throat, working that whiskey down. *Fuck me. Imagine if it was something else she was sucking.*

And then I couldn't get the image out of my head.

And then I hated her for it.

Claire would be so ashamed of me.

Of my behavior.

My heart pounded with rage.

"Enough!" I barked. "I don't want you completely wasted, and you're a quarter of my size."

She wiped her mouth with the back of her hand.

Valerian grinned at her. "I'm impressed. You didn't even choke."

"I just swallowed." She shrugged.

I groaned into my hands. Why the hell was I shaking? "Swallowing is good."

"You okay?" She asked in her sweet innocent little voice.

"Yup." *Nope.* "Perfect." I stood, "Let's get this over with so he can go sleep with my sister." I just shook my head. I would never get over it.

I snapped my fingers at her. Didn't she know that meant to come?

She put her hands on her hips.

"What?" I growled. "You. Here. Now."

"Say, please." Her voice trembled.

I squeezed my eyes shut for a brief second, then stomped over to her, wrapped my hand around her hair, and tugged her against my chest. "Please."

Her lips parted.

I pulled her hair a bit harder.

Her lips parted more, her eyes grew hooded.

I kissed her.

It wasn't a nice kiss. It wasn't a kiss you tell your friends about. It was dominant. Mean. It was a kiss that bad men give bad women because they know that the kiss means nothing.

It wasn't a kiss she deserved.

But I did it anyway.

Because I was pissed that she looked pretty.

I was enraged that I couldn't stop looking at the innocent sparkle in her eyes when I might as well have blood on my mouth like my hands.

She tasted like the light I used to have.

And I hated her more for it than she would ever know.

The fire in my soul fanned into an inferno of need for something I no longer experienced—something that felt good.

"Well." Valerian cleared his throat. "Maybe be less angry, Ash, or at least look less angry. And, Annie, I'm pretty sure that's not your first kiss."

I almost shoved her away. My fingers shook with the need for violence as I dropped her hair and stole the bottle of whiskey from Valerian, then downed a few shots.

I slammed the bottle back on the table, grabbed my phone, and texted my dad.

> Me: I may be drunk and making bad choices. Is Mom cooking dinner? I stole one of "Valerian's" old whores.
>
> Scary Dad: Son. I'm home in ten minutes. If you as much as let one of those women into this house, I'm waterboarding you... because I can and because Mom is cooking, and I would kill you for more helpings. I'm a good dad like that.
>
> Me: Oh Dad, I'm not an idiot... she's not in YOUR house.
>
> Scary Dad: Nine minutes. I know you're... I know you're upset, but fucking random girls who want you for your money—not a good call.

> Me: Dad, don't be ridiculous. They want me for my cock.
>
> Scary Dad: If she's there when I'm there, I'm going to do more than waterboard you. I'm going to turn you over to Mom. Now, who's cocky?

I actually shook a bit as I typed my response. "Valerian, you owe me more than you will ever know."

> Me: Okay byeeeeeeee
>
> Scary Dad: Ash?

I grinned at the phone but made no move to answer.

> Scary Dad: ASH!

And then.

> Scary Dad: Seven minutes, I decided to speed.

"Shit!" I dropped my phone on the table and grabbed Annie's hand. "Okay, man, he's going to come out here from the garage. Sneak in through the kitchen. If my mom sees you, just give her the eyes and beg—if you must, on your knees. Run up the stairs and let Violet do the rest." My heart was racing. Why the hell was my heart racing? "Oh, and hide in the bushes by the sliding glass door. He hates those bushes a spider that lived in them bit him once—"

"If a spider bites my ass…" Valerian jabbed a finger at me.

"You'll live," I bit out. "Now go, he's probably almost here!"

"And you." I tugged Annie toward the door with me. "I hope you're ready to get wet."

Her eyes widened. "Wh-what? Wet? Why would I?"

I turned, slowly, and licked my lips. "The real question is, why wouldn't you when you're with me?"

Her eyes narrowed. "I thought—"

"That's the problem." I pulled us outside; she stumbled

behind me. My grip on her wrist was probably too hard, but I was too frustrated to care, too confused, and not as numb as before.

I hated it.

"Stay." I put her right next to the pool, ran behind the wet bar we had there, grabbed another full bottle of Jack Daniels, popped it open and took another swig, handed it to her, and made a hurry motion.

She took a swig, and I honestly thought I could watch that smooth throat swallow all night long.

She handed it back, and then I took another swig, then pulled her into my arms and licked her up and down her neck, making her smell like me, like whiskey, like my tongue.

She stood still.

I set the whiskey down. Her blue eyes focused on me completely. She didn't even look terrified that my dad, the scariest man alive, was talking about torturing his favorite son for letting a girl on his property.

"You ready?" I gripped her wrist as we faced the deep end of the pool.

"Uh, for what—"

I wrapped my arms around her and pulled her into the pool, taking her down with me, down into the deep, down into my darkness, I baptized her in it, and I wasn't sorry when she came up for air and shrieked at me. If anything, that made me want to pull her deeper, beg her to drown with me. Maybe it wouldn't be so lonely if I had someone dying with me.

"Come." I gritted my teeth.

She shook her head and started to swim away, which was when I lost my fucking mind, swam after her, grabbed her by the arm, and with a giant splash, pushed her up against the tile wall, my hands bracing on either side of her head. "You don't get to run when you volunteer."

"You're angry," she whispered.

"I'm fucking furious!" I roared right in her face.

I hadn't expected to yell.

And I didn't expect her to slap me.

But she did.

Twice.

It stung like heaven.

So, I decided I needed more.

I shoved my body up against hers, and then I stole a kiss and another, and then I couldn't tell who was pushing who, or who was moaning, or who was dying.

Both of us, maybe?

She captured my tongue with her lips.

And I gripped her thigh with one hand as I shoved my tongue farther into her mouth, needing more of her taste needing to feel anything but like myself.

She wrapped an arm around me, then her legs followed.

I groaned against her lips. "Told you, you would get wet."

"This is cheating," she panted back.

"And this is you." I slid my hand up her shirt and cupped a heavy breast. "Not complaining."

She rocked her hips against me.

What was happening?

In the back of my mind, I was screaming to let her go, but in the forefront, it translated wrong; it translated to a scream of desperation for the exact opposite, for her not to let me go.

"Come on." I pulled her with me toward the shallow end, and when I could actually touch, I sat on one of the side steps and pulled her on top of me, her legs on either side as

I basically dry—or wet—humped her where I'd first learned how to swim.

"You're huge." She squeezed her thighs around me. I winced from the pain of it, from knowing nothing would be the same, none of this, not even sex.

Not even meaningless sex with a person who I barely tolerated.

I captured her mouth again, biting down in a painful kiss that reminded both of us what this was.

What it would never be.

She rocked her hips even harder into me, pinning me against the side like she liked it like she wanted me to bleed.

I tugged her hair back, already addicted to the way her lips parted like she wanted more.

And then a throat cleared from overhead, and I got the distinct eerie feeling you get when you know multiple guns are trained on you.

I kissed down her neck, murmuring, "Kinda busy, Dad."

He sighed. "I can see that. Hello, Annie. I take it he lied about you being one of Breaker—or sorry, Valerian's old sluts."

"Breaker?" She said in a confused voice.

"Dad…"

"Shit." He looked away and then looked back at me, his expression unreadable, like he was doing really hard math and needed a little bit of extra help with the last equation. His smile wasn't cruel; it was damn calculating as he nodded at me. "Annie's been vetted a while, so you two… just clean up when you're done…"

THE HELL?

I gaped at him in both frustration and terror. "Dad, aren't you—"

"Oh, and make sure your mom doesn't see, or you will really be dead."

And then he fucking started whistling as he walked into the house, most likely right after Valerian had.

I peered over at the bushes.

My dad stopped whistling and caught my glance. "Looking for something?"

My sanity?

And maybe a condom?

Ha-ha.

Where the hell did that come from?

"Nope." I quickly went back to kissing Annie, hoping he'd disappear, and when he did, I shoved her off me, got out of the pool, and started walking back toward the pool house with a hard-on from hell and soggy clothes.

I could hear her footsteps behind me as I jerked open the pool house door. I could somehow smell her lilac perfume too, which was disconcerting, to say the least.

"Hey." Serena was drinking straight from the bottle. She really should have been born a dude, pretty sure Junior would still be obsessed. "Your dad let you go."

"He's too smart." Junior plopped onto the couch and flipped on the TV. "Also, we ordered pizza. Go clean up before you ruin your own floors."

"Yeah." I stomped up the stairs, and again she followed. And it pissed me off, the loyalty, the barely asking any questions, the lack of just anything unless I pushed her.

I wanted someone angry like me.

I wanted someone sad like me.

I wanted someone to yell.

And I wanted to pick a fight so bad my fists burned with it.

I stripped out of my wet shirt once I reached my bedroom and tossed it to the bathroom floor. Annie stared at me through the bathroom mirror, her eyes were so wide like she was trying to drink in every detail and lacking the ability to do it.

"What," I barked, slamming my hands down on the tile. She jumped, and then she just stared.

I counted the beats, the seconds as her eyes locked onto mine. What was she thinking? Why was she staring? And why the hell was she still here?

"Go," I said through clenched teeth.

A frown stretched across her pretty face, and then she pulled her top over her head, leaving her completely topless and me completely helpless not to stare. "I need some clothes for home."

"Don't get pissed when I say, I prefer you naked. Khaki skirts do nothing for you."

Her eyes narrowed. "They're comfortable, and at least then guys don't give me attention."

This surprised me even though I didn't want to have any sort of conversation with her. But the words seemed to tumble off my tongue uninvited. "You don't want guys' attention?"

"Maybe just yours." That damn swallow again.

"Trust me, you don't." I grabbed a towel, then she grabbed a towel. Was she really going to just mirror everything I did?

Ignoring her, I gave her my back and turned on the shower, almost tempted to jump into the chilly water to cool off my anger.

To cool off the fact that for the first time in over two weeks, I felt like I was responding to a woman. Guilt hit me so hard I wanted to die.

This was wrong.

What the fuck was I doing?

How dare she.

A hand touched my back.

I flinched.

And then another hand touched my bare back sliding down to my wet jeans, her breasts slid against my skin.

"I don't want this," I whispered.

"At least lie to my face." Her hands shook as she tried to tug my jeans down. "And sometimes need trumps want."

I squeezed my eyes closed. "Leave before I lose my temper… again. I'm serious, Annie, you don't belong here." In this house, with my demons, by my side, in my shower naked.

I shuddered, kicked off the remaining clothes, and stepped into the shower pressing my forehead against the white tile, my thoughts a blur, my chest heaving even though I was standing still.

I felt her behind me even before she opened her mouth.

Shoving aside every rational thought, I turned around and picked her up, slamming my lips against hers in another kiss of warning, pain, and maybe a little bit of release.

She clung to my biceps, her lips parting, allowing me and my mean kisses relief that we hadn't even known we needed.

She didn't moan. She didn't do anything except hold on to me and return my kiss with a wild one of her own. I tasted her, going back for more again and again as our bodies slid into one another.

With a groan, I picked her up and shoved the glass door open, only going as far as the sink.

Both of us were drenched as I dug my fingertips into her ass. Her hand wrapped around my length, pumping me once.

I almost yelled for her to stop.

It had been no one but Claire for so long.

What the fuck was I doing?

She gripped me so tight again, it was almost painful; my eyes rolled back as she scooted closer to the edge of the counter and tore her mouth away.

Panting, I gripped her by the shoulders and ground out, "This means nothing."

"I know," she whispered, uncertainty in her eyes. "Think of it as my thank you."

"Thank you?" I frowned.

"For not killing me after everything when I know you still want to when I know you still think about punishing me—"

"I think about punishing you every second of every day, and this is not even close to being a penance for what you really deserve." I glared and then thrust into her in one abrupt movement.

Her head fell forward, resting against my shoulder as her fingernails dug into my skin.

I wasn't gentle.

I was rough.

My next thrust was so hard her body slid back across the tile, and her head hit the glass mirror.

"Not." I thrust again. "Even." She moaned. "Close."

I gripped her chin with my hand and jerked her head toward my mouth, biting down on her lip and then rained kisses down that perfect neck.

Annie tried to wrap her arms around me tighter as I lifted her off the counter still inside her and walked us toward the bed.

I set her at the top near the headboard. "Hold on to this."

Eyes wide, she grabbed the edge of the headboard near the pillow as I drove into her again and again.

My bed.

Our bed.

Claire's.

Tears filled my eyes, tears I couldn't wipe away as the memories surfaced to the point of being so painful I let out a scream. "Your fault! This is your fault!"

"I know." A tear slid down her cheek. "I'm sorry, Ash, I'm so sorry."

I was so close, but I didn't want to stop.

I didn't want this to end.

Because she would go.

Because I would yell at her even though she had given me exactly what I needed.

Because something was wrong with me.

Broken.

"It's okay," Annie said softly, and then she hooked her heels behind me and sucked me in deep, held me prisoner. "You have to let go."

"No." I clenched my teeth.

"You must." Tears slid down her cheeks.

We locked eyes.

And I let her go.

I tried.

But the minute I finished.

I pulled her back.

I couldn't do it.

I would never be able to do it.

I pulled out of Annie and gave her my back. "Leave."

"Ash—"

"Fucking leave!" I thundered, knocking over the lamp, breaking it on impact.

She swiped her cheeks and then reached for one of my T-shirts from the floor and a pair of sweats I'd worn the night before.

Without even asking, she dressed in my clothes.

Shot me one last look of pity. I would rather die than see that in her eyes.

And left me like I'd asked.

If only she could read my mind.

My heart.

Because now it was sobbing in the corner like a little kid, just wishing she would fight hard enough to stay.

Broken. That's what I was.

The sound of a door slamming downstairs made me flinch, and then I was back to taking my shower and washing the innocent girl with her khaki skirts and wide eyes down the drain while clinging to a dead woman who was never coming back like she was a lifeline.

"I'll see you soon," I whispered. "Soon, baby... soon."

CHAPTER
Twenty-Eight

The darkness calls not once but twice, it demands I
answer regardless of my strife, I say the words let me
go, the answer is always the same, a resounding no.
—Valerian Petrov

Violet

My hands shook as I held them in my lap, picking at my
pink fingernail polish. I didn't have remover, but I needed
it to be gone, the pink was one of Dad's publicist's idea. It
made me look innocent.

And I'd kept it on.

But I wasn't that girl anymore.

I hadn't been that girl for a long time, no matter how many
times I tried to fake it. And Breaker, he'd always seen through
that facade, pushed me until I lashed out, and then rewarded
me when I was myself again.

Breaker.

I hung my head as a tear slid down my cheek.

Valerian.

The same, but so very different. My brain told me I was in love with Breaker, not Valerian, but my stupid heart soared whenever he was in the room; it demanded I run into his arms, get on my hands and knees, and beg him to hold me and never let go.

But how do you get past that sort of betrayal?

How?

A soft knock sounded at my door. Mom was probably checking up on me. She'd been worried, everyone had been worried when they realized what Valerian and I had gone through.

What he had done.

"Come in." My voice was soft, and I hated it because I wasn't weak. I just had no energy left, and I knew that even if I promised Valerian one more night, it would be impossible for him to even make it inside the house, let alone my room.

I hated the disappointment that coursed through my veins. I hated him for making me like him.

Mom poked her head in. She didn't look a day over twenty-five, with her sleek shoulder-length black hair and sculpted jaw. She could have been a supermodel, and even though I know Dad can be scary, she somehow tames him in a way that seems impossible. "You holding up?"

"Yeah," I lied.

"Well…" She winked and then grabbed something or someone behind her and shoved him in my room. Valerian.

He shot me a cocky grin. "Your mom likes me."

My eyes narrowed, even though my heart leaped in my chest. "All females like you—must be a curse."

"A gift." He turned around and gave my mom, MY

294

MOM, a hug and kissed her on the cheek. "Thank you for understanding, Luc."

"Any time." Her gaze swept over to me as the downstairs door slammed. "I'll just go distract your father for the next few hours—in fact, it's a great night to go out to dinner. I'll just put away what I was making."

I gaped after her as she closed the door to my room with a silent click.

I was in my childhood bedroom.

But I wasn't a kid anymore.

I lifted my eyes to meet Valerian's hard stare.

I was his.

I was a Petrov.

It was like my tattoo burned on my finger.

I was his queen.

And he was a boss.

So many things had happened in this room, our first kiss, followed by a very inappropriate make out session that lasted until five a.m. and resulted in Breaker—Valerian hiding under my bed until my dad left.

I was fifteen.

And he was horny.

"I fell in love with you here," he whispered. "Remember the Cinderella tent you used to have set up in the middle of your room?"

I scowled. "You swore."

His smirk was so damn sexy that I had to look away or lose my resolve. Already I could feel my heart warming. I hated that I wanted him.

He had ruined everything.

And sex wasn't going to fix this.

"We lay in it for two hours. I asked if I could kiss you again and you said yes, but only if you could see my—"

"I was young!" I said defensively.

"So was I." His voice deepened. "I don't think I've ever gone so embarrassingly fast in my entire life, all because of innocent little Violet Abandonato's tight squeeze and what was it, two pumps? Three?"

"Two and a half." I chewed down on my lower lip. "It was over before it started."

I squeezed my eyes shut at the double entendre.

He got up from my bed. I focused on the wood floor, on my leopard print rug, as he took a step toward me. His brown boots came into full focus along with jeans that molded to powerful thighs. Slowly, I walked my gaze up his body. He was wearing a white V-neck shirt; it was a deep enough V that I could see the swirl of the Campisi tattoo poking out from underneath.

"Why did you get the tattoo when you're a Petrov?"

He sighed and then peeled his shirt over his head, giving me an eyeful of a muscled six-pack, tan skin, and bulging biceps that I wanted to hold on to, to squeeze.

Why did he have to be so damn pretty?

"Here." He pointed to the bottom of the tattoo, and there, hidden in plain sight but camouflaged, was the mark of his true Family. "The Petrov Sickle. The only way to get this tattoo is to be born into the Family—or married into it."

"Did you know they would bind you to me?" I finally asked, my curiosity getting the best of me despite my anger.

His face fell. "Vi, I already told you, I had no idea, but it—damn, it makes sense when I think back on how easily Andrei agreed, how he and Phoenix orchestrated everything.

One thing I know for certain, Breaker and Violet would have never been able to be together."

I wanted to scream. "You don't know that!"

"Vi…" His eyes burned into me. "The adopted son of Tex Campisi, one who has no supposed bloodline, one who was set to guard you at political events? One who was ordered by your father never to touch you? I know you love him, but Chase isn't… He's strategic, and marrying me would have been the opposite of that. Somehow, he would have convinced you; somehow, I would have fought for you, and I know for a fact I would have ended up dead. Serena and Junior made sense and were willing to die for each other. We were more than a secret. You were this untouchable thing—he would have chased me down until I was out of the picture, of that, I'm sure."

"You don't know my dad like I do. If I would have gone to him, told him I loved you."

He flinched at the past tense.

"He would have let me."

Valerian's face fell. "Ask him next time you see him."

"I will." I gritted my teeth. "I think you should leave."

"You promised me one more night." His easy grin was back. "And it looks like we still have ohhhhh, at least five hours until midnight."

"Then you go." My chin wobbled.

"Then I go…" he whispered. "Back to Seattle."

"Alone," I confirmed, hating how desperately I wanted to fling myself into his arms because he was alive, and he was talking to me, but he was different, and he'd told so many lies, and we were supposed to be something not like this. "Say it."

He locked eyes with me. "Alone. I go back alone, but not forever, because one day…" He approached then. "One day you'll realize what a colossal mistake it was watching me walk out of your life when all I ever wanted to do was be by your side. I lied to you. But I sacrificed everything so we could be together, so while you're sitting there feeling sorry for yourself that Breaker's dead, remember, I'm still him, and I'm standing right in front of you, alive, breathing, begging to taste my wife's lips, begging to love her, begging to touch her skin and feel her heartbeat with my mouth."

"You always were so good with words," I grumbled and swiped a tear from under my eye. "Is that how you got so much action?"

His grin was lopsided as he shrugged. "I got action in order to forget about the only girl I wanted to bend over the table every time we had family dinner. I don't think you realize how many fantasies I've had about just your mouth or pulling your hair just to see you gasp. And now I get you for one night, and you can't say no. I get you for the first time without lies, masks, without wondering who you loved more, Valerian or Breaker. Tonight, I'm just me, and I'm going to fuck the hell out of you."

Breaker would never talk to me like that because he had known he'd get slapped.

But I liked it.

I liked it way too much.

And suddenly I was reminded of the time he'd spanked me, first the anger, then the embarrassment and then the need for more pain mixed with the pleasure he promised.

"You can try to hide behind that defiant lift of your chin and your perfection, but I know something else nobody does." He started to circle me as I tensed under his perusal, and then he stopped behind me, grabbing the side of my neck with his hand and pulling me back against him, his fingers digging into my skin lightly as he whispered in my ear. "Violet Abandonato likes to get dirty. Tell me."

I swayed back against him, my eyes unfocused as his hands moved to my soft blue cotton shirt and jerked it over my head, causing my hair to fan out around my naked shoulders.

I had no bra on.

He trailed one finger down my neck and then across my ribs toward my jeans. Both hands moved to my hips as he held me in front of him. I could feel his hard length throb against my ass, even through his jeans. He was ready. I moved my hips against him.

He bit out a curse as my mouth parted, needing to taste him but not wanting to beg him for it.

"It will always be you, Vi. Only you," he whispered, and then he was almost violently pulling my jeans down to my ankles. I stepped out of them and stood still, clad in a pair of black silk underwear, topless, waiting for his next move.

But he did nothing.

He just held me against him again, this time, I could hear his heavy breathing, I could feel his restraint.

And I wanted him to snap.

I wanted him to take me.

And I was too afraid to ask.

But the longer I stood there with his arms wrapped around me, pinning me against his body, the more intensely mine pulsed with need, making it impossible to stand still.

I shook with it.

And there we stood.

My back to his front.

No words were spoken.

And then his teeth tugged at my right earlobe, his lips wet as he spoke against my ear in Russian. I had no idea what he said, but for some reason, it made me hot, because it sounded hot. I was so screwed when it came to him, literally.

"Beg."

"No."

"Beg." He tugged harder, "Your time's running out. If this is really our last night, I'm going to make it so memorable that you can't help but think about me every second of every day, that you physically hurt for my touch, that you think of my fingers inside you, you think of my mouth sucking you, my tongue devouring you, my dick filling you…"

I let out the breath I'd been holding, my voice was shaky. "Please."

I almost whimpered when a ripping noise had my underwear falling to my feet in a flutter, my ass bared to him, my entire vulnerable body bared to him. And then he was flipping me around, ducking his head and my legs wrapped around his face.

Down I went.

Down he went.

I fell across the bed, and his mouth managed to stay lodged between my legs as he gave one brutal swipe of his tongue. But then he drew back and said, "Not good enough."

I clenched the sheets in my hands, desperate to grab onto something. "Please!"

"Please, what?" He had a full view of all of me, and he looked like a man who'd just won the lottery.

I gulped at his full mouth, glistening from me, from what he had done to me just by standing behind me. It would be embarrassing if I wasn't in almost physical pain to have him keep going.

"Please." I locked eyes with him. "Valerian."

Eyes wild with a feral glint, he lowered his head, and I nearly lost consciousness as he swiped his tongue, then used his fingers, finding every single sensitive spot that could drive a woman insane.

"More, please more!" Maybe begging wasn't such a bad idea if this was the outcome over time?

Valerian stopped.

"Why the hell are you stopping?" I was going to murder him dead!

He grinned up at me. "Because I like you angry."

"I will literally pull a gun on you!"

I had one in my dresser.

He smirked.

I narrowed my eyes.

And then I lunged for my dresser, but he tackled me to the floor. The gun went tumbling, but I noticed that the knife I kept hidden under my bed beckoned.

"Oooo…" Valerian pinned my wrists above my head. "Not so fast, we wouldn't want to get blood on the carpet."

"Oh, we really would." I clenched my teeth.

He leaned down to kiss me.

I fought him.

But it was impossible not to respond as he covered my body with his heavily muscled one. And then he was shimmying out of his jeans, tugging them down with one hand while holding me in place.

I squirmed beneath him and glared when he stopped

kissing me for a few minutes and whispered, "You're glorious. You know that, right?"

"Because I fight you? Or because you piss me off?"

"Because I see you." He sobered. "I've only ever seen you, not the girl you want others to see, but the angry one who just wants to be heard, who wants her own life, the life I can share with her." And then he was kissing me again, and my mind grew more muddled.

Because he was right.

He was hot and hard against my thigh, I tried to move my body to inch closer, but he just laughed against my mouth and then. "Do you need me?"

"Yes." I tried to move my arms.

"Good." He released me, and all hell broke loose, between me scratching his back in a vain effort to get closer, and him kicking off the rest of his jeans while still trying to claim my mouth in between.

We joined in an ugly tangle of moans and bodies sliding together. His first thrust filled me completely, his second almost sent me over the edge, and then he moved faster like he couldn't help himself, his eyes almost frenzied as he leaned over and kissed me.

Closer, I needed to be closer.

But we were as close as two people could get.

And still, I craved more.

"You're mine, Violet." His voice was hoarse, his eyes drilling into me. "No matter what happens, you'll always be mine."

I moaned as his hips drove forward.

Gazes collided, locked.

I watched him own me.

And I felt a small part of myself give in.

And that small part was enough for me to experience the most mind-blowing orgasm I'd ever had.

And enough for me to scream his name.

"Valerian!" It was out before I could stop it.

He went over the edge so hard that I felt him pulsing inside me like a million tiny heartbeats.

He didn't know. He was mine too. I was just too scared to say it, and too broken to confirm what he already knew.

I loved him.

I loved Valerian Petrov.

The new Petrov king.

And I only had four more hours to show him before he went back alone, and I stayed in Chicago with my distrust and broken heart.

I was a fool if I ever thought he would let me go.

CHAPTER
Twenty-Nine

Falling in love with your best friend is distracting, it's terrifying, like falling out of an airplane and hoping they remembered the chute.
—Valerian Petrov

Valerian

I always had a taste.

Most people focus on smell.

But the way she tasted always felt like home to me; even when I took her virginity, it was what I focused on.

The fact that she tasted like she always did.

Like she was mine.

Like she was just waiting for me to love her.

I could give her a million reasons why I'd believed it had been okay to hide my secrets, but the one truth that remained was that she was right—I should have trusted her with this a long time ago, but a part of me wondered if she would have hated me even then just like King did. For knowing that one day I would go away.

And come back different.

One day, I would have no choice.

I'd had to live with that sword hanging over me, but I'd wanted our friendship to be pure, untainted by a future I'd despised.

I sighed and pressed a kiss to her neck then slowly pulled out of her. Her chest was heaving, her eyes filled with tears like she wanted to cry or maybe just scream at me for loving her.

Good, let her scream.

Instead, she just stumbled to her feet and mumbled something about needing a shower.

I followed her.

Didn't she know? I would always follow her.

She turned on the spray, and even though I'm sure it was freezing, she stepped under it. With a sigh, I opened up the glass door and followed.

Her back was to me, but her shoulders were shaking.

"I'm sorry," I whispered. "Does it matter that I love you? That I would die for you?"

"It used to." She sniffled. "And now I just… I think I need time. Time to process the last two weeks of my life, time to process a future with you, time to just… have a day where my heart and my head aren't at war with each other."

"I can give you time." Slowly I reached for her, turning her around until she was facing me, even with her teeth chattering, tears streaming down her cheeks, and her wet hair plastered to her face; she was stunning.

I pulled her into my arms. Kissing my way down her neck. Thankful that she was letting me love her with my body since she no longer trusted my words. Her soft sighs were all the encouragement I needed as my mouth moved to hers. The water finally started to warm as it poured over us like a summer rain. My tongue slid past her parted lips as she clung to my shoulders, her breasts pressed against my chest.

I broke away from her just long enough to move my kisses down her neck to her chest, and then I knelt in front of my queen. Gripping her hips with my hands, mentally begging her to tell me to stay, pleading with her to get in that car with me and never look back.

I held on to her hips for what felt like hours, nothing but the sounds of our own breathing and the splatter of water in the steam-filled the shower. I rested my head against her stomach as she ran her hands through my hair. My submission didn't matter, did it? My worship? My dedication? I would always be the man who had been baptized in fire, hidden away and resurrected at the wrong time, for a purpose that was necessary in order to be with the one person who didn't see it that way.

I sighed against her skin. The water was starting to chill again. Slowly I rose, wishing she would have chosen that moment to say something that told me things were going to be different. Instead, tears slid down her cheeks in rapid succession as I pulled her in for a hug.

She laid her head against my chest.

And I knew, in that moment, if this was all I got from Violet, I would take it. Just her resting her head against my chest, trusting me to hold her, to love her, to protect her.

And just like the Polar Bear King, if I only had her nights, if I only had her body. If I only got fractions of her love—I would be satisfied, and I would fight every single war to make it to her during those times, to steal those minutes of her love and hold them in my heart forever.

She pulled away from me briefly, her eyes searching mine, and then she cupped my head between her hands and pressed a chaste kiss to my mouth. "I do."

"You do?" It hurt to breathe, it hurt to exist.

"I do," she repeated, "take you…" Her lips were swollen from all of our kissing. "Valerian Petrov…" Her voice shook. "…as my husband." She moved to her knees and took me in her mouth briefly before pulling back and whispering. "As my king."

My heart fucking burst in my chest as her mouth covered me, her head bowed to me, her lips claiming me.

And just like before, when she first touched me.

I didn't last long.

Maybe it was the hunger mixed with innocence in her eyes, or maybe it was just something about her.

"Vi—" I shot down her throat. My knees sagged, and I steadied myself with a hand on the wall.

She licked her lips and then looked up and whispered, "My Valerian."

"My Violet." I rasped.

"In the story…" She rose and wrapped her arms around my neck. "After the queen saved her king, did they live happily ever after?"

"Happily ever after's boring, Violet." My lips tugged into a smile. "Don't you want an adventure?"

Her blue eyes locked on to me. "I think I'd be happy with a little less adventure, after all of this."

I smiled, tracing my fingertip over her lips. "Yeah, I can see why."

"So?"

"So, I promise to give my queen whatever she needs."

"Violet Petrov." She said it like she was testing the name.

"Mine," I said simply.

Her jaw flexed as I reached behind her, turned off the water, and then opened the shower door to grab her a towel wrapping it around her shivering body and then grabbing one for myself.

"I gave you four nights," she said in a small voice. "So, give me three days."

My heart jumped in my chest. "Three days?"

She smiled slowly. "Give me three days to say goodbye to my family. I never got to before. I need to pack, I need to process like I said, but after three days, after I talk to my dad…"

I was ready to fall at her feet in worship. "After all of that…"

"I'll see you in Seattle."

I let go of the shaky breath I'd been holding, and then I was jerking her towel from her body and tossing her onto the bed as my own towel dropped to the floor.

She smiled against my mouth.

It was going to be okay.

We were going to be okay.

I pulled the covers up around her body and held her close.

She fell asleep in my arms, exhausted.

When midnight struck, I kissed her on the cheek, put on my clothes, and made my way back down the stairs.

I should have known he would be sitting there.

Glock in one hand.

Serrated knife in the other.

The kitchen light was dim over his head as he tapped the knife against his thigh like he was counting the seconds until

309

he could slit my throat.

"Chase." I gritted my teeth and pulled out a chair and sat.

Luc and Ash weren't going to save me from this one.

I was in this alone.

And if he wanted blood.

He would get blood.

"How is she?" He didn't look up, just kept tapping his knife against his thigh. Shit.

How to answer? Satisfied? Smiling? Fucking delicious? "She's better."

"That's not what I asked." Slowly he lifted his head, cold blue eyes locked onto me. "How. Is. She?"

"Strong," I said in a clipped voice. "Beautiful." I crossed my arms. "Claimed, and no longer yours."

He jumped to his feet, kicking his chair back in the process, chest heaving.

I tilted my head. "Are we doing this here? Now? How much of my blood do you think you need to spill to feel better about all of this? She's legally bound to me, and you can't do shit about it."

"You little shit!" Chase spat. "Do you know what you've done? You've taken everything from her! Everything I've built! Her life was not supposed to go in this direction! She had a plan, she had—"

I held up my hand. "You mean you had a plan, and I ruined it."

He gritted his teeth. "You gave her no fucking choice!"

"I saved your fucking life! Not to mention your family!" I roared, jumping to my feet and gripping his shirt with my right hand, knowing he had his gun trained on me, and the knife was at my throat. "You would be dead if I didn't do what

I did. So maybe stop with the theatrics and the yelling and say thank you. Then again, you don't have a humble bone in your body!"

He sneered. "Humility gets you killed, you know this just as much as I do, Petrov."

"I can't help what I am, Chase, but I do love her, more than anything, because, at the end of the day, I was the one willing to make the sacrifice to have her, and sometimes I wonder if you would do the same. Or is your precious career more important? Your connections? What people think? I didn't steal her, I protected her when you couldn't. I didn't destroy her future, I made sure she fucking *had* one."

I let go of him.

Slowly he lowered the knife, his eyes haunted.

The gun clattered to the floor, and then he slumped into his chair, resting his head in his hands like he was broken. "She's my baby."

"And now she's mine," I whispered. "But that doesn't make her any less yours; she's still Abandonato through and through, as proven when she tried to beat the shit out of me earlier today."

He lifted his head and smiled. "Violet's too tame for that."

"Tell that to my throat after getting punched."

His grin widened. "Good girl, I taught her that."

"Yeah, it felt like it."

He looked away. "I didn't want you for her."

It stung, but I knew the truth. "Sometimes I don't even want me for her. She's too good for me for this life."

He nodded and then pulled out another knife.

Great. My nerves were already shot. People didn't just talk back to Chase and live to tell about it. Already I knew I wasn't going to escape out something broken and was bracing for the pain.

Shock rippled through me when he sliced across his hand and held it out. "My loyalty…" He lifted his head, voice firm. "To the new Petrov boss."

He handed me the knife with his other hand.

The knife was sharp, and I felt little more than a quick sting as I made the same cut the bosses always made when showing fealty to the other bosses. I waited for the blood to well along the thin line, and then I shook his hand, our blood mixing, our loyalty no longer divided.

Out of all of the men that I now called equals, out of all the powerful men, I didn't expect Chase to be the first to humble himself and show me his allegiance.

Then again, I hadn't expected him not to kill me.

My throat felt like it wasn't working as we both dropped our hands to our sides, and then he was pulling out a bottle of whiskey and pouring us both small glasses. "I was going to kill you tonight."

"That's a fun story, please tell me more," I said dryly.

His lips pressed into an amused smile. "The night's still young."

"Cheers." I lifted my glass and clinked it against his, but we both knew, it was an empty threat. Now that we had shaken hands, he would die to protect me, and I would die to protect him.

It was the first time in my life, I realized, that I felt like the king I was, as I dusted off my dirty crown, and took my seat next to the powerful Abandonato line, no longer hiding in the crowd, but sitting on my deserved throne.

And damn if it didn't feel good.

CHAPTER
Thirty

Love feels like something inside of you is breaking at least ninety percent of the time, and the only ointment is usually the person that's doing the breaking.
—Valerian Petrov

Violet

I woke up to the smell of bacon, eggs, and coffee. My body was sore from Valerian, and for some reason, that brought a smile to my lips. In the bathroom, when I glimpsed myself in the mirror, I paused and studied my reflection. I looked... different.

My mouth was swollen, I had a few bruises on my hips from where he'd grabbed me, but they were light, and I liked that his hands had been on me, marking me, holding me, making me beg.

I shivered at the thought.

My brain was still a mess.

My heart was still trying to process everything.

But my body was ready for another round.

Talk about confusion.

I quickly dressed and made my way downstairs, ready to have the hard talk with my dad that I didn't want to have but knew was necessary.

He was reading the paper, and it almost looked so normal I wanted to laugh; he was anything but normal.

Even sitting in a chair with his leg crossed, he was lethal.

He probably knew how many steps it took to get from the kitchen door to the bedroom and had at least a dozen weapons hidden by the cereal.

I remembered when I was a kindergartner finding a gun inside the Fruit Loops and frowning at what a shitty prize it was.

That... was a childhood in the Abandonato household.

"Dad?" I poured myself some coffee.

He slowly lowered the paper. His eyes were soft as he took me in, a small smile tugged at his lips. "You were up late."

Kill me now. I slid down into a chair and then slid farther down as embarrassment washed over me. "Yeah, well... I noticed we're out of bagels again."

He choked on his coffee and rasped. "Touché."

I clinked my coffee mug with his as we both grinned at each other.

"I have something to ask—" I frowned. He had a bandage wrapped around his hand. "Did you get hurt?"

"Merely a flesh wound." He winked. "What did you need to ask, sweetheart?"

Ash chose that moment to bounce into the room, but he took one look at Dad and me and turned around.

"Sit," Dad barked.

Ash sat as far away from us as possible, scowling. He had dark circles under his eyes, and his hair was all messy on his head. He looked like he'd either had a ton of sex the night before or spent it drinking and trying to forget his demons. Maybe it was both.

I was instantly worried.

But we all mourned differently.

And I felt guilty that at least the love of *my* life was alive—different, but alive—and his wasn't coming back. Not now, not ever.

"Violet." Dad folded the paper and set it on the chair next to him. "What's your question?"

I chewed my lower lip. "If I would have come to you, honestly come to you and told you I loved Breaker, would you have let us be together?"

"No." His eyes softened. "Because Breaker Campisi could have never married Violet Abandonato and lived to tell about it. I wanted something better, someone better. I wanted you to choose, yes, but I didn't want you to choose someone who couldn't give you everything that you were born with, and while I know how privileged that sounds, remember, his past was a secret to all of us, a mystery, something that I couldn't trust when it came to marrying you. Protecting you was one thing, being your friend another, but marrying you? I have to be completely honest; I still don't know how I feel about it, but things are…" He released a sigh. "…different now."

"Just because he has a different name?" I wondered.

"Not just that, but he…" Another sigh. "…he saved you, he saved me, Luc, Ariel—and he took his rightful place. He's where he belongs, and I agree with him that you would have always been a target married to Breaker, and he would not have had the resources to adequately protect you. He would have most likely died young doing that. Now that he's a boss—"

"He has a fucking army," Ash finished for him. "Sorry, you were just monologuing so long that I thought I'd help."

My dad's eyes narrowed in on Ash. "Care to share with the class why you were dry humping Annie in the shallow end of the pool?"

I nearly spit out my coffee. "You did what? To who?"

"Tell me you at least dumped a gallon of shock and chlorine into the pool afterward, you know Mom likes to do laps there and I highly doubt she wants to swim through your—"

"Dad." Ash clenched his teeth. "We didn't… I didn't… Why does this always happen with us? Must you be so invested in my sex life?"

"Must you be such an exhibitionist?" He shrugged.

Ash tore his gaze away from us. "I pissed her off, she left, I hate her, end of story."

Dad burst out laughing, shocking me so much I nearly dropped my mug. "Damn, that's exactly what I was thinking while she rode you like her favorite pony, while she screamed your name and while you nearly bit sucked off her neck multiple times while sucking on her lips… how much you hate her. Sure, I'll buy it."

Ash flushed.

He actually flushed.

I looked between them.

Dad shook his head slightly, like silently warning me to leave it.

But how did a person leave that?

"Ash, you know it's okay to…" I licked my lips. "It's okay to be happy."

"No." He shoved his chair back. "It's actually not." He stormed out of the room and ran up the stairs, most likely to find Mom and say good morning like he did every day when he came over for breakfast.

I was the daddy's girl.

He was a total mama's boy.

It's probably why the girls all loved him—he knew how to get them to eat out of the palm of his hand even when it wasn't on purpose.

"As I was saying…" Dad ignored the outburst. "The only reason he gets to keep you is because he's a boss, a powerful Petrov boss. He would burn the entire world to keep you safe. He would use every resource, every cent he has, and now he has it all, and he's able to do it, I wouldn't be surprised if he doesn't already have men trained on you."

I flinched at the thought. "Breaker would have had men too, right?"

"No." Dad shook his head. "That's up to the boss. You know how the hierarchy works. At best, he would be a made man, at the worst, he'd be a captain on the Campisi payroll—" He held up a hand. "I take that back. if someone died, he was second in line, but we don't hope for death in our families, we hope for life, so I wouldn't have taken that into account."

I exhaled. "All right then."

"So." He folded his arms. "You've made your choice?"

"Dad…" I sighed and walked over to him. "You make it sound like I'm choosing him over you."

"In a way, you are." Dad's smile was snide. "But that's what marriage is." He stood and pulled me into his arms. "I'm so damn proud of you."

I sniffled. "I leave in three days."

His arms tightened around me, and then he whispered, "Sweetheart, if you love him like I know you do, there is absolutely no reason for those three days. You think time will heal, but more often, time just makes us overthink decisions that have already been set in stone." He kissed my temple. "Go to him."

"But I have to say goodbye, and I have to pack, and I have to—"

"New life." He drew back without completely letting me go and winked. "New things. Let him take you shopping, I bet he'd love it, let him help you start your new life in Seattle." He squeezed my shoulder. "Go to him."

I frowned. "It's so confusing when you're not scary and suddenly make sense."

He winked. "It's part of my charm."

Mom's snort came up from behind me. "Yes, oh so charming, do tell your daughter how you fell asleep drinking with Valerian last night, woke up and stumbled to bed, and snored all night long."

"Luc," Dad growled out her name. But then he reached for her, tossed her over his shoulder, and carried her out of the kitchen, calling back, "Good talk, Vi, I've got a busy day." He slapped Mom on the ass.

I could never unsee the blush on her cheeks.

And then Ash was storming back into the room like an angry tornado looking for houses to break.

"Who pissed in your Cheerios?" I crossed my arms.

His fists were clenched, eyes glazed over.

I sighed. "Are you high?"

"No." He gritted his teeth. "I wish."

"Do you need to get away for a bit?"

His jaw flexed. "What did you have in mind?"

"A little trip to Seattle with your favorite sister?"

"*I'm* his favorite, but nice try." Stepping into the kitchen, Izzy yawned and smacked him on the back of the head as she walked by.

I froze. "Izzy, is that a hickey?"

Ash's eyes widened as the kitchen fell silent. "Iz?"

"Uh…" She gulped, and then Maksim lazily walked into the room, his hair poking out every which way.

Ash lunged.

Izzy screamed.

And Maksim used me as a human shield.

Perfect.

"The hell, Maksim!" Ash roared. "How the hell did you sneak in? We nearly had to put on a porno to get Valerian by!"

"Oh, that." Maksim winked. "I had impeccable timing."

Izzy rolled her eyes. "He's good with his fingers."

"WHAT?" Ash looked ready to murder.

"Chill." Izzy grinned. "He's a climber, duh, he climbed the tree by my window."

"That tree's nearly impossible to climb." Ash glared in my direction as Maksim still hid behind me.

"That's what she said." Maksim's voice lowered. "I have really, really strong fingers, some might say magic."

"Keep talking, ask me what happens next," Ash growled.

Junior and Serena walked into the kitchen, and I stared. Had everyone stayed the night last night?

They took in the scene.

Serena's grin was pure evil while Junior crossed his arms and jerked his head toward Ash. "We killing him or torturing?"

"I'm leaning toward torture." Ash smiled.

Serena rubbed her hands together. "You know, I slept on your shit couch last night, Ash, and woke up ready to kill you, and you give me this gift? You're my new favorite cousin."

"Hey!" I protested.

"Sorry, not sorry." She winked. "Oh, also word on the street, is Valerian left early this morning. Something happened in Seattle, and Nikolai sent his jet…" Her gaze flicked around the room. "…and why is everyone looking at me like someone died?"

"He left?" The blood drained from my face, and I gulped in a couple of huge breaths. "Already?"

Maksim forgotten, I went and slumped into the chair. "I was going to try to catch him and go with him and—" I stopped talking and then perked up. "You think Dad would let us use his jet?"

Ash's eyebrows shot up to his forehead. "No, but we could always steal it."

Junior sighed. "Last time I walked with a limp for two weeks, no thanks."

"Right, but that was because we went to Vegas," I pointed out. "Not because we chased after the man I love."

"Aw…" Serena's face softened. "I like happy endings."

"Same." Maksim chuckled and winked at Izzy.

"I would stop before your blood gets sprinkled over the eggs, bro." Junior patted him on the shoulder.

"Well?" Ash shared a look with me. "We doing this?"

I stood. "We're doing it. Plus, Dad's extremely distracted right now."

From upstairs, Mom screamed Dad's name.

We all exchanged looks of sheer horror.

And I've never seen so many people scramble out of a kitchen with hot food and coffee in my entire life.

It took us exactly an hour to go grab King, despite his protests, and Tank, despite his grumbling that our dad was going to kill him—but he was like having really good FBI back up, plus he was in this now, because we'd adopted him into our family. Now his allegiance was toward Ash and only Ash. Meaning if Ash said we needed him, he had to drop everything.

I thought Ash was going to shit himself when Annie arrived with Tank by her side, but they were close, and where he went, she went.

Annie looked like she was ready to hurl when the plane took off, and then she looked ready to hurl again when she locked eyes with Ash.

What the hell happened last night?

I looked around at all my family, my friends, and everything suddenly felt right in the world.

This time when we went to Seattle, there were no secrets, no lies, only celebrating in Valerian's insane mansion.

"So, it's right on the water?" Ash asked, strategically ignoring Annie while she tried not to steal glances at him. "Does he have a yacht? Because I could really go for that right about now, you know, along with a shit ton of pot so I can pass out and forget last night."

Annie flinched.

"Ash," I whispered. "What are you doing?"

"What I must." He sighed and then put on his noise-canceling headphones and closed his eyes.

He missed the tear that slid down Annie's cheek.

Just like the murderous glance Tank shot in Ash's direction

as he wrapped an arm around her. He handed her an iPad and headphones like it would distract her from Ash's meanness.

He'd always had a mean streak because he had to out of necessity, but now… now it felt like he fed off his own cruelty.

Sometimes I didn't recognize my brother anymore, and it broke my heart. How many more deaths would he cause, or survive before I lost him completely?

With that haunting thought, I closed my eyes and tried to sleep, because when I saw Valerian, I expected to be up all night.

I fell into a deep sleep with a smile on my lips, imagining his face.

CHAPTER
Thirty-One

Most enemies hide in plain sight, waiting for the day
to step out and fight.
—Valerian Petrov

Valerian

I'd been back at the house for a few hours, wondering what the hell was so important that I had to fly back ahead of schedule. I'd sent out a text to Violet, but it wasn't the same, and it got me thinking, this was why I needed to be in Seattle and yet another reason the men were probably angry that Andrei had been in Chicago.

They needed leadership here.

At their home base.

In their city.

I sighed and looked around my empty office, the couch where Violet had kissed me might as well burn a hole into my skull as memories washed over me.

I had been so afraid that first day when I walked in here,

afraid that the memories would be too much. But I should have known Violet would be like a breath of fresh air, and she had been. Every room she walked into, even when she hated me, even when she was scared, it was like she'd been helping me build new memories without even realizing it.

I tapped my cell against my thigh and then tossed it on my desk, next to the picture of my mom that was staring back at me.

I picked it up, my fingers dancing along the front of it like I could still touch her soft face, smell the berry shampoo she used on her bright blond hair. Her smile was huge in the picture like she knew one day I'd need that smile to remind me why I was doing what I was doing.

Because she'd died.

And I'd lived.

"That's my favorite picture of her," Sancto said, walking into my office with two glasses of whiskey. He set one in front of me and took his, throwing it back in one full swallow.

Still holding the picture, I looked up. "She was beautiful."

"She was." A muscle ticked in his jaw. "It's such a shame when such beauty gets stolen."

He stilled. "Why don't you have a drink? You look stressed."

I set down the picture and leaned back in my chair, my shoulders tense. "I'm stressed because my wife isn't going to be here for three full days, and I miss her, so what's so important that you needed to speak to me in person?"

He eyed my whiskey and then me. "There's a reason for the alcohol."

"Perfect." I gritted my teeth and reached for the glass, downing it just like he did and then wondering why I felt the need to chug it like him, remembering my early training about mimicking others when you're tired.

Shit.

Something was off with him. His eyes were suddenly wild as he got up and started to pace.

"I always knew you would be loyal, I just never realized how easy all of this would be when the time came." His smile was sad, and then something flickered in his gaze over my head, the other picture of my mom. "Too bad that loyalty will kill you." He pressed his hands against my desk and leaned over it as my vision blurred. "You couldn't just stay hidden with the Italians; no, you had to rise up and take everything from me! The minute the men knew you were alive, they cheered, they celebrated like you came back to life! Like you deserve this!" He pounded his fist against the desk baring his teeth.

I tried to stand and fell back down into my chair, panic rising in my chest as I realized I really was going to lose this one.

I had left early.

Violet wasn't coming for three more days.

Why the hell didn't I bring backup?

Nobody expected me back for hours.

My men weren't here because they thought I was still in Chicago.

Nobody was here but me and Sancto.

Sancto and the ghosts of my mom, my dad, my childhood.

My eyes felt heavy.

He'd drugged me.

I shoved the glass away from me, but my eyes blurred again as whatever he'd given me coursed through my system. The more erratic my heartbeat, the more the drug spread. The more I panicked, the less time I had.

I had to focus.

"Why?" I ground out with difficulty. "Why do this?"

"You killed her!" He roared. "And I loved her! You were a spoiled little shit who couldn't live without his horse blanket. You made her go back in that house! She would still be alive if it weren't for you! And then, you come back from the fucking dead and take over the Family when I was this close to stealing the crown from Andrei! I had loyal followers. Loyal men who are now taking your side! The great Valerian Petrov! Back from the dead!"

"Thought you... wanted... this." Keep him talking, find a way out. But I was starting to see spots in my line of vision; it was like taking a billion Benadryl and then losing all function of my arms and legs.

"So." He lit a match and grinned. "I figured the only way for you to truly know what she suffered that night, what I've suffered for years is to baptize you into the flames and let them finish the job!" He grabbed the white horse blanket my mom had given me from the drawer I always kept it in even though I tried to slap his hands away in a vain attempt to get him to stop. "You need your blanket? Well, fucking take it." The smell of kerosene was almost sickening, I almost blacked out as he did something and then my blanket was on fire, and he was throwing it in the corner next to the curtains. "I hope you rot in hell. And now your last few memories will be of me, taking back what's mine, and avenging your mother's death!"

"She loved... me," I whispered, my voice almost completely gone.

"She loved me too," he said with a chilling voice. "And she's gone."

"Wait."

The door to my office slammed shut.

I needed to fight, or I was going to die. I couldn't succumb. I tried to get up and fell back down in the chair, and then I crashed to the floor, as flames licked up the curtains of my office and danced up the ceiling threatening to swallow the room whole.

I reached for the chair and tried to drag myself across the floor, but it was useless, my body felt paralyzed, my vision was going dark.

My brain told me to pull myself to the door, but my limbs weren't responding, and my eyes were so heavy it was painful.

Smoke filled the room at such a rapid pace that I was suffocating, and I couldn't even cough. With the combination of not being able to breathe from the drugs and the smoke, I would die before I would feel the first burn.

She wouldn't see me like this.

Nobody was going to save me.

But at least she was safe.

At least she was home.

My eyes burned as I squeezed out a few coughs, gasping for air.

And then I saw her.

Of course, I did because I was dying.

Really truly dying.

"I'm s-sorry," I whispered, reaching out to Violet. "Love you..."

My last thoughts were for God to keep her safe from monsters like Sancto.

Monsters like me.

CHAPTER
Thirty-Two

Heaven feels like her touch. I imagine Hell feels like
the loss of it.
—Valerian Petrov

Violet

"Something's wrong," I murmured as the SUV pulled up to
the house. I'd had a bad feeling ever since we landed.

Sancto ran out of the house.

He never ran.

Everything about him screamed purpose and control.

And right now, he looked—out of his mind, crazed, and
just a bit evil as he made his way toward one of the black
SUVs.

"Ash, stop him. I don't know why, but—" An acrid odor
teased my nose as we got out of the SUV, and I sniffed then
gagged. "Oh God, that smells like smoke!"

A gunshot tore the air, and something pinged off our SUV.
Sancto stood holding a gun, aiming it at our group, at least the

ones already out of the car. I knew that Junior would see what was going on from the driver's side and do what he usually did, mess people up.

"It's too late!" Sancto's eyes dripped with hatred, shocking me to my core. He'd always been so kind, so gentle. "He should have died! He killed her!"

I knew what he was talking about.

Valerian's mom.

I held up my hands. "Sancto, think about this, you can't kill the Petrov boss without consequences."

"Hah! You know they were going to vote me to take over from Andrei next? And it would have worked if you hadn't whored yourself out!"

I glared. "You know what else is going to work?"

He waved the gun like he didn't care.

"I'm legally his wife, and I'll fight you to the bitter end for control of this Family. I'm sure it'll help that I'm his successor according to our marriage contract." I was lying through my teeth, but I needed to give the others time to take him down as I slowly walked toward him. The smell of smoke was getting worse, and everything in me wanted to race into that mansion to get to the man I loved. But for now, I just needed to stay calm and get to Valerian—if he was still alive. I would not cry. Not now.

He needed me now.

He needed his partner, his queen, to be strong.

I jutted my chin out at Sancto.

Eyes demented, his hand shook as he pointed the gun right at my forehead. "You're a lying bitch!"

The gun aimed at my head one minute; the next, a gunshot

rang out, and blood covered my fingers and part of my face as Sancto went down.

Junior rushed toward me. "You okay?"

"Nice shot." Serena grinned like there wasn't a dead body lying down in front of me. "I mean, you were a little to the left but, we can't all be perfect."

Junior rolled his eyes. "It *was* perfect, and you're just mad I got it first."

"True," she grumbled.

My family was insane!

Smoke billowed out of the house. "Valerian!" I screamed, and then I ran. He was in there, and he had to be alive. He had to be.

Ash ran in with me because, of course, Ash would run toward danger. That was how both of us were programmed, Dad's fault.

I coughed and turned toward the billowing smoke coming out of the closed office door.

"Wait!" Ash felt the knob and snatched his hand back with a curse. "Vi, I don't know if this is a good idea."

"KICK IT OPEN BEFORE I KILL YOU!" I shrieked.

"Fuck, you're insane!" He shoved me behind him, then kicked open the door and jumped back. Black smoke roiled out in waves, quickly filling the hallway. The flames were just getting to the ceiling after climbing up the curtains.

And my husband was lying lifeless on the floor.

"Valerian!" I rushed toward him.

"I'm s-sorry," he croaked. "Love… you."

Ash shoved past me and felt for a pulse. "It's slow." He coughed. "But he's alive." As some of the others rushed into the room with us carrying fire extinguishers we kept in the

SUV, Ash grabbed Valerian by the shoulders and dragged him out of the smoke into the entry hall. "Time to be the doctor you were born to be and save your husband, Vi."

I gave him a shaky nod. "Um… umm. Gr-grab one of the med kits from the car, and search the house for where they keep their emergency supplies. Most of the Italian families have them in their training rooms, but I never saw his. You have to hurry; I don't know how much smoke he's inhaled he needs oxygen."

I swear I lost years off my life in the minutes it took for Junior to bring me one of the med kits we always traveled with. I pulled out the small O2 tank and covered his mouth and nose with the mask then tested his oxygen levels.

My hands shook as I checked his eyes; they were dilated, was he poisoned by something?

Junior left me and joined Tank, Annie, Izzy, and King, where they were hopefully able to put out the fire. Then Ash was back with another med kit, a larger one that looked like it belonged in an emergency room. Without waiting for instructions, he tore open the IV.

"Vi," he barked. "What next? We need to know what next?"

Abruptly my sense of calm kicked into gear. "I-I think he should be responding. His oxygen levels are still in the nineties, so he didn't get too much smoke. I think he's going to recover. He wasn't in there long enough to pass out from lack of oxygen. There's something else! I glanced toward the door where the smoke drifting out had slowed and now looked more grayish white. "Look at his desk, see if there's anything he touched, a syringe, anything that can help me figure out what's in his system."

I searched Valerian's arms for any puncture wounds, then his neck, behind his ears, but nothing was there. His pulse was strong, but it was slow.

Maybe not poison; maybe drugged.

Drugged. That was it. If Sancto wanted him alive enough to die in the fire or pass out, he wouldn't kill him with poison first.

Ash ran back with a small glass. "This was on his desk; it smells like whiskey but—"

I took the glass from him and sniffed inside. Something was off, and if my guess was correct, he either dumped in a shit ton of sleeping meds or added a cocktail a true doctor would give...

"Nikolai," I murmured.

Growing up, we had all seen way too much, but something that had stuck with me was seeing Nikolai in action, and he'd pulled off some strange medical miracles without blinking an eye. One of which was to kill a man while he remained alive.

Ash stared at me. "Nikolai?"

"Don't you see? It's a particular expertise of Nikolai's, drugging—" I grabbed Ash's arm and tugged. "It's something Sancto would have had access to. He flew in Nikolai's plane—Ash! Call Nikolai now. I think this is his drug, it's his own special concoction. He calls it JR88. It paralyzes you but makes it possible to feel everything; too much of it causes shallow breathing, hallucinations, and you can even pass out from it. If I'm right, he should know what counteracts it because right now, the only thing we can do is hope his body processes it."

Ash was already on his cell before she finished speaking, and within minutes Nikolai was on his way. He stayed on the line with Ash holding the phone on speaker as Nikolai told me what I needed to do.

"Adrenaline," he said calmly as though the love of my life wasn't dying in front of me. "A good old fashion shot to the heart should do it."

I glanced up at the others who were surrounding us.

Every face paled. Heads shook as if to say, *"not it."*

"What?" I snapped. "You guys can shoot a guy in the head, but when it comes to stabbing them with a needle, you pass out?"

Junior shuddered. "I hate needles."

"I can't even give blood," Ash reminded me.

I rolled my eyes. "Good thing you have an almost doctor on your hands then." I reached for the adrenaline and told my hands to stop shaking; I didn't like Nikolai saying it "should" work. I clenched my teeth. It *had* to work because shooting someone with adrenaline wasn't exactly safe.

Especially if they were healthy.

He could easily have a heart attack and die.

"Damn it, you better come back to me, Valerian Petrov. I love you." I added a quick prayer under my breath, pulled the cap off the needle, then jabbed it directly into Valerian's chest. And pushed down the plunger.

He immediately sucked in a breath and started coughing. "The fuck is that?" He rasped. He squinted like he was having trouble focusing. "Is that a needle?" Then he sagged, his head lolling to the side.

"I think he passed out," King said from his quiet spot in the corner. He'd helped everyone as much as possible and was actually the one who was starting the process of cleaning out Valerian's office like he couldn't stand to watch his brother lying there lifeless. "He also hates needles. I think it's a family trait."

Seconds later, Valerian woke up, after I'd removed the needle and the trauma that went along with it.

"Is this real?" His voice was hoarse, and he still spoke a bit slowly.

"It's real." My eyes filled with tears as I pulled him into my arms; I couldn't stop shaking as I held him tight. "I'm sorry we were late."

Everyone burst out laughing just as Nikolai made his way into the house with about a dozen associates.

I was too focused on Valerian to even care how pissed everyone looked as they searched the house and moved toward the office.

Servants and staff, some of whom I recognized, appeared as if out of thin air. Where had they been when Valerian was attacked?

"Clean up," Nikolai barked. "And once the boss is up and walking, we find any more traitors and shoot them on sight, no excuses. And spread the word to his 'staff.' He will spill as much blood as he needs to, don't make me torture it out of any of you."

A chill swept over the room as Valerian slowly moved out of my arms and to his feet. I wanted to pull him back down then slap him for thinking he could just get up and walk after nearly dying.

"Valer—"

Ash nudged me. "He's the boss. He needs to show strength, let him go."

I wanted to cover him with my freaking body like a shield. Instead, with shaking hands, I helped Valerian stand, he took two steps toward Nikolai. Two other men I didn't recognize joined them.

And then I watched my husband take a gun from Nikolai, walk with authority toward three men who were hovering by the door, and shoot each of them in the head, no questions asked.

"Shit." Ash hissed next to me.

Even Junior looked stunned.

Because this wasn't Breaker anymore, was it? This was the new Petrov boss. This was Valerian.

And Valerian Petrov shot first and asked questions later.

I never thought I would be the type of person who was proud of someone for killing. I was training to be a doctor, my job was to save lives, not take them, but I had a certain respect for Valerian then, for the way he had nearly died then took care of business.

Protecting his Family.

Protecting me.

Whatever the cost.

He leaned a hand against the wall for support. I was certain he was still dizzy from the drugs, but he stayed upright as he handed the gun back to Nikolai and turned to the remaining men in the room.

"Cross me, and I kill you. Threaten my Family, and I'll turn you over to The Doctor." He nodded toward Nikolai. "Only so I can bring you close to death, revive you, and do it over again, and when you're close to your last breath, I'll bring in your family and shoot them while you watch, while I release you and let you live a life without everything you love, while you beg for death. That's your future if you don't follow me."

One by one, the men approached him, each of them

reaching for his left shoulder, they braced arms, and it continued until every man in that hallway pledged their allegiance.

To the untrained eye, Valerian might appear fine, but I could tell his actions were taking a toll on him. He needed to lie down and not worry about getting stabbed.

"Go." Serena shared a look with me. "We'll help clean up and let the dads know what went down, which probably means we'll have at least one of them on a plane headed in this direction." She drew in a long breath. "Most likely, Tex."

"Good." I sighed. "He hasn't spoken to him since…"

King shoved off his spot on the wall and left us.

I wanted to cry.

This wasn't the future Valerian should have had.

But it was ours now. We just needed to pick up the broken pieces.

Together.

As husband and wife.

I took a deep breath, walked over to him, and then pulled him in for a hug. "You need to go lie down," I whispered for his ears alone. "Doctor's orders."

He clung to me, breathing me in then releasing a dark chuckle. "I've always had a doctor-patient fantasy—ouch, I nearly died!"

I rolled my eyes. "I pinched you, it's not like I stuck a giant ass needle in your chest to revive you—oh wait, I did do that. Weird, it's almost like I saved your life."

He kissed my forehead. "I hate that we're even now."

I smiled at that. "Nah, it's kind of perfect, almost like a happily ever after."

His eyebrows shot up as we both looked around the entryway at the dead bodies, lingering wisps of smoke and blood. "Well, I can honestly say I'm wrong. Guess happily ever afters aren't boring after all."

"We literally have to step over a dead body to get to the stairs." I pressed a kiss to his mouth. "Let's go."

"I'd throw you over my shoulder and run if I could." He wrapped an arm around me as I helped him up the stairs.

And when we finally made it into the master bedroom, I wanted to cry with the rightness of it.

"I'm home." Tears filled my eyes.

Valerian turned to me, cupping my face with his hands. "You'll always be home as long as you're with me."

Our mouths met in a harsh kiss, one that was almost painful as he reached for my shirt and jerked me closer.

I tried breaking away, but he held me tight. For a man who had nearly died, he seemed pretty freaking strong.

He angled his head, deepening the kiss.

He tasted like fire and smoke.

It was perfect.

Like he was refined by the flames, stronger because of the struggle.

And he was mine.

"You need to sleep," I whispered against his mouth.

"I nearly went into a forever sleep, so let me have you. I'll even lie down and let you take complete advantage." His smile was so beautiful, I couldn't say no. "Ah, I can see the excitement in your eyes. Does innocent little Violet want to be... on top?"

I smacked him and then realized I probably looked crazy with blood and smoke on my skin; I moved away only to have him pin me down again.

"Blood is blood, I'm giving you my soul, my life, and erasing it right now."

He grabbed one of my boobs and pinched a nipple, earning him another slap.

And then I was slapping, he was pinching, and we somehow ended up on the bed. I tugged away his shirt. "Don't move."

"Wouldn't dare." He grinned, putting his arms behind his head as I unbuttoned his pants and tugged them down past his feet.

How was it possible for him to look so damn sexy? Smelling like smoke but lying there in nothing but golden skin, perfect muscles, and black boxer briefs.

"No commando today?" I asked, dipping my fingertips inside the band of the briefs.

He jerked beneath me. "I was trying to be professional, you know, boss and all."

"Screw professional." I winked.

"Mmm, how about you just screw me?"

I leaned over him and licked just below his belly button, gazing up at him as a tsunami of heat rushed over my body. With my tongue, I drew small circles, causing his hips to pump into my chest; he was hard beneath me, hot, needy. That made me smile as I locked eyes with him and whispered, "Beg."

"I hate you." Eyes wild, he reached for my hair and twisted it around his fingertips like he'd always done. This time it was almost painful as he tugged and then clenched his teeth. "Fuck me."

"Say please." I bit down on my lower lip.

"Please, Violet, make me yours…"

I pulled away from him long enough to strip naked as he kicked off his briefs and waited for me.

"You were mine as him, and you're mine now. You've always been mine," I said, voice strained. "Always."

He reached for me.

The minute I gripped his hand, he was pulling me on top of him. Our mouths met in an explosion of fireworks as I straddled him and then positioned myself on top of him.

He let out a satisfied groan when I sank onto him and started moving my hips. "This…" He gripped my hips, slowing my movements. "This is what I want every second of every day. You and me like this."

"We'd never get anything done." I smiled down at him as his hands slid up from my hips to my breasts and down again like he couldn't decide what to focus on.

"That's completely—" His lips parted with a curse. "Fine."

"You okay, Valerian?"

"No." He swore again. "You're perfect, and I'm dying all over again. This is… everything." He gripped my ass and squeezed as he thrust into me like an animal unleashed.

"Right there!" I yelled. "Please!"

With strength he shouldn't have, he flipped me over with his legs, so he was on top as he kissed me. "You feel so good, Vi. Almost like you were made for me."

Tears filled my eyes. "Maybe I was."

Our tongues tangled as our bodies clashed into one another in a beautiful mess of sweat and smoke.

My orgasm hit so hard and sudden that I couldn't speak. Feeling him inside me, feeling the tremors of his body with his release was like being reborn, and when he collapsed on top of me and then rolled over onto his back, I really did think he had died as he whispered my name and closed his eyes.

I checked his pulse just in case.

Death by orgasm.

He would never live that one down.

I kissed his cheek and smiled.

His pulse was strong.

He just needed to sleep off the rest of the drug.

I grabbed one of the blankets draped across the chair in his sitting room and covered him with it. In a sudden move, he jerked and then grabbed my wrist. "Stay."

"I should probably get everyone set up in rooms, figure out dinner—"

"See? I knew you would be the perfect wife. You gonna clean for me too? Or are—"

I lurched away from him and smacked him in the back of the head. "Oh, I'm sorry, did that hurt?"

"Italians," he grumbled. "Always with the slapping."

"Russians." I leaned over and kissed his full, lush mouth. "Always with the vodka."

"Vodka is life," he whispered and then repeated what I assumed was the same phrase in Russian.

"I know you're trying to sleep."

"Uh-huh."

"And that it's been a long day."

"Yup."

"Are you even listening?"

"Totally." He yawned.

I sighed. "I'm just curious. Are you completely fluent in Russian? Is the accent even real? And I'm assuming that you didn't really have a sight problem and were wearing contacts to dull that emerald green?"

Without so much as opening his eyes, he responded with a Russian accent that reminded me of our first days together.

"It comes and goes; I grew up around it so I can talk like all the men that used to come to the house. As far as being fluent, I've known Russian, Italian, and some French since my mom made me take lessons in all of them starting at the age of three, and you're correct."

"And yet you still suck at English? Crazy…"

His eyes flashed open, and then he was pulling me onto the bed and trapping me next to him. "Less talking, more cuddling."

"You hate cuddling." I smiled against the mattress as his arms held me against him.

"Only because every time I cuddled with you I got so hard it could have become embarrassing, so I lied and said I hated cuddling—the last thing I needed was your dad cutting my dick off because, at the tender age of fourteen, all I could think about was pinning you to the mattress and screwing you."

"Fourteen, huh?"

"I would have probably gone off like a bullet if you as much as grazed my zipper."

"You mean like you do now?"

"Viiiiiiiiiiii…" He drew my name out. "I was drugged, you know."

I smiled. "Fine, sleep, and then we talk."

"We always talk; it's what we did, so we didn't fuck."

"It's what you did."

"You liked it."

I sighed happily. "I loved it."

"Goodnight, Mrs. Petrov."

"Good night…" I kissed the top of his head. "My Russian Polar Bear King."

CHAPTER
Thirty-Three

I knew the day would come when the sun would set, and darkness would run, I hoped for it, I believed, and finally, it's as if I can see the road ahead, the path I took, the life I had once overlooked.
—Valerian Petrov

Valerian

It took me eight hours to sleep off the fun little drug that Nikolai had created a few years ago.

I'd heard rumors about its effects, and now I could easily say they were true, and I never wanted to experience that sort of helplessness ever again.

During my naptime, I'd gone from having my cousins and friends downstairs with a few associates to every damn man that worked for me, stopping by to check on me, most of them left with a bottle of vodka, meaning I needed to host a party and soon.

And we would as soon as I did the thing I didn't want to do

but needed to do in order to gain that last shred of forgiveness that was cowering in the corner of my heart.

The sound of classical music filtered through the living room as Ash and Serena poured drinks for themselves. Phoenix stood on the far side of the bar, eyeing me along with Andrei, who looked the most relaxed I'd ever seen them. After finding out about my brush with death, they decided to come down, along with my dad, to make sure everything was okay.

I told them I had it handled.

But I knew, in the back of my mind, I would still need them as mentors. I was young, everyone knew it, and I'd almost been taken out by one of my own.

"Hey." I pulled out a barstool and stole a bottle of vodka from Phoenix's grip.

I guess it wasn't really stealing since he let me take it. Phoenix rarely let anyone do anything, though, so I counted it as a win.

"I have questions," I finally said.

Andrei's lips curled into a tiny smirk. "I wondered if you'd figure it out yourself or if you'd need us to draw you a little scenario map."

Phoenix shrugged. "It goes something like this. You and Violet already had sex, the Russians saw you were alive, and what was the word you used, Andrei?"

Andrei cleared his throat. "Sad kicked puppy dog eyes."

"That," Phoenix snapped his fingers. "That's how you looked at each other and then boom, messy hair, swollen mouths—"

"Get to the point." I ground my teeth.

"He's angrier now that he's a boss." Andrei nodded. "I like it."

"You're annoying." I glared at him.

He lifted his glass into the air, looking every inch like one of my family members with his light hair and haunting eyes. "Thank you."

"So." Phoenix shrugged. "It was a good plan. There were rumors you were still alive, so we decided to just... quicken the process. That's really all you need to know."

"Oh, and dying wasn't part of our plan." Andrei patted me on the shoulder. "Truly sorry about that one. We thought Sancto was loyal." He shrugged. "And sane. Then again, we're all of us a little bit insane." He chuckled into his glass, giving me totally creepy vibes, while Phoenix just looked upward like he wondered why he was cursed with a friend who talked in riddles. Then again, it was Phoenix. Some might say he deserved that and more.

"Well, good thing I'm alive then," I grumbled.

"There is..." Phoenix cleared his throat. "One more thing..." He nodded his head toward the outside patio.

My adopted dad, the friggin' Capo of the Italians, was standing there, arms braced against the balcony with King standing next to him looking so much like him that it was almost hard to tell them apart except for the extra muscle and height Dad had on King still.

"This is going to hurt." I took the bottle with me and made my way outside. Standing next to them made me feel like a liar, and I hated it.

"King knew," Dad murmured, emotions held carefully in check. "And you didn't tell me?"

"I couldn't." I looked away. "I made a promise to Phoenix. He knew King was lonely, wanted another brother. But not only that, you're powerful, the most powerful man in the

Cosa Nostra. Nobody even blinked when you announced my adoption."

I turned toward him, expecting anger in his eyes. Instead, all I saw was sadness, and it felt like a million knives getting driven through my chest one by one.

"Trust me, son. I need you to trust me the way you trust Phoenix, the way you trust Chase despite your irritation over him wanting to murder you. The way you trust Ash with your life, Junior, Serena, hell, even Maksim. I need you to trust me in that way, not just with your brother because you're a terrified ten-year-old who's afraid he's going to die just like his mom. Those are the things you tell your parent. Maybe not immediately, but when you're ready, so if you want my allegiance as the Capo, you're going to have to prove to me that you can trust me despite your fear. Because if you can't, then I can't align with you, and if I can't align with you, then I can't suggest that the bosses do it." He angled his head to the right and studied me. "Are you hearing this?"

"Trust you, huh?" I rocked back on my heels. "So, you want me to just confess everything I've ever done to you right here? Right now? Is that going to make it better?"

"It's a damn good start." He crossed his arms.

"Fine." I grinned. "King and I both lost our virginity at the tender age of thirteen."

"Son of a bitch!" King said from the other side of him. "Dad, I swear we were older. The hell, man! Throw yourself under the bus, don't take me with you!"

"You. WHAT?" Dad bellowed.

I grinned. "Oh, and we stole pot from one of the drug rings you guys busted and got so high that we wandered into a strip club—King made ten dollars, I've never been so proud."

King just groaned into his hands, then slumped into one of the outdoor chairs. "I hate you, I hate you, I hate you."

"When I was fifteen, Violet gave me the best blow job of my life. King found out about it then asked—"

"I swear if you keep talking, Valerian, I am going to murder you in your sleep." King jumped to his feet. "And it won't be slow!"

"Hey, at least you're talking to me again." I shrugged at him then looked back at Dad. "King and I also decided to skip school one day just so we could go drink at one of the lakes. We took the girls with us, and everyone skinny-dipped. It was totally fine until Violet started stripping, and then I had this huge problem, so King started dancing naked on the dock, giving me time to run to the shore and jack off shamelessly behind a tree while Violet swam like a fucking mermaid through the water. I think it's why every Usher song gives me a semi—though I really don't want anyone knowing that."

"It wasn't Usher, you idiot. It was T-Payne!" King stepped closer and gave me a shove. "Plus, it wasn't my fault you had zero control of your hormones. A swift wind would have given you a semi!"

"That's probably true." I winked.

"Boys." Dad pinched the bridge of his nose. "These— er, confessions, not really what I was talking about."

"But I have a point." I crossed my arms. "Everything I did, I did with King. He was and still is one of my best friends. I told him because I was afraid, and I burdened him with that truth, but it was and still is one of the only things I kept from you, and *that's* the truth."

Dad's eyes locked onto me, and then he was pulling me

into a hug. King tried to escape, but Dad grabbed him by the collar of his shirt and pulled him in too.

I thought he was going to say something emotional.

Instead, he held us so tight it was hard to breathe. "Mom never hears a word of any of this, are we clear?"

"But Dad, you said to be truthful—"

"Damn it, I know what I said!" He shoved us away, jabbing his finger between the two of us and then back to me. "It's for my own sanity. She'll make me sleep on the couch, and you know that hurts my neck. She hears not a word of this. And for the record..." His eyes darkened. "Never, and I do mean *never* tell Chase that you jacked off watching his daughter swim. *Ever.*"

I held up my hands in innocence. "He actually tolerates me now. No way would I let that get out."

King let out a little chuckle. "Hmm, seems the tables have turned. Maybe I should shoot off a little text to... what's Ash's name for him? Scary Dad?"

"King." Dad glared. "No."

"Fine." He rolled his eyes.

Dad took one last look at us then made a beeline for the bar where Phoenix and Andrei had set up camp.

"Is there a reason Phoenix is showing Andrei pictures of an RV?"

I shuddered. "Sure hope not."

"Cool." King exhaled and then started to walk away.

"Wait." I grabbed him by the shoulder.

He froze.

"I'm sorry," I whispered. "I'm sorry I didn't prepare you for this, I'm sorry you had to keep this secret, sorry you had to watch everyone mourn. I'm just... I love you, and I'm sorry."

"See, that's all you needed to say." He hung his head and then turned back around. "You made an impossible choice, I get that. But you made it for both of us. You made a liar and betrayer out of me too, and that's not me, that's never been me. Yeah, we kept a lot of shit from Dad when we were young, but it was always because I was with you, not because I was strong enough on my own." He gulped. "Sometimes, I still don't think I am. Sometimes, I don't know who I am without the great Breaker— or sorry, Valerian by my side."

"Bro." I pulled him in for a tight hug. "I'll always be by your side."

"In Seattle." He grumbled.

I let him go. "Then move up here for a year. It's not like you wouldn't be safe."

His eyes lit up, and then Violet walked out to the patio. "Newlyweds… Maybe I'll wait for a few weeks before I bring it up to Dad. Hopefully, by then, you'll be bored of all the sex you're getting, and I won't want to cut my own ears off and bemoan the fact that I'm not getting any."

I rolled my eyes. "You were literally sleeping with your tutor all semester."

His grin turned sloppy. "She gave me an A+."

"Wow." Violet shook her head at him. "And here I thought this one was the whore. Congratulations, you've just earned a new badge for banging the tutor who's how many years older than you?"

"Three." King waved her off. "What can I say? Sex helps me focus."

"King!" Dad roared from inside. "Something you need to tell me about Miss Turner?"

"Fuck." King hung his head and then slowly turned around. "She's a really good tutor?"

"You. Little. Shit!" Dad yelled.

And then King ran for the door.

He was, of course, tackled by Ash, who was mean enough to want King to suffer. At least Ash wasn't drinking himself to death anymore or banging his head against the wall because, according to him, the pain made him feel better.

"So." Violet reached for my hand. "Everything good?"

"Everything is…" I narrowed my eyes. "Weirdly normal."

A gunshot rang out.

A lamp fell.

Neither of us even looked.

"Yup." She smirked. "Weirdly normal."

"Geez, Tex, he's turning purple!" Ash yelled.

"Oh God, I'm going to puke," Maksim announced.

"What the hell is wrong with you people?" Tank joined in as more loud noises commenced.

"And you?" Violet pressed a kiss to my mouth before talking. "How are you?"

"Deliriously happy that last year, I brought a girl to a club, lost her, found her again, saved her, lost my soul, only to have her bring me back to life again." I smiled at her. "So, I'm feeling pretty fucking good right now."

"Good." She chewed her lower lip. "Because I'm pretty sure that mood is about to change when you find out…"

I felt myself pale. "What happened?"

"Annie needs a place to stay. The dorms aren't safe for her anymore. Her parents are dead, courtesy of Ash and—" She sighed. "I may have brought it up to your dad, who then took matters into his own hands and—"

"Oh shit, don't tell me."

Violet winced. "My dad offered to take her in."

And there it was.

The bomb exploding as we both turned to see Ash on his phone, his face pale. It was like slow motion as he stomped up to Annie looking ready to murder her even though she probably had no clue why he was so pissed.

He threw the phone onto the ground, breaking it nearly in half, then turned and looked at Violet like he was going to kill her.

I stood in front of her and shook my head slowly as Junior came up behind Ash and took him down.

"He's not himself," I whispered.

"He's not even human anymore at times." Violet hugged me from behind. "But blood is blood, so we'll get him through it. One way or another, we'll get him through."

I had my doubts this time, but I didn't voice them. I just focused on the woman holding me and the fact that I knew I could finally lead this Family not because I was strong enough, but because I had a partner who was.

After all, you can't deny Abandonato blood—it fights for what's theirs.

"Come on." I tugged her hand. "Let's go clean up the blood."

EPILOGUE

In vain I have struggled it will not do, My feelings will not be repressed, You must allow me to tell you how ardently I admire and love you.
—Jane Austen, *Pride and Prejudice*

Ash

They were already married, so I wasn't quite sure why they wanted to have another wedding and reception, other than Violet said she wanted her father to walk her down the aisle.

It took every ounce of strength I had to stand up there with Valerian while Violet walked slowly down that aisle—that and a shit ton of whiskey that Junior kept plying me with so I'd be numb enough to keep my anger in check.

I was self-medicating more and more.

And then I just stopped.

Because it made me dream of her.

If I drank too much, I saw her face, and then the nightmare would occur; I'd be in that emergency room with Nikolai by my side telling me to say goodbye.

I never got the words out, though.

They refused to pass my lips.

Because that would make it true.

She's gone.

But I still felt her in my soul.

How was that even possible?

Annie eyed me from her spot next to Izzy. They were bridesmaids, and even half-drunk, I could appreciate the way her black dress hugged her small, curvy body.

And that was the fucking problem.

I was attracted to her.

I begged God, literally anyone but the girl I blamed for Claire's death, anyone but the person I hated more than I could ever possibly love.

And yet every single time I saw her.

I burned.

"You may now kiss the bride!" Tex announced, hilarious that he was ordained; yeah, maybe I was a little past drunk if the thought of Tex holding a Bible made me chuckle and sway on my feet.

"You okay?" Junior nudged me.

"Never."

"Oh good, you're past the point of drunk, and now you're going to get the sads again? Buck up, your family needs you."

But who wants me?

I moved through a haze as I walked with Junior toward the reception at Valerian's mega-house.

A white tent was set up in the backyard, and there were enough Italian and Russian associates to start an all-out war in the Pacific Northwest.

But everyone was smiling.

Even the ones that had tattoos on their faces.

Freaky as hell.

Savages.

Phoenix walked by then with Cruz Martinez, I tried not to gape, but the guy didn't visit often which in my drunken state did not cause warm fuzzies to erupt. If anything, it meant there was trouble, and where there was trouble, there was Phoenix Nicolasi.

He held a black folder in his right hand.

Cruz snatched it away and opened it just as one of the Sinacore made men sauntered over; the guy had slayed half the bridal party—sexually, not actually killed them.

My lips twitched. Damn Sicilians, they knew how to score, I'd give them that much. All blue eyes, dark skin, and slicked-back hair, but this one? He was about our age; he had nothing but easy smiles and winks for the ladies, but now? Now, he looked lethal as he grabbed the folder and paled.

"Spying?" Junior whispered.

I sighed. "Let me spy in peace."

"You're slurring, and you don't even know it."

I shoved him away and stumbled to an empty chair that looked out onto the Puget Sound, laying my head back against the wood.

It didn't take long for me to start spying again out of pure anguish, drunkenness, and boredom.

A guy I'd never seen before was currently making out with one of the cousins from the Alfero side, he was making her laugh, and it pissed me off that everything he did looked so fucking easy.

Every small caress of his fingertips.

Every lick of his lips as he leaned down and whispered something in her ear.

"He's hot." Izzy plopped down next to me. "Like so hot that I felt the need to point it out to every single girl in residence, where the hell did he come from?"

"No." I jabbed a finger at her. "Just. No."

"But—"

"—No," I barked, earning the attention of a few people around us, including the mystery dude my little sister was currently checking out. He whispered one last thing to the girl he was flirting with; her smile fell, and then he turned his lethal eyes toward Izzy.

Oh, hell no, he was dying today.

He didn't walk—he sauntered toward us, and I swear to all that's holy it was like Izzy was watching him in slow motion as her jaw hung open.

The minute he was in front of us, I shot to my feet. "She's taken."

He held up his hands. "Wasn't offering."

My eyes narrowed. "Do I know you?"

His smile was slow, calculated. "Romeo Sinacore."

Izzy let out a small gasp next to me.

Yeah, I knew of him, like the fucking black widow of the Sicilian mafia, he had just as many kills under his belt as I did, possibly more, but rumor had it they only sent him in to either go undercover or when he needed to flirt with some guy's wife in order to gain intel.

Most made men shot first asked questions later.

Not Romeo Sinacore—no, he was rumored to use his body like a weapon, and his victims? They begged for death if only he kissed them, touched them, fucked them, one more time.

"You're Ash, right? Ash Abandonato?" He crossed his arms in amusement like he didn't literally have what looked like blood splatters on his hands; what the hell?

I plopped back on my seat, my eyebrow arching as I jerked my head toward his hands. With a curse, he shoved them in his pockets. Amused, I plopped back in my seat. He'd fit in just fine around here. "Yup, that's me—look take your Casanova ways and point them in any direction away from my baby sister—feel me?"

"Unfortunate—" He winked down at her. "I've heard Abandonato women are great in be—"

I jumped back to my feet, ready to swing at him.

He jerked back, hands up, and burst out laughing. "I'm kidding, and that's fine; I'm not here for pleasure anyway..." He eyed Izzy up and down one last time before whispering out, "Pity."

And then he was gone.

Izzy had gone still as a statue next to me.

I wasn't sure how long we stayed like that, but soon we were surrounded by my friends, my cousins, all of them trying to cheer me up as we swapped stories about growing up.

"Remember the time Ash stole all that beer from his dad?" Maksim laughed. "I came home so drunk, my dad refused to speak to me for a full week. I think it was worse than getting shot at."

"Bro, you're just pissed because he took away your calculator." Junior laughed, and everyone quickly joined in.

"True." Maksim nodded. "I was working on a love potion, sue me."

"Is that the same one that gave you hives?" Serena asked.

"Yup." Maksim nodded and took a swig of beer. "On my ass."

"And his dick." Valerian came over and sat. "Oh wait, was that a secret?"

"Duuuuude!" King burst out laughing. Even he was happy after being pissed off at the world for a week. "Did you scar?"

"Ask Izzy," Serena teased under breath.

Izzy glared and then looked away, wringing her hands.

Even Maksim went quiet.

"Oh, come on," Serena whispered. "It's not like it's a secret."

"Andrei found them." Violet sighed and sat on Valerian's lap. "And let's just say we're all lucky they're still alive."

Ah, it made sense why she was checking out Romeo—she wanted to forget the heartache. It never helped when you jumped into bed with someone who wasn't your other half; all it did was make you feel even more like shit. I'd have a chat with her later.

"I'm out." Maksim stood. "I need more beer."

He didn't as much as look at Izzy.

She scowled after him then flipped him off.

"Easy, tiger." Serena wrapped an arm around her. "Do you wanna talk about it?"

"If that annoying, little, brat Kartini, wouldn't have ratted us out, things would have been different."

At the mention of Kartini, we all turned, just as the music started, and wouldn't you know there she was dancing with Sergio like the princess she was.

She was in the second half.

What we called the younger kids, because they never hung out with us, mainly because we were a really bad influence, and they were underage, but now that she was eighteen…

Things were about to change.

It didn't help that she was drop-dead gorgeous.

"I'm surprised Sergio hasn't locked her in her room yet," I

muttered and then cursed as Annie made her way over to us along with Tank.

I was just getting up when Junior snapped me in the thigh with the back of his hand. "Don't be rude."

I clenched my jaw.

"Nice party." Tank clinked his beer with Junior's. "Congrats, guys."

"Thanks." Valerian beamed.

I nearly choked on his happiness.

It should have been me.

Married.

With a family.

Her in a white dress.

"So how are things at Scary Dad's house?" Valerian asked Annie.

Her body stiffened, and tension hung on the air. She gave a too-bright smile. "Perfect. Absolutely perfect."

And in the back of my mind, all I kept thinking about was what we'd done, what I'd done, how I'd ruined her, and any chances I would ever have.

How I had done it on purpose.

How I'd hurt her.

How she let me.

And how I wanted nothing more than to keep punishing both of us just so I could feel something.

"Good, I'm so glad you have a safe place." Violet smiled.

I almost snickered.

Safe?

She was living with a fucking monster.

And as I looked up into her eyes and saw them widen, I was beginning to think she preferred it.

WANT MORE *Mafia Royals*?
CHECK OUT *Destructive King*,
ASH AND ANNIE'S STORY,
COMING JANUARY 12, 2021!

WANT TO SEE WHAT *Romeo Sinacore* IS UP TO?
CHECK OUT *Mafia Casanova*
COMING THIS NOVEMBER FROM
RACHEL VAN DYKEN & M. ROBINSON!

ACKNOWLEDGMENTS

I'm so thankful to God that I'm able to write books that make me feel all the things. This has been a hard year for everyone, and it was like my own brand of therapy being able to write and escape into this world!

Thank you so much to my amazing husband, who, during quarantine, took the little man and played with him all day every day while I got work done. Seriously, Nate, you're a lifesaver!

Thank you, Nina and Jill, for holding my hand through this release, from edits to marketing, to plotting to making sure I don't jump from a cliff because I haven't figured out what to do yet and then BINGO (Jill lol)!

Becca, Angie, you always help so much, and I'm so thankful to have you guys on my team!

To my beta readers, Tracey, Jill, Georgia, Stephanie, Candace, Yana, Krista—you guys are incredible and always offer the best feedback. I'm so blessed to have you!

To Melissa and Serena, GAH, thank you for taking an early read and making me cry; I think we're all even now, right? RIGHT? Are you still making voodoo dolls? Not cool. I'll send wine!

It would take me forever to name all the authors who read this early, who helped me, who held my hand and told me I wasn't crazy. Thank you for being so supportive in this community, thank you for being anchors during the storm; you know who you are. Kristen, Corinne, Kristin, Audrey, Monica, Lauren, Nana, Jessica—See, I'm just starting my list, and I'm like I'm missing so many people who have been my rocks along the way, so it's so hard to list! But thank you, guys!

To Liz Berry and Jillian Stein, thank you for helping when I'm stuck or need marketing advice even when it's not a 1001 Dark Nights book! You guys are epic.

And to the readers and bloggers, I am only able to do this because of your support. I don't think you will ever understand what it means to get reviews, commentary, to see you share things, to see you react, it makes my world turn, and I will forever be in your debt for letting me into your worlds and being able to share mine.

Thank you, Rockin' Readers, for putting up with all my crazy excerpts because I have no self-control, and if you want to join the friendliest group on Facebook, please be sure to go click Rachel's New Rockin Readers! And join the family, blood in no out.

HUGS RVD

ABOUT THE
Author

Rachel Van Dyken is the #1 New York Times, Wall Street Journal, and USA Today bestselling author of over 90 books ranging from contemporary romance to paranormal. With over four million copies sold, she's been featured in Forbes, US Weekly, and USA Today. Her books have been translated in more than 15 countries. She was one of the first romance authors to have a Kindle in Motion book through Amazon publishing and continues to strive to be on the cutting edge of the reader experience. She keeps her home in the Pacific Northwest with her husband, adorable son, naked cat, and two dogs. For more information about her books and upcoming events, visit www.RachelVanDykenauthor.com.

ALSO BY
Rachel Van Dyken

Eagle Elite

Covet
Stealing Her (Bridge & Isobel's story)
Finding Him (Julian & Keaton's story)

Ruin Series
Ruin (Wes Michels & Kiersten's story)
Toxic (Gabe Hyde & Saylor's story)
Fearless (Wes Michels & Kiersten's story)
Shame (Tristan & Lisa's story)

Seaside Series
Tear (Alec, Demetri & Natalee's story)
Pull (Demetri & Alyssa's story)
Shatter (Alec & Natalee's story)
Forever (Alex & Natalee's story)
Fall (Jamie Jaymeson & Pricilla's story)
Strung (Tear + from the boys POV)
Eternal (Demetri & Alyssa's story)

Seaside Pictures
Capture (Lincoln & Dani's story)
Keep (Zane & Fallon's story)
Steal (Will & Angelica's story)
All Stars Fall (Trevor & Penelope's story)
Abandon (Ty & Abigail's story)
Provoke (Braden & Piper's story)
Surrender (Andrew & Bronte's story)

The Consequence Series
The Consequence of Loving Colton (Colton & Milo's story)
The Consequence of Revenge (Max & Becca's story)
The Consequence of Seduction (Reid & Jordan's story)
The Consequence of Rejection (Jason & Maddy's story)

RACHEL VAN DYKEN
www.rachelvandykenauthor.com